THE DEADLIEST FALL

CHARLIE COCHRANE

Riptide Publishing
PO Box 1537
Burnsville, NC 28714
www.riptidepublishing.com

The Deadliest Fall
Copyright © 2023 by Charlie Cochrane

Cover art: L.C. Chase, lcchase.com
Editor: Carole-ann Galloway
Layout: L.C. Chase, lcchase.com

ISBN: 978-1-62649-981-2

First edition
June, 2023

Also available in ebook:
ISBN: 978-1-62649-982-9

THE DEADLIEST FALL

CHARLIE COCHRANE

RIPTIDE PUBLISHING

Sometimes the most dangerous question is the one you don't ask.

TABLE OF
CONTENTS

CHAPTER ONE

Hampshire, 1947

"Come back, you menace!" Leslie Cadmore broke into a run, but his dog was fleeter of foot than him and absolutely determined, it appeared, to stay at a distance from him. He shouldn't have let the hound off the lead, although wasn't it easy to be wise after the event? "Max! To heel."

Leslie might as well have tried to catch the wind in his cap. The black Labrador was evidently under the impression that this was an incredibly enjoyable game, given the way he repeatedly looked back to encourage him to come closer, before setting off again. Thank God the common was wide, provided good visibility and was always kept clear of livestock at this time of year.

"Max! If you don't come here, so help me, I'll—" He never managed to finish the threat, a pair of young women having come into sight. They'd rounded a stand of trees and would soon be within earshot. *Damn it.*

The dog, still capering about, spotted the newcomers and made for them, slowing to a respectable trot and no doubt putting on his most friendly expression, the devious little sod. The swing of his tail gave every indication of a happy, amenable hound.

"You swine," Leslie muttered, annoyed that the women had clearly worked the kind of magic he couldn't, although grateful that Max's interest in making new friends might allow him to be put back on the lead.

By the time Leslie reached them, Max had transformed into the most well-behaved pet a man could wish to own, sitting compliantly at the women's feet and letting himself be stroked.

"I'm so sorry." Leslie raised his cap. "He's such a pest. Oh." He paused, breaking into a grin and holding out his hand towards the taller of the women. "I didn't recognise you, Marianne. How lovely to see you again."

Marianne warmly clasped his hand in both of hers. "I thought it was you, Leslie, although this fellow made me think I had to be mistaken. Where's Towser?"

"Gone to his long home, I'm afraid. Four years ago." He turned to the other woman, who was owed an explanation. "He was my retriever, Miss . . .?"

"Geraldine Simpson." Marianne's friend extended her hand. "So pleased to meet you. I've heard about Towser already and the fun you all used to have walking him on the common, although Marianne told me less about his owner."

"She would." Marianne Sibley had always given the outward impression she was fonder of Towser than she'd been of *him*, although for a while Leslie had suspected that had borne an element of subterfuge. "I'm far less interesting than my dogs. Leslie Cadmore, late of this parish and a very old friend of the family Sibley."

"Your mother still lives here, I believe?" Geraldine made such a contrast to Marianne. Compact where her friend was willowy; cheery faced where Marianne always seemed so cool and aloof; brightly dressed in contrast to the autumnal shades the other young woman had always favoured. Leslie had valued his friend's calmness in those younger days and how different she was to many of the local young women.

"Mother does live here," he replied. "In Larkspur House, where I was born and grew up. Marianne knows the place well. Do you remember the tennis parties?"

"I do. Towser always had to be tied up, poor lamb, because he wanted to join in. I hope this chap is better behaved." Marianne bent to pat Max, who was wearing a saintly expression.

"He's an absolute scoundrel, although I couldn't guess how he'd conduct himself at a tennis match, as he's never had the opportunity to experience one. He's a town dog, Miss Simpson, so doesn't know country manners." Strange, though, that Marianne wasn't aware of what had happened to Max's predecessor, because Leslie would have expected her and his mother to pass the time of day on occasions. Had the Sibleys also moved away—his mother hadn't mentioned it, if so—or was there something else that had prevented the doings of Leslie Cadmore being passed on to her? And Geraldine knowing that Mrs. Cadmore was still a local proved she must have been discussed. Marianne's expression was no help, her face, as it had been from a child, proving unreadable.

"Did I hear you calling him Max?" Geraldine asked.

"Yes. After a distant cousin who once came to visit Larkspur with his family. It's proved an apt name."

Marianne burst out laughing. "I remember him. He was what my mother would call a spoiled brat. If he was my child, he'd have spent more time confined to his room than out of it. Any idea what he's doing now, Leslie?"

"Working his way through the ranks at Scotland Yard, believe it or not. Perhaps he's seen the light, or it's a case of poacher turned gamekeeper."

"He could be paying off the sins of his childhood. All I have to do is think of him pulling my pigtails and my scalp hurts. Worse than your brother was, Geraldine."

"Oh, George isn't that bad. Settling down with Victoria and finding himself articled has bridled any wild tendencies." Geraldine cast her friend a sidelong glance that could only be described as sly. "Like Patrick."

"How is your brother, Marianne?" Leslie had anticipated Patrick would be mentioned sooner or later and was pleased *he* hadn't had to raise the topic. Despite being twins, Patrick and Marianne were as different in personalities as any siblings could be. Chalk and cheese didn't come near it.

"Working too hard. Throws all of his time into his practice." She patted the dog's head. "He'd like you, boy. Prefers his patients with a bit of character."

Leslie nodded. Patrick had always liked dogs to be dogs and not pampered lap pets. He'd also appeared to prefer animals to the majority of humans. *"You can trust them,"* he'd say, *"unlike much of the human species."* Even as a child, Patrick had seemed to be a veterinarian in the making. He'd no doubt have a successful practice and that wouldn't simply be a testament to his skills or training. Patrick had the same lean, dark, handsome looks his sister was blessed with. Looks that would see a stream of female clients bringing their pampered pooches to his door.

"You're right about the hard work. He never seems to be available, that's certain." Geraldine's voice bore a distinct hint of annoyance. "My mother has invited him to a number of events, but he pleads pressure of time. She's rather given him up as a lost cause."

"Many people have." Marianne tossed her head.

"He'll settle down one day," Leslie said, not sure that he believed that any more than Patrick's sister would do. They both knew him too well. *Had* known him, in Leslie's case, given how long it was since they'd last spoken. Suddenly, Leslie was filled with a fleeting memory of the three of them as children, the last time they played hide and seek: him, Marianne, Patrick, all of them around twelve years of age. She'd said afterwards they were getting too old for such childish things, possibly because she'd taken umbrage at Patrick being so slow at finding her. Best not to mention that, since it probably still rankled, and the day itself had ended sadly, with a tramp being found dead of exposure in the church porch. Mr. Cadmore had been called on to handle the affair, being churchwarden and with the vicar away on holiday. Still, such rare instances apart, those had generally been very happy days.

"Give my very best to your mother. I do feel guilty for not having kept in touch with her as I should." Marianne fixed her eyes on Max. "Like you, Leslie, I don't get down here as often as I would like."

That provided a partial answer to some of his questions, although moving away from an area didn't mean she couldn't send a letter if she really wanted to. Perhaps, like Patrick, Marianne was simply busy. Leslie's mother had told him that she worked as a legal secretary in Winchester, and he'd assumed—evidently mistakenly—that she travelled there from the Sibley home.

"I will pass on your regards, with pleasure. Are you here for long?" Leslie added. His mother might be pleased to have Marianne over for tea in order to talk over old times.

"Until Monday morning, when my nose goes firmly back to the grindstone. Albeit returning to work will make a pleasant escape from Father's hunting stories. His enthusiasm hasn't dimmed over the years." Marianne gave the dog a final stroke, then took her friend's arm. "We must get back. Terrible trouble if we come in late for luncheon."

"Blame me and my wretched hound." Leslie tipped his cap again. "Nice to have met you, Geraldine. Fond regards to your parents, Marianne, and to your scapegrace of a brother."

"I'll tell them all that I spoke to you. Although I'd always assumed you'd have kept in touch with Patrick." Marianne waved her hand airily. "It shows how mistaken we can be." She set off slowly, pausing after a few steps to turn and say, "It really is lovely to see you again. We shouldn't have let it be so long. All of us."

"Indeed." Leslie watched the women go, momentarily unable to move himself and not only because he was thinking about the assumption Marianne had made about him and Patrick keeping in touch. Her gait bore the same easy grace as her brother's, bringing to mind the last time Leslie had seen him. At Waterloo station. Walking away and out of Leslie's life.

"We're back," Leslie called, entering the hall of Larkspur House and letting Max off the lead from which he was clearly anxious to be freed.

"In the drawing room, dear." His mother's voice sounded as sweetly as a woman's half her age.

Alexandra Cadmore was still a handsome woman, despite the events of the past few years. Not for her, however, the lot of so many of her friends during wartime, a telegram bringing the news no wife or mother would wish to receive. Leslie had been based at home, doing something he could never divulge the details of, apart from hinting that it had been vitally important. "Logistical and extremely boring if crucial to the war effort" was how he'd described his work, and that was what his mother had told her friends. He wasn't convinced she believed the "boring" part, although she'd always kept up the pretence. So, he'd remained physically safe, returning to civilian life tired but intact, if a touch emotionally battered.

It was his father, Jerome Cadmore, who'd been torn from her and not by death. Unless finding a vocation and entering a Benedictine monastery could be defined as crossing into—or having one foot on the doorstep of—one's eternal rest. It was marginally better, she'd confessed to Leslie when the news had broken, than his having run away with a WAAF, which had happened to one of her old school friends. Worse in some ways, though, because anybody could understand the attractions of a woman in uniform; the attractions of God weren't so obvious. It had been the third year of the war, so Leslie hadn't been on hand much to give her support, but she'd coped, as she always did.

"Did you have a nice walk?" His mother glanced up from her knitting.

"Very, apart from Max exhibiting wanderlust. I ran across Marianne, out taking the air with one of her pals. I didn't realise she no longer lived here with her parents." Leslie flopped down into his favourite chair.

"I'm sure I told you. I daresay you weren't listening at the time." She grinned. "How is she?"

"Not a jot different from how she was at nineteen. Or indeed nine. I was surprised that you haven't kept in touch with her."

"I see her parents at church. They keep me abreast of all things Sibley. Marianne's doing splendidly at work and has a little flat of her own, now." She paused to count her stitches. "They worry about her living alone, but that's a cross all parents bear. Which friend was with her?"

"A girl called Geraldine something-or-other. Simpkins. Simpson. Max was most taken with them both." The dog, who'd sprawled himself on the fireside rug, glanced up at the mention of his name. "Thank goodness they came along or I'd still have been out on the common, trying to get this wretch back on his lead."

"Marianne always had a knack with animals. Her father's daughter, every bit, although she's a better hand with a rod and fly than he is."

Leslie chuckled. Mr. Sibley had been continually vexed at the fact. "She's better at taking a trout than *most* of us. Some zoologist chap once told me that women have a natural unfair advantage when fishing. A natural aroma they produce that attracts their prey."

"Does it work with men, dear? Is that why some women appear to be irresistible?" She held her handiwork up to the light, nodding approvingly at it before resuming knitting. "Although in Marianne's instance, I'd say it's likely a case of her not rising to the male fly. Not yet, anyway."

Leslie wasn't sure she ever would. Not every mare had a hankering for the stallion.

"Should we invite her and her friend to tea today?" She continued, with an air that was a little too nonchalant to be entirely convincing. Was this a repeat of the getting-my-son-in-a-room-with-eligible-women ruse? "I'm sure that young Edwin would take an invitation across, on his bicycle. Would sixpence be over-generous as payment?"

"I couldn't say, not having a housekeeper's son to run errands for me and so being oblivious to the going rate." It wasn't spoken unkindly: Mrs. Edwards was an absolute treasure, a war widow without whom the running of Larkspur House would no doubt grind to a halt. Leslie's mother was lucky to have her and to be able to keep her. At least his father had only dedicated *himself* to God and not included his considerable worldly wealth, so his wife had been left with enough to live comfortably.

"But should I invite her? I noticed that expression of disdain at the suggestion, dear." How his mother could have seen any expression on Leslie's face, given the way her eyes were fixed on her knitting needles, was a mystery of the arcane maternal arts.

"I wasn't aware of feeling disdain. Perhaps it was indigestion. Invite her by all means. It's not like she'll have that rogue of a brother with her, to drop a teacup or trip over the rug." Leslie wasn't sure why he'd felt the need to mention Patrick. Maybe it was simply to divert his mother from any further discussion of Marianne and her matrimonial prospects. It was a topic she'd aired on many an occasion over the years, and one that had subtly featured Leslie as a possible candidate for the woman's affections, although not so often recently. Could this be her idea of reviving a notion that was always doomed to fail?

"Patrick was certainly the clumsiest child I ever met. He must have grown out of it, or else he'd not have anyone bringing their animals to him. With the exception of women of my age who should know better." There was very little that escaped the notice of Leslie's mother, despite the fact that she didn't do much socially anymore, outside of the church or the local causes she supported. "Is he staying with his parents too?"

"Not that I'm aware of, although to be honest I didn't ask Marianne the question." Nor had she offered the information. "I don't think he works locally."

"He's based in Surrey, I believe. Near Epsom, so he can work with horses as well as his beloved dogs. I'd have thought you'd have known that." That remark was evidently worthy of a direct glance, over the top of her spectacles.

"I haven't spoken to Patrick in years. Same as I've not spoken to Marianne." Leslie shrugged. "You know what it's like. People knock around together and are great pals, then they go off in different directions and suddenly find they've not spoken in ages. And the longer it goes on, the harder it is to get out one's pen and paper to jot down a line. It takes an errant hound and some good fortune, like this morning on the common, to re-establish communication."

It wasn't just a matter of the length of time. Somehow, the closer you had been to somebody, the trickier it was to make that first move and the more awkward that reconnection might prove. The conversation with Marianne had felt stilted, to say the least.

"Then perhaps a chat over a pot of tea and a scone is exactly what's called for. I'll compose a note to Marianne. Was the friend called Geraldine? I shall invite her too."

Leslie confirmed the name, accepting his fate. He excused himself, saying that a short turn around the garden would be pleasant, before luncheon, although he insisted Max should stay inside, as punishment. The dog snored happily, oblivious of what was being said about him.

Leslie lit a cigarette, hands cupped to protect the match's flame from the wind. No sooner had he taken the first draw than he heard Edwin leaving the house, heading for the garage where he kept his bicycle. Once Leslie's mother got an idea in her head, she lost no time on it. Marianne would no doubt accept the invitation, unless she had another engagement that couldn't be broken. Leslie should use the next few hours preparing himself to be a welcoming host, which was longer than he'd had to gather his wits on the common.

He strolled along the path, glancing with pleasure over the rolling Hampshire countryside. Whoever had laid out the gardens at Larkspur House had known their business, making the most of the south-facing aspect. People were said to have lived in this area for thousands of years, probably enjoying the same view from their villa or roundhouse. When Leslie was a boy, he'd turned up pieces of pottery in the local mole hills, pieces that his father had assured him were Roman. He'd believed it at the time and it might have been true, although Mr. Cadmore did have a plausible way about him.

It was a skill that he'd developed further in the running of his business, gently planting ideas in other people's heads when it would prove useful, such as the time he'd employed a young man only to find him unsuited to his role. Via a couple of seemingly innocuous conversations, focussed on the young man's ambitions and happiness, they'd soon reached the point where he'd decided he'd made the wrong choice and would be joining a local brewing company. Leslie grinned in remembrance of the tale.

He'd reached the Larkspur orchard—if half a dozen apple trees and a similar number of both plums and pears could be given that title—which was the place where he'd always been happiest. Sitting in a deckchair in the dappled light or swinging in a hammock, when reading, dozing, studying for exams, or simply enjoying the thrill of being alive in a world untouched by the fingers of war. As a small child, carefully scribing his name and address in his little notebook. *Leslie Simon Cadmore, Larkspur House, Kinebridge, Hampshire, England, The World.* That world had changed, as so many had warned it would, although some people had still retained the over-optimistic view in 1939 that this time it really might all be over by the first Christmas. Would people ever learn from the past?

The hammock had long since been taken down, and as Leslie wanted to rest his limbs, he had to make his way to the rose garden, where a sturdy wooden bench had been well placed to benefit from any sunshine. Today's light was watery but bore a hint of warmth to come, and though it would be too early in the year for buds or blossoms on the roses, it wouldn't be unpleasant to finish his cigarette there, coat wrapped around him.

The bench seemed to fit his shape. When younger, he'd found it too hard, smacking of self-punishment, but now the solidity of it was better suited to his tastes, after years of getting used to discomfort. Bletchley chairs in Bletchley huts. Strange to think how he'd assumed back then that he could easily put the war years and all they'd brought behind him, to return as quickly as possible to his previous life, only to find that the time he'd spent in that place couldn't be unspent. It would always be part of him.

Be grateful you made it through in one piece—thousands of men and women would have given their right arm to be home for another spring. Some of them did.

It could have been Patrick's voice in his ear, saying those words, rather than the voice of conscience, but he hadn't spoken to Patrick in ages and couldn't even say with certainty when the man had last visited Larkspur House. Yet his presence somehow still seemed to fill the garden, this place where they'd played so often as young children and later as boys on the cusp of manhood. The mentions of Patrick that morning rang accusatorially in Leslie's ears. How the hell could they have let so much time pass without making contact?

Because you're a coward. One who didn't have the guts to ask Patrick either of the two questions you wanted to, afraid that the answers would be too hard to bear.

How easy it should have been to frame the first. "Do you really love me, Patrick, as I really love you, despite everything?" Seeing Marianne had brought that more clearly into focus, had reawakened the need to have Patrick at his side again, whether it was out on the common walking a dog or sitting in the orchard or lying in a bed between cool linen sheets.

The other question would have been trickier, as impossible to ask Patrick as it would have been for Leslie to tackle his father about why he had gone into Combe Abbey. Either question would have risked receiving an answer full of peril, in terms of how it might have irrevocably changed a relationship. Leslie often wondered if *he'd* somehow driven his father into leaving, perhaps unconsciously forcing the man to consider what it would be like to live a family life in the knowledge that his son was different, and all the disgrace that might bring were it made public. It might have been a safer choice to cut himself off from continually dealing with that. It was easy to love your neighbour—or your family—if you didn't have to live with them.

But if that hadn't been his motivation, what had? He must either have been running towards a life of contemplation or running away from something in his secular life that could no longer be borne. Leslie couldn't shake from his mind the great scandal of 1938, when there'd been an attempted strangling in one of the nearby hamlets. A farmer had given himself in at the local police station, confessing that after fourteen years of constant nagging, he'd snapped and nearly killed his wife. Surely that sudden outburst of violence could never have happened with Leslie's parents?

There had only been one instance when Mr. Cadmore had shown real aggression, and that had been when on a holiday. He'd killed what had appeared to be an otter with a heavy blow to the skull, much to young Leslie's horror. It had turned out to be an escapee from a local—illegal—mink farm, about which Mr. Cadmore had been warned.

"Evil creatures, Leslie. Best to get rid of them quickly, before they can cause any harm." Most anglers would have agreed with him.

More comically, there was a family story about him having boxed the ears of a rival for the love of Leslie's mother. Yet Mr. Cadmore could be so soft he'd wept at a sermon about the massacre of the innocents.

On the way home he'd explained his distress. *"If it's true—and you take all these Bible stories with a pinch of salt because men wrote them down—then it's beyond wicked."*

He'd always shown a similar desire to protect his family from harm. Until, of course, he'd broken their hearts by his act of retreat into the life of the cloister. That decision had been so out of character—assuming they had really understood what the man was like and what he wanted. Maybe some part of his father was, and always would remain, hidden and unknowable. Leslie had spent many hours brooding on the subject, having nobody he could discuss such personal things with. Had his father harboured a self-denied yet lifelong devotion to God, one that he was always going to manifest at some point or else be driven mad? He'd left no clue behind when he'd made his abrupt departure, his final note to them, *I've left you well provided for money-wise. I can't let you suffer*, ringing hollow. Emotional anguish was as hard to bear as financial.

If Leslie was unclear about his father's motives, he had still less clarity in his thinking about Patrick. The other question Leslie had left unasked was more serious by far. It was almost unthinkable to air, no matter how close the two men had been. Leslie whispered it now, the calm of the garden—as well as the knowledge that nobody could hear—bringing him courage.

Did you murder Fergus Jackson? And how the hell did you pull it off?

CHAPTER TWO

The guests arrived right on the stroke of four, as Marianne had stated they would in the note she'd sent back with young Edwin. As a girl she'd always kept her promises, especially regarding punctuality, and she'd retained that courtesy into womanhood. She'd brought a bunch of flowers from the Sibley glasshouse, which she presented to Mrs. Cadmore with a beaming smile and apologies for not having been a better correspondent over the past year.

"No need to apologise, my dear." Leslie's mother kissed Marianne's cheek. "It's all too easy to lose touch, no matter how strong one's determination not to do so. You're here now."

She ushered her guests into the drawing room, where the table was already laid, Leslie following in their wake, having done barely more than smile and say hello. He couldn't shake off his unease, a highly illogical feeling of impending disaster that had grown over the previous few hours. They went through the innocent rituals of pouring the tea, sharing the cakes, and engaging in chitchat about the doings of Marianne's parents, but that didn't help his apprehension subside. Everything felt like one of those scenes in a film where the tension in the music ramped up and the action led into a terrible event.

Seeing Marianne had roused so many memories, some of which would have been better left dormant. If she raised the matter of why Leslie no longer kept in touch with Patrick, how could he convincingly explain why that had happened, why the two inseparable friends no longer even exchanged a card at

Christmas? Would she accept the explanation he had given his mother, the simple attrition of a relationship, caused by time and the separation of war? Come to that, had his mother accepted it?

Some adept steering of the conversation by Leslie's mother in the direction of Geraldine brought a moment of respite and elucidated plenty of information about the woman. She and Marianne had been at school together, although not great pals in those days, being in different years. The friendship had developed since Marianne had moved to Winchester, where they'd unexpectedly found themselves close neighbours. To his mother's possible disappointment—and not a little to Leslie's surprise—Geraldine turned out to be engaged to a chap called Bobby who'd flown Lancasters during the war and was now in the final stages of qualifying as a doctor. That would take another potential candidate off the maternal list of eligible young women if Mother hadn't given up all hope on that front. It also forced Leslie into reassessing his assumptions about the relationship between the two guests.

During the war, his mother had stopped dropping hints about what a lovely couple Marianne and Leslie would make. The remark she'd made earlier about the girl not rising yet to a male lure had suggested that his mother had reached the same conclusion as he had: that Marianne preferred the company of her own sex. Marianne and Geraldine walking arm in arm on the common had led Leslie to believe they might be romantically entwined, which was clearly the wrong conclusion, because the story about the Lancaster pilot appeared to be genuine. Geraldine being simply a friend didn't make the conclusion about Marianne incorrect, although her single status might simply be a matter of her not having met the man for whom she would give up her independence.

Once Geraldine's fiancé's war record had been properly discussed, alongside that of both women—and as much of Leslie's wartime service as could be covered under the umbrella of "administrative duties"—matters inevitably turned where Leslie had dreaded.

It was Geraldine who first mentioned Patrick. "Didn't your brother work with animals during the war? I can't remember if you said he was fully qualified by then."

"He was by the end of the conflict, when he got himself involved in the army," Marianne replied. "I hadn't credited quite how many dogs were needed for service in Egypt."

"It was something to do with controlling looters out there." Leslie immediately regretted his answer, because how could he dare admit that he'd been taking a keen interest, albeit from a distance, in what Patrick had been up to? "What was he involved in before he went out to Africa? I know he'd been putting the final touches to his studies and cutting his teeth in proper vet work at the start of the war, although I can't imagine him being content with that when the country was in such peril."

Marianne shot an unreadable glance in Leslie's direction. "He was initially doing some stints as an air raid warden, as and when his work allowed. Burning the candles at both ends, although that was nothing new to him, as you well know." A rather waspish remark, although the others appeared to take it as a jest. "He occasionally got himself involved in training servicemen, although what he did with them was on a need-to-know basis and we as his family were told we didn't need to know much. All he said was that somebody had spotted him at work and decided he'd be usefully employed in preparing soldiers for combat or some such thing. So animals were involved, possibly in training soldiers to fend off dog attacks or avoid the beasts entirely. I could, mind you, be getting the wrong end of the stick."

"If you've misunderstood, then I've done the same. Patrick told me something broadly similar." Back when they'd still been talking to each other. "I realise his account might have been subterfuge, to cover for activities he was sworn never to mention, not even to a—" He'd nearly said *lover*. "—lifelong friend, although it sounded like the truth."

"Then it probably was," Marianne observed. "Patrick was never a very efficient liar."

Which was another reason that Leslie hadn't dared asked his questions. Patrick wore his emotions on his face and had struggled to hide how much he hated Fergus Jackson. The latter must have realised the fact, unless he'd been completely oblivious. Which was entirely possible, since Fergus had seemed to count other people's feelings as far less important than his own needs and desires.

"I've heard that Patrick used to mix with rather a wild crowd, before the war. Oh, yes, please." Geraldine held out her cup in response to her hostess's offer of a top up.

Leslie's mother nodded. "Leslie rubbed shoulders with them too. A little clique of what we'd have called 'fast' chaps in my younger days. Mind you, having seen what some of the local airmen got up to during the war, such behaviour might appear to have become the norm. Although there's probably more excuse for it in time of battle, I'd say."

"Indeed. I wouldn't blame anyone for eating, drinking, and making merry if your next sortie could be your last." Marianne's tones effectively put a stop to any argument. Given Mrs. Cadmore's apparently open-minded attitude, it had to be Geraldine she was protecting: maybe the Lancaster pilot had been rather profligate with his wild oats and his fiancée was either upset at or unaware of the fact. "Perhaps Patrick's friends could see which way the wind was blowing and guessed we were due for another conflict, one they might not make it through."

"If they did, it wasn't consciously. There's also a world of difference between making merry on your own account and dragging others along for the ride." Leslie really didn't want to discuss the matter or the people involved, but it would appear strange if he didn't chip in at all. Leading younger men astray had been a Fergus speciality, whether they wanted to be led or not, and that debauching of innocents had particularly riled Patrick in the same way that cruelty to animals had.

Marianne snorted. "Don't get me started on that or we'll be here all evening."

Leslie took a drink of tea. His instinct had been right about disaster on the horizon, and this conversation had sailed into perilous waters. "That 'clique' was made up of hedonists rather than fatalists, I'd have said. And I wouldn't describe them as either

Patrick's crowd nor mine. They were too wild by half for us to be anything other than on the fringe."

The Retainers, they'd called themselves, from the London club they had all belonged to, whose motto broadly translated to, *Retain the aim less noble.* Leslie had always wondered why such an organisation, with its origins supposedly in philanthropy, should have such an immoral motto on its coat of arms. An act of whimsy on the part of its founders back in the time of Pudding George? Or had it been a completely different organisation then, hiding a milder version of the Hellfire Club beneath the altruistic exterior?

"Well, whatever they were, two of them didn't make it through the war." Marianne sipped her tea. "One was killed on a bombing raid and another on the convoys."

"Only two?" Leslie's mother frowned. "I'm sure there was another chap in that group who also died in service."

That would have been Fergus, whom Marianne would surely have known about, so why hadn't she included him? Could it be that she bore the same suspicions and reluctance to air them as Leslie?

"I met them all together on one occasion," Mrs. Cadmore continued, "at that lovely party your parents gave for Patrick's twenty-first birthday. I'd heard about them in advance, but at the time I couldn't see what all the fuss could possibly be about. Why those young men had gained such a reputation, I mean. They seemed quite delightful, to me."

Marianne gave the nearest thing to a snort suitable for polite company. "That's because they'd all been warned by Patrick to be on their best behaviour. You should have been there, Geraldine, to see the performance. Quite as convincing as anything you'd see in Drury Lane. They were all absolutely charming, especially to the maturer females. Begging your pardon, Mrs. Cadmore."

"No offence taken." Leslie's mother inclined her head. "Charming *and* dashing, any hostess would have been pleased to welcome them."

Leslie remembered her making a similar observation the day after the party. How the men concerned had paid such polite attention to her and to Mrs. Sibley; possibly more than they'd paid to Marianne and her friends. It had certainly been a lovely evening and the clique had been an ornament to it, in complete contrast to how they normally were. Fast indeed—much faster than his mother could have imagined—and wild, but all of them ready to behave themselves if the occasion demanded.

"It all sounds a bit mysterious, how a group of nice young men could be regarded as such rogues," Geraldine said.

Marianne snorted. "If you'd met them, you'd have realised. The five horsemen of the apocalypse, Patrick sometimes called them."

Leslie wouldn't have gone that far. They couldn't have been the first group of men in various stages of their twenties who'd been handsome, debonair, and overfond of the pleasures of the flesh. Especially those who indulged at places like their private club in London and the Turkish baths nearby.

"Five?" Geraldine's brow puckered. "You've only mentioned two and I don't think you told me their names?"

"Donald and Dougal were the pair who bought it during the war," Marianne said.

Mrs. Cadmore took up the account, with a note of pride. "Another was Eric Hazletine. He appears to have changed his ways since those madcap times. I heard he's tipped for parliament at the next election."

Eric had always spoken about wanting to enter politics, although nobody had thought him serious. Nowadays, he was making a positive campaigning point out of turning his back on his wild-oat-sowing past. A charming wife, his wartime heroics, and a semi-miraculous recovery from meningitis in 1945 involving the British wonder drug penicillin weren't hurting his prospects at the ballot box, either.

"That's still only three." Geraldine counted them off on her fingers.

"James Lyth," Marianne said. James—who was said now to be living in Wales—had been easy to get on with. "The fifth was Fergus Jackson. I wouldn't say that's a case of saving the best for last. Not a popular chap, Fergus. He seemed to have a talent for rubbing folk up the wrong way."

"Popular with the ladies?" Geraldine asked.

Marianne shook her head. "He didn't have much time for them. Now, Eric and Dougal always had girls in tow."

Dougal had not long been engaged to a WAAF at the time he'd been killed while protecting a squadron of bombers in 1944, and Eric now had a child on the way. Patrick had been certain that neither man's interest in women had been the kind of charade that men of their type typically indulged in. Dougal had probably been itching to "taste of the fruit of all the trees in the garden of world" when he'd been hanging around the Turkish baths and would subsequently have settled down to be a model husband if he'd had the chance. As Eric now seemed to be, despite having slept with any and everyone in his wild days. It was a surprise the meningitis that had threatened his life hadn't been syphilis.

"Leslie, your mother asked you a question." Marianne's voice—loud and exasperated—cut into his thoughts.

"I'm sorry, I was miles away." Leslie smiled sheepishly. "Thinking what a change of character Eric Hazletine appears to have undergone. Pillar of the community."

"Collector of lame ducks, as well. Quite literally in the case of his secretary, who's halt in one leg." Marianne raised an eyebrow.

"That seems rather harsh, Marianne," Leslie's mother said.

"Sorry. I was being waspish. Thinking that the secretary's injury having been acquired during war service doesn't hurt Eric's image, either. Nor do his independent means, which allow him to get a head start on his rivals. You'd better ask your question again, Mrs. Cadmore."

"Please. I promise this time I'll listen properly." Leslie adopted his most alert expression.

"I was asking you if you ever heard from James. I remember him being most attentive and fetching me a plate of food from the buffet at that party, because there was rather a crush in there and he said he'd have sharper elbows to fight his way through the crowd. As we ate, we chatted away about his studies at Oxford.

Theology, perhaps." Her brow wrinkled in thought. "Or Classics. Something rather surprising."

"I believe it *was* theology, with a view of going in for ordination, although that didn't happen. Last I heard, he was working as an accountant, somewhere in Wales. I think the war rather changed his view on joining the church." Leslie hurried on, since he'd inadvertently touched on matters he didn't want to explore. "I suspect it was for the best. He was too soft-hearted to be a clergyman."

"Isn't that the very quality one needs?" Geraldine asked.

"Leslie's right," Marianne said. "Poor James would have been ridden over roughshod by the average PCC member, let alone every scrounger and stray dog who turned up at the vicarage door. Like that tramp who came begging round here. If the vicar had been here at the time, no doubt he'd have welcomed him into the vicarage with a fatted calf."

"What tramp?" asked Geraldine.

"Our seven-days wonder." Marianne rolled her eyes. "Some vagrant who died of exposure in the churchyard."

"Hardly a seven days wonder," Leslie's mother said, in clipped tones. "I know it was years ago, but some of us still remember. And feel guilty because we didn't show him proper Christian charity when perhaps we should have done."

Both Leslie's parents had been upset at the man's death, wondering if they should have given him at the least a bowl of soup or an old blanket when he'd come knocking at the door. It had been a higher level of remorse than most folk had shown.

"I hope James is happy." Mrs. Cadmore, having markedly changed the subject, laid down her cup. "I felt he was rather a sad chap. A little boy lost."

That was remarkably perceptive, given that she'd only met James that one evening and couldn't have spoken to him for more than a quarter of an hour. How much else had she deduced about the group from that party and any references that had been made about them beforehand or afterwards? Could any woman of her respectable background have spotted their sexual preferences—for example the fact that Eric would have had it off with anyone who offered or that James had a penchant for older men? One of whom was said to have drawn him to the principality?

"I've not heard anything to the contrary. About whether he's content." Not an informative answer, but the truth. For the moment, that was all he was willing to say. That whole part of his existence seemed a lifetime ago, if still horribly painful in parts.

"And what about the other chap who didn't make it through the war?" Geraldine evidently wanted to tie up every loose end of the conversation. "That had to be Fergus. What happened to him?"

Leslie glanced at Marianne. She should have been able to supply that answer, but she was keeping her eyes fixed on her teacup. Was she waiting, forcing Leslie to respond, or was that reading too much into what might simply be a moment of forgetfulness? Perhaps Patrick had never discussed the matter with her, as he'd avoided discussing it with Leslie.

"Such a shame about Fergus. He struck me as a jaunty sort, Geraldine, and the handsomest of the bunch, as far as I was concerned." Leslie's mother smiled: Had she also been taken in by the Apollo-like face, the apparently beautiful manners and the charming repartee or had her astute perception come into play? "Reminded me of what one of the old-fashioned knights might have been like. Marianne, your mother told me he'd joined the RAF, but I don't think that's right. Leslie?"

"No. I have a feeling that was a story people put about to cover up the fact he was involved with something hush-hush. Probably being dropped behind enemy lines. He was the first of them to give up his life in the service of his country." Whatever else could be said about Fergus, nobody could have accused him of lacking courage and a desire to serve his king. Indeed, none of the five men could have had those charges brought against them.

"Aha. I see. Yes." Mrs. Cadmore nodded brightly. While she wasn't entirely aware of how Leslie had served his country, she often dropped hints that it had involved a similar amount of subterfuge. Although her present air suggested she was feigning ignorance about Fergus. "But I was told on good authority that he was killed in action. I think your mother mentioned that too, Marianne. She always wanted to keep up with the news about her children's friends."

"Mother has always had particularly efficient ways of keeping tabs on things," Marianne said drily.

"How did this chap Fergus die?" Geraldine asked. "Was it out in France? I ask because I remember hearing stories about the Great War and families not getting their loved one's body home because it had been crushed in the mud and never found. My aunt Maud went out to Flanders to lay flowers on as near the spot of Uncle Fred's death as she could find. It beggars belief such things could be happening again."

The corollary to the question allowed a little longer for those who needed it to compose themselves, although Leslie had anticipated the story of Fergus's death arising from the first moment the group of five had been mentioned. He, too, could play the pleading-ignorance game. "The Jacksons certainly got him back. He was killed over here, in a horrible training accident, I was told, although I could be wrong. Your mother hasn't mentioned it, Marianne?"

"If she knows anything further concerning what happened, over and above the official story, she's not shared it with me." Marianne shrugged. "I doubt anyone knows except those directly involved."

Delicately put, if she was referring to Patrick. The whole incident had been shrouded in secrecy for all sorts of reasons, not least because of the effect on morale of such incidents, yet Leslie would have put money on Marianne having similar suspicions to his. Or at the very least wondering how much her brother was involved, because surely they both knew how close he'd been to the death. And if she had understood her twin as Leslie had always suspected she did, she'd have understood that he had the motive to kill Fergus.

Patrick hadn't been alone in that. Fergus was said to have left a string of chaps with a sour taste in their mouths, stretching back to before he'd reached manhood. He'd always had the sexual morals of an alley cat, not fussed about who or where or when, so long as the other party was male and the chances of them being caught at it were minimal. Sometimes not even the latter. The thrill of danger had clearly appealed.

One or two of the men Fergus had coupled with hadn't been as free and easy as him—Dougal had once mentioned he'd had chaps crying on *his* broad shoulders because they'd made the mistake of falling too hard for the lothario or had let him draw them into activities they'd later regretted. Had those men been upset enough about it to kill Fergus if they'd had the opportunity? Possibly, despite that seeming a bit far-fetched as a motive for murder. Although Fergus had gone through so many lovers, he'd no doubt have encountered some for whom a logical motive wouldn't have mattered, jealousy or rage being enough.

Although the problem remained—how could said lover have engineered being present in that place on that day?

If Fergus had known how many people held a grudge against him, would it have made much difference to his behaviour on that training course or indeed anywhere? He was brave, he was said to have believed he was leading a charmed life, and he must have doubted that anyone could do something to him in such a public setting. Yet died he had. And Leslie knew that Patrick had been present when it happened.

"A training accident? How ghastly," Geraldine said. "My Bobby reckons that's a necessary risk of war, people being killed in training exercises, although he also reckons a lot of it gets covered up. It would unsettle the public and add to the worry of wives and sweethearts who'd have had quite enough to fret over. Probably that's what happened with this Fergus chap. All covered up for the noblest of reasons."

"Not quite the same with self-inflicted wounds, unless the soldier involved had a lot of influence. Quite a thing during the Great War, I understand, although perhaps less so in the one just gone." His mother's statement generated a startled look from her guests and a thoughtful one from Leslie. He'd need to follow that up once their guests had gone.

Geraldine shivered. "That's ghastly. Would people really do that?"

"They would, especially if they'd been conscripted and didn't want to be there." Marianne launched into an account about a friend of a friend of her father's, who'd come home from somewhere near Mametz Wood with an injury that most people who knew him suspected hadn't been caused by any of the Kaiser's men. From there, the topic of conversation moved to Bobby's father, who apparently had rows of medals from where he'd seen service at Ypres.

"He was a boxing champion too," Geraldine said.

"I remember your father teaching us three the rudiments of boxing. Wasn't he a capable featherweight at university?" Marianne asked, then flushed fiercely.

"He'd boxed a bit when younger. Came in useful when fighting off his rivals for Mother's affection," Leslie said with feigned lightness, aware of the pain on his mother's face at the mention of her husband. He'd been about to make a joke about an old photograph in which his father sported a black eye but decided against it.

Before Geraldine, who seemed genuinely unaware of the awkwardness in the air, could reply, Marianne took a theatrically alarmed glance at her watch and said, "Lord, is that the time? We need to go, Geraldine."

"Oh, that's a shame." Geraldine rose and offered her hand to first her hostess and then Leslie. "Thank you so much for having us. It's been a delight to meet you, Mrs. Cadmore."

"My pleasure. Marianne, you must let us know when you're here again and I'll invite you over." Whether his mother meant both women or only the one, Leslie couldn't say: she was too polite to have made anything obvious.

"I will do. I promise." Marianne gave her hostess half a hug and an affectionate peck on the cheek, although *he* only got a handshake and a smile. "And don't you be such a stranger, Leslie."

"I'll try not to be." He escorted the women to the door, watching them go with not quite as much relief as he'd expected. The moment of peril had come and passed, although cans of worms had been opened and memories stirred. Some folk had observed the passage of wartime by the usual procession of months and years, others had seen it less in terms of the calendar than in major events—disastrous and triumphant. The retreat from Dunkirk, sinking the Tirpitz. For Leslie, the record of occurrences had been more personal, focussing on 1942. Fergus's death, his father's departure, the rift with Patrick—all in all, it had been the year from hell.

Once he and his mother were alone again, Leslie felt he'd two new questions to add to his list of those needing asking. Perhaps if he tackled them now, when his mother seemed eager to talk, the answers might help him when the time came to attack one of the others. He'd still have to tread warily, though, and summon up his courage. "Mother, two things. Earlier, was that a pointed reference you made to self-inflicted wounds? And how much *do* you know about Fergus Jackson's death, because I don't believe you're as uninformed as you make out."

"Funny you should ask that, because I've been trying to decide whether to mention it." His mother nodded towards the sideboard. "Pour us a sherry, there's a good lad, and we'll talk."

Once they were settled with their drinks and with Max—who'd been confined to his kennel while they had guests—sitting sweetly at Leslie's feet, she said, "Fergus. I thought of him the other day, but I didn't want to upset you by raising him out of the blue. That's why I asked Marianne over to tea and then tried to bring the conversation round to him as subtly as I could. I'm not sure how well I did."

"You played a blinder. And Marianne played a straight bat. What made you believe I'd be upset talking about him? I never liked the man."

"Oh, I know that, dear. I'm not so oblivious as you might think." She took a sip of her drink. "It was the manner in which he died. That's what brought him to mind, because a couple of months ago we had someone in the village trip and fall on a knife in their home, although in this case the cut wasn't so deep they couldn't be saved. It brought that terrible time back to mind. You won't have known, but when I heard Fergus had been killed my heart bled. For you and Patrick, rather than *him*, I'm ashamed to say. How terrible to have that happen to a friend."

"It was certainly a shock to us all."

His mother nodded. "And then to discover later there'd been all sorts of rumours flying around, saying that he'd somehow managed to contrive his own death. That's what I wanted to discuss with you, because I can't believe he'd have done such a thing. That group of young men were too fond of life."

Leslie couldn't have felt more stunned if Patrick had walked into the room at that instant and kissed him. "Where on earth did you hear that he'd killed himself? You're right, of course, that rumours bred like flies after his death, but I didn't realise they'd become common currency."

"They hadn't. The River Test gossiping network didn't pick that story up on their radar. James came to see me one day and told me all about it."

Now the level of shock was almost equivalent to Patrick having walked in unannounced and given him a jolly good rogering. "James? We exchange cards every Christmas and he's never mentioned seeing you. When was this? And how did he know where you lived?"

"Patrick told him, naturally. They'd both got a spot of leave and met at that inn on the river that he always liked, The Gadfly, after which James called in here. To pay his respects to me, he said, it being not long after your father went into his cloistered life, although James was too polite to mention that. I suspect he really wanted news of you, perhaps to pass on to Patrick." She took another sip of sherry. "Anyway, I talked about the twins' birthday party when we'd all met and how sad it was that some his pals hadn't made it through the war. He said it *was* sad for two of them, although in Fergus's case he couldn't say it was any great loss. I was rather surprised at him making that harsh a remark, James coming across as such a well-mannered young man."

The sort of man that many a mother would have approved of if he'd been dating her daughter. Too easily led, though, and perhaps too honest. "Harsh perhaps, yet completely correct. Fergus Jackson may have been a good soldier, but he wasn't a nice man and I can name several people who would have been pleased to see him gone."

Leslie's mother gave him a shrewd maternal stare. "I won't ask you to elaborate on that if you don't want to, although it adds weight to my belief that he didn't contrive to get himself killed."

How long had she been mulling this over? "Why have you never asked me about Fergus before? It's been so long."

"I was too scared of what I might hear. Mr. Sibley said that Patrick had been present when the accident happened, although I don't think he was supposed to have told me, so I was worried that if we spoke about it, you might tell me some awful tale. About how Fergus had cut his own throat or something equally horrible. But I've decided to stop being a coward."

"Oh, Mother. It's not as bad as all that." Leslie went over to perch on the arm of her chair. Now he knew where he got his indecision from. How long had she turned the accident over in her mind, thinking only the worst? "I'm happy to elaborate about Fergus and his history, up to a point. He may have had a charming way with him, but plenty of people didn't like him. For a start, I can tell you he had a habit of trying to get people to invest in dubious schemes. Not that *he* thought them in any way doubtful, because he had money to burn and not much of a head for business, which is a dangerous combination. Some people, however, lost a lot of money they couldn't afford to lose."

"He swore it was a gilt-edged investment." Leslie could hear the mutual acquaintance's voice as loud as day, despite not recalling his name. *"I've sunk a packet in it. I could murder the swine."*

Fergus's gall had extended to an attempt at inveigling both Leslie's and Patrick's fathers into making risky investments, but he had been given short shrift by Mr. Cadmore, who'd also persuaded Mr. Sibley not to take the bait. Leslie's father had always been good at convincing others to do the right thing.

"I heard a similar story from your father. About the schemes, not the losses. Is that all he did?"

"Not quite. He left a string of broken hearts in his wake and not all of the owners were happy to be cast aside." Leslie took a deep breath, other voices sounding in his head, although not discarded lovers this time. A friend of Patrick's retching over a toilet basin. *"I should have told the bastard no but he wouldn't have taken it for an answer. God knows what he persuaded me to try."*

Patrick's bitter response. *"He'll try it on the wrong person one day and end up with a dead body on his hands."*

"There's other stuff, as you can imagine. Drink. Drugs. Mixed himself up in every vice under the sun and took other folk with him."

"I see. James told me he felt the simplest explanation for Fergus's death—the accident—was the right one, rather than the bizarre theories people were muddying the waters with, but perhaps he has too trusting a nature."

Too trusting where Fergus had been concerned, certainly. Leslie patted his mother's shoulder. "He might have a point. But you still haven't told me why you should have thought I'd have got upset discussing how Fergus died."

"Because of Patrick being involved in running the training course. I assumed he'd have told you all about what happened." Her voice faltered. "I'm sorry if I've spoken out of turn."

"You haven't. You should know that Patrick refused to talk about the matter. I first knew about it from Eric Hazletine. He'd heard somehow, I guess from a pal who was involved in what passed for an enquiry, so the news was third-hand by the time it got to me. It sounds like you're as well informed as I am." That wasn't entirely true, but it would have to suffice. Especially since a remark his mother had made earlier suddenly registered. "And what exactly did you mean about the fact that Fergus was unpopular added weight to your belief that he didn't suffer a self-inflicted wound?"

She exhaled slowly, clearly gathering her words. "Ever since James visited, I've been wondering whether there was anything to Fergus's death other than accident or suicide. Not that he said anything outright, and I'm probably just being a silly old woman who spends too much time on her own mulling things over, but the whole story strikes me as odd."

"You're neither silly nor old, both of which you know very well. And you're not alone in speculating about Fergus's death because I've been thinking much the same. If there's something James said that's relevant, the most subtle of hints for example, I'd be grateful to know what it was."

"Get us both another sherry, then, because *I'd* be grateful to have the chance to talk about it." She smiled wanly.

Leslie was halfway across the room heading for the decanter when the telephone rang.

"Could you answer that, dear? I'm nice and settled."

"Will do." Leslie went into the hallway, picked up the receiver, and gave a cheery, "Hello?"

"It's Marianne." Those tones had been unmistakable.

"Long time no speak." The girls couldn't have been long in her home after walking from Larkspur House. Had they forgotten something?

"You daft thing. I suppose you're wondering why I'm calling."

"Naturally. I'm guessing you left your hockey stick behind, like you did when you were thirteen?"

"Stop being silly. I've got to get back to Winchester tonight, and I don't have time to muck around. Are you free tomorrow and could you get yourself into London?"

"In the evening, yes. Why?"

"Patrick rang, five minutes ago. He'd like to see you."

Fortunately, there was a chair beside the telephone table, because Leslie's legs had caved.

"Hello?"

"Sorry. The line went crackly. Patrick. Where did he suggest we meet and when?" With only half a mind on the job, Leslie took up the paper and pencil his mother kept by the telephone for taking messages, to make a note of the location and time Patrick had suggested. Seven o'clock at a well-known hotel where they could probably find a quiet table at the bar. He asked Marianne to repeat the details—using the bad-line excuse again—afraid he might have got it wrong given the state he was in. "Thank you for this. Can you let him know I can make it?"

"I'm not your secretary. Or his." Marianne laughed. "We left it that if he didn't hear from me, then you'd be there. Make sure you don't forget."

Or get cold feet.

After he'd put the telephone down, Leslie sat staring at the piece of paper, before folding it and carefully putting it into his pocket. If he'd been a superstitious man, he might have wondered if his earlier sense of impending doom hadn't concerned Marianne's visit. Whether it had been a premonition of the two shocks he'd received in the space of the last half an hour.

Still disturbed from raising the subject of Fergus's death, it seemed as though he'd be forced to discuss it yet again in the space of a few days.

CHAPTER THREE

"Who was it, dear?" His mother's voice snapped Leslie out of his thoughts.

"Marianne." How long had he been sitting here since putting down the phone? He rose and returned to the sitting room.

"Not bad news, I hope."

Leslie must have appeared more shaken than he'd realised. "I *hope* it doesn't turn out to be. Classic case of talk of the devil and all that. She was saying that Patrick had rung her to say he wants to see me. I have no idea what it's about."

"I could never read Patrick's mind so I won't even attempt a guess." She raised her hand. "Just remember that life's too short to go leaving things unsaid."

Leslie retook his place on the chair arm, a position that gave him the advantage of not having to face his mother. "You're being remarkably candid this afternoon."

"You can blame Marianne for that. Or maybe praise her, because it might be no bad thing in the long run. Seeing her again brought so much back to mind. You and the twins here, playing. Your father teaching the three of you to putt on the lawn." His mother sniffed back a tear.

"Don't get upset." Leslie put his arm around her shoulders.

"I'm fine, dear. It's not your father I'm getting teary about, honestly. Only you three youngsters and the many like you who never came home." She dabbed her eyes with her handkerchief and blew her nose. "Now, before we get back to discussing Fergus, that second sherry won't pour itself."

"Quite right it won't. You should put me on a fizzer for dereliction of duty." Leslie went and topped up both glasses, then settled himself in the seat opposite hers. "I'll tell you what I know and you can do the same. It's not much, I'm afraid, and some of what I've found out I probably shouldn't pass on."

"Anything at all would likely help me see things clearer."

Leslie steadied himself. "Fergus was among a group of men being taught a range of self-defence methods. Not the usual sort but ones you might have to employ if you were behind enemy lines. That included dealing with dogs, which is why Patrick was there. He told me all this."

"Ah." She nodded. "James said he thought it was a course about *using* dogs, but that makes more sense."

"Yes. I can't see Fergus as a dog-handler. Towser hated him, and I suspect that was mutual." The dog had always been an astute judge of character, unlike Max, who wanted to be everyone's friend. Had James got the wrong end of the stick about the training, or had Patrick told one of them an outright lie? If so, he'd told Marianne the same one. "The official story, apparently, is that Fergus stumbled over, fell on the knife he was about to use, and it cut into an artery. One of those freak accidents where if he'd fallen an inch or two to right or left, there'd have been no particular harm done, but because it stabbed him where it did, he lost a vast amount of blood and died within minutes. Unlike the lucky person you mentioned earlier. Fergus wasn't supposed to be carrying a knife, though—let alone using one—which raised questions about the way the training was being run. Security and all that."

"That could explain the rumours about his injury being self-inflicted, I suppose, if he was breaking the rules in having such a weapon on him. It could also be why the details might have been covered up, especially if he was well regarded or had friends in high places. Did he, by the way?"

"I believe so." Leslie held something stronger than a belief: he was aware of a lover in a particularly influential position who might not have wanted Fergus's death—or character—gone into too deeply. Although how said lover could have exerted his influence from a desk in the Admiralty would take some explaining. "Whether they produced an official report to ensure lessons were learned for the future, I couldn't say, but Patrick was livid and wanted to make sure such an incident was never repeated. Although I doubt he was as much worried about the welfare of the soldiers as that of the dogs. Don't ever say that to him, by the way."

Max raised his head, giving Leslie a dirty look.

"Perhaps you shouldn't mention it to Max, either, dear. You've offended him."

"He's only cross at being woken—usually he's oblivious to anything that doesn't concern food or being a menace to me." He patted the dog, who murmured contentedly and settled back down. "I'd better go and wash my hands. They're all doggy."

The activity would give him time to compose himself, because his last conversation with Patrick kept playing in his head. It had started with Patrick offering his condolences about Mr. Cadmore and then Leslie—who'd been a mass of confused emotions at the time—had stupidly remarked that his father might as well have died as far as he was concerned. That had provoked an unexpected burst of temper from Patrick, after which the discussion had escalated into a blazing, and ruinous, argument. The strength of Patrick's reaction still shocked Leslie. What else had been going on to make him so angry?

Once he felt ready to face his mother again, Leslie entered the room with a breezy, "Anyway, I have no doubt that Fergus didn't hurt himself deliberately. I *do* have doubts about it being an accident, though. No evidence, only suspicions."

Mrs. Cadmore, sherry still in hand, nodded slowly. "It seems so wicked to say I'm pleased to hear that, but I am, because I believed I was the only one who'd thought such things."

"And why did you harbour suspicions? I mean, my misgivings were because I knew what Fergus was really like and how many people held a grudge against him. People who'd been taken in by his dubious investments, for a start." Let alone the others he could list now.

"It was a remark James made when he called here. He'd seen Fergus a fortnight before he died. They were both unwell after that meeting, apparently, which I took as a euphemism for having a roaring hangover after drinking too much." She eyed her own glass, then took a large swig.

"That's quite possible. An excess of whisky was one of Fergus's innumerable vices. I shan't go into detail on the others."

"I'm grateful for that. Anyway, after they met, because of something Fergus said, James wondered if he'd been having a premonition of his death. He told James that if he heard stories of him falling on his sword, they'd probably be exaggerated. He'd asked Fergus what he meant, because it sounded so odd, but he'd refused to elaborate. Now, to me, that sounds less like a ridiculous premonition than a reference to an actual threat, only James was too nice to see it that way."

"Falling on his sword." Leslie shivered. Maybe he was reading too much into everything, but that sounded horribly like the threat Patrick had made back in 1939, on a day he'd become too exasperated at Fergus's latest escapades. This one had involved some poor dupe called Frank who'd been so high he'd wandered through a gate at a level crossing and had nearly been hit by the down express.

Leslie remembered how close a call it had been. Him and Patrick rushing to catch up with Frank, scared they'd be too late.

"Grab him, Leslie!"

"He'll be fine." Fergus's slurred voice sounded behind them. *"Drunks never come to harm and neither do junkies."*

"Shut the hell up." Leslie tugged Frank's left arm while Patrick yanked the right. The man was inches from the rails, intent on heading straight across them, oblivious of the speeding train that had appeared further up the line.

Afterwards, Patrick, still shaking, seized Fergus by the lapels and pushed him up against a tree. "You'll go too far one day, and somebody will run you through with a bayonet. It might turn out to be me, so help me God."

That warning, and its resemblance to the way Fergus had died, was one of the slender threads by which Leslie's suspicions about his ex-lover's involvement hung. Yet Patrick hadn't been the only one: Donald—or was it Dougal, or both?—had said he'd swing for Fergus, although everyone present at the time had taken that as being a typically casual remark that people made with no intention of following through. Dougal, in particular, had been a man of great probity, probably more suited to parliament than Eric, and unlikely to have attacked the man.

"It wouldn't surprise me at all if somebody had threatened to stab him," Leslie remarked to his mother, as lightly as he could. "If we were talking about who might lose their temper with him and strike the man in the heat of the moment, I could write you a list. But if we're talking about killing in cold blood, which is what we're speculating this is, then that list would get narrowed down."

"And then narrowed down further still by who could have been there at the time?"

"You are quite scarily perceptive. Yes, I think you can eliminate Marianne, for example, or anyone else who would have stuck out like a sore thumb if they'd been hanging around where the course was taking place, unless they'd got someone to do the deed on their behalf."

"Is Marianne one of those who'd have been pleased to see Fergus dead, or did you simply pluck her name out of the air?" Perhaps there was something magical about his mother's sherry that was prompting such candour and insight.

"A bit of both. She had no more affection for Fergus than I did. Didn't trust him and got almost as angry as her brother at the way he led some of the others astray." Not just in terms of sex or booze. Patrick had told her about Fergus taking drugs, either for sheer pleasure or to give him the ability to party until dawn broke. Leslie gave a rueful smile.

"Is 'no more affection' a polite way of saying you both hated him? I saw how you all interacted at the twins' birthday party, and Marianne isn't always good at hiding her feelings."

Then Leslie's mother must have noted Patrick's barely disguised hostility. The three friends had wondered if Fergus—or any of them—had been high on the occasion of Patrick's birthday bash. He could imagine the man using an artificial stimulant to get him through an event that risked boredom. Fergus had appeared unnaturally bright and breezy that evening.

"You miss very little, Mother. Although I honestly can't see her in the role of femme fatale, and if she was, she wouldn't have acted underhand. If she wanted to deal with anyone, she'd do so in a direct manner. I can remember her belting some chap who'd made rather too forceful a pass."

"Good for her. I hate women letting themselves be trodden on." Which was an odd thing to say, considering how little fight his mother had appeared to muster when Mr. Cadmore had upped sticks. At the time, Leslie had considered that pragmatic, her not wanting to get into a fight she was likely to lose, but perhaps she'd not been entirely unhappy to see him go. Leslie would have to add that to the list of questions he was reluctant to ask.

"I wish women in general agreed with you."

"Most men wouldn't like it, dear. Now, do we know the exact circumstances around this tumble Fergus took on his knife? I must sound like Miss Marple in the Christie books, but it's relevant, isn't it?"

"For me it's the crux of the whole matter. If what I've heard is correct, it didn't take place in a melee where it would be simple to push a man over—or stumble into him 'accidentally on purpose' and nobody be any the wiser. Fergus was on his own, on the edge of the woods, trying to avoid the tracker dogs. Laying a false trail with aniseed or whatever people do in the circumstances."

"Oh." His mother's eyes widened. "But if he was on his own, doesn't that mean he could easily have been attacked? By someone who lay in wait for him?"

"Ah, there's the rub. There was a reliable witness stating that Fergus simply tripped over and that nobody else was close by enough to have engineered it happening."

"Reliable or not, the witness could have it wrong. People do. People also tell lies."

Leslie ran his hand through his hair. "That's what's so damned difficult, Mother. Patrick was the witness, according to Eric. And *he* was in plain sight of another person all the time this was happening. So, if it *was* murder, irrespective of who had a motive or managed to get themselves into those woods, how did they do it?"

Unless it was Patrick himself who'd done the deed and the person who vouched for him was collaborating on covering up his guilt. Or there'd been a third party and Patrick had covered for them. Leslie hoped his mother wouldn't want to discuss either of those ideas.

A knock on the door, heralding the arrival of the housekeeper to discuss when they wanted their cold meat and salad brought the conversation to a timely end.

Given the form his mother was showing, it might be too dangerous for them to delve too deeply into Patrick's role in Fergus's death. After all, what Leslie knew and his mother couldn't fully appreciate was how much Patrick had hated Fergus and why.

Miss Marple would surely have appreciated the combination of motive and opportunity Patrick had possessed. Had he acted on it?

CHAPTER FOUR

I t was a long twenty-six hours between Marianne telephoning and Leslie meeting her brother.

After the phone call, Leslie had dined with his mother—refusing to discuss Fergus's death any further that evening as he needed some thinking time—then bundled Max into his car and set off for his little house in the western suburbs of London. He'd gone to sleep minutes after his head hit the pillow but had woken at two in the morning with thoughts whirring. Did his mother suspect what Leslie and Patrick had meant to each other? Why had Patrick decided he wanted to talk to him now?

"If I see you this side of hell freezing over, it'll be too soon."

Patrick had said that at Waterloo station, before turning on his heels and stomping away. Like the idle threat of swinging for someone that Leslie had remembered, those words might have signified nothing, but it had been clear that Patrick had meant every one of them. Yet something profound must have happened recently that had made him want to talk.

Waterloo. If Leslie had been asked what had happened straight after the event, he could barely have answered. They'd met there to go for a drink, both being in town, but it had turned out to be a dreadful mistake. They'd both been tense, Leslie because of his worries about his father, whose character had appeared changed, and his doubts concerning Fergus's demise. Patrick, presumably, had also been anxious over events surrounding that death. As with dry tinder, the smallest spark had been bound to cause a blaze.

Are you going to be able to have a civilised conversation this time, and have you really got the guts to tackle Fergus's death with him? Are you somehow expecting this to be the reignition of your affair or has that flame been put out, never to be relit?

Eventually Leslie had got back to sleep, for what only seemed like a few minutes before his alarm sounded. He'd needed a strong cup of tea before going into work, and then he'd had to struggle all morning to get his brain into a productive condition. When the working day at last came to an end, he'd gone through the usual routine of travelling home, getting changed, making a fuss of Max and eating the dinner his daily woman had left for him. Although everything had been done with his mind elsewhere, his attention focussed on how he could apologise without sounding abject—which Patrick would hate—and still manage to discuss Fergus's death. This would be a make-or-break meeting: if he and Patrick couldn't reconcile this evening, what hope would there be for any future meeting happening?

The hotel bar turned out to be Monday-evening quiet, but it was warm, welcoming, and neutral territory, at least for Leslie. Although, for all he knew, it could have become Patrick's favourite haunt, giving him the advantage of home turf. Unready as yet to settle himself with a drink, Leslie perched on a chair, feeling the need to be able to spring into action.

Patrick arrived exactly when he was due, almost to the second, striding purposefully into the bar, giving Leslie a nod, and extending his hand.

"Leslie."

"Patrick."

They shared a brief handshake, like two company directors meeting to discuss a deal might, not like two men who'd been long-term lovers and whose fingers knew every inch of the other's body.

"Would you like a beer?" Patrick asked briskly.

"Pint of best bitter, please. I'll find a quiet table." That would allow Leslie a few moments to regather his thoughts. He'd been tense in anticipation of that first physical contact in years, but the touch of palm on palm hadn't provoked the same spark it had when first their hands had met. Maybe their intimate knowledge of each other had taken them past the tentative chemistry of the early steps in a courting dance. Or possibly the spark had truly gone, never to be recaptured.

Or is it simply that there's no chance of taking a single pace down that road while your questions remained unasked?

Patrick brought the beers to the table, carefully laying the glasses down. As Leslie's mother had said, he'd always been clumsy and as he'd grown older, he'd learned to take extra care to compensate. "It's been too long."

"It has." Leslie raised his glass. "Cheers."

"Cheers." Patrick took a long draught. "How's work going?"

"Busy but enjoyable, I'd say. You?"

"Potentially more work than I can deal with solo." Patrick nudged his head to one side, a gesture that had always indicated deep thought. "I've taken another vet into the practice to ease the burden. Good-looking lad, so he'll probably generate enough new business of his own to ensure his time's filled."

If this had been when they were still lovers, Leslie would have made some riposte about women—and men—beating a path to Patrick's door with their sick animals for exactly the same reason, but the time didn't feel right yet for such remarks. This conversation was completely bland and transactional. Was that a necessary part of their reconnection, keeping things light to overcome the awkwardness they both must feel? Or was it a sign, like the handshake, that things between them had changed irrevocably?

Isn't that what you came to expect while you tossed and turned half last night away?

It might have been what Leslie expected, but it wasn't what he'd hoped, although he would have denied it. The love he bore Patrick had never disappeared, and seeing the man walk into the bar had reawakened other feelings—lust, anger, fear—that were making a mess of the plan he'd been wrestling over all day about confessing his own stupidity and confronting the bloke about Fergus. There'd be no bloody point if it didn't give him a chance of getting Patrick back.

They shared a couple of pleasantries about work and family, Patrick asking about Mrs. Cadmore with what appeared to be genuine interest rather than mere politeness. Finally, Leslie could hold back no longer. He laid down his pint and faced Patrick square on. "I really don't think we came here to talk about our families. We can hear that news from home."

"So, what did we come here to discuss?"

"You tell me. Marianne said you wanted us to meet up but she wouldn't elaborate."

To Leslie's surprise, Patrick broke out laughing. "The devious little cow." The insult was spoken with affection. "She told me that she'd been to yours for tea and that *you* were the one who wanted to talk to me. We've been had, Leslie Lad."

The unexpected use of that nickname—one that had graced their tenderest moments—momentarily wrong-footed Leslie, although he grinned at how he'd told his mother that Marianne wouldn't do anything underhand. Still, she'd always been a problem-solver. "It appears we have, Patrick."

Patrick smiled. "And there was me assuming you wanted to discuss your father upping sticks and whether I had a hand in it."

"Why the hell should I think that?" For an instant, Leslie wondered if he was still asleep and in some extended dream that had conflated his two main concerns.

"Because—as you surely know—he came to see me, the week before he made the announcement that he was off to the cloistered life. I still don't know whether he wanted advice or simply a neutral ear to pour his thoughts into." Patrick stuck out his lower lip. "The morning of our argument, I got a letter from him asking for a meeting. He pleaded with me not to let on to you as he wanted to tell you himself. Don't say he never mentioned it."

"He didn't. Not to me and not, I'm certain, to Mother." Leslie was about to add, *And neither did you*, but that would have been unfair, because the blazing row at Waterloo had left Leslie unwilling to get in touch in the short term, and Patrick must have felt the same. And then, the longer they'd left it to make contact again, the harder it had become.

Patrick took a swig of beer, then scratched his head. "This makes no sense. I thought . . ."

"You thought what?" Leslie was struggling to take this in, more surprised at this revelation than at learning James had called on his mother. Exactly what had transpired in the conversation between Patrick and Mr. Cadmore and had it settled his decision? "What did he say?"

"I'm afraid much of it I can't tell you. He swore me to secrecy, and while it wasn't quite like signing the Official Secrets Act, I took the promise I made him as binding. I'm sorry. I know that's a useless answer."

Leslie opened his mouth to protest, angry to think that Patrick might have a better grasp of the matter than he and his mother did. But such an argument would probably get him nowhere: Patrick would hold by any vow he'd made, having always had a highly developed sense of both honour and right versus wrong. "I suppose it's the best I'll get."

"I'm afraid so." Patrick stared at his drink.

Leslie remembered other conversations about moral codes. Back in 1939, they'd discussed whether the evil of taking a man's life could be outweighed by the good that might ensue from such a death. The vast majority of men or women would have killed Hitler if they could go back in time and do so. Patrick had confessed to being one of them, so would he have also seen Fergus's death as justifiable? Better to stick with Leslie's father at the moment. "What *can* you tell me? I promise you I won't mention anything to Mother unless I'm allowed to."

Patrick blew out his cheeks. "It's difficult. You see, it didn't sit well with my conscience, him telling me what he should have had the decency to discuss with you and her. I'd hardly call it Christian behaviour suitable to a man about to devote his life to God. His excuse was that he didn't want to hurt you both. I pointed out that it would be a greater hurt if he merely left without a decent explanation, but he was determined. He had a secret, which he told me a bit about, although not the whole thing." Patrick paused. "He thought I might have some understanding of it. I did. I can't say other than that, so please don't probe me."

"I won't. Don't I know what it's like to have to bear the burden of something you can't discuss with anyone, not even people who work at the same place but in a different section? It makes you feel so useless." Leslie hadn't meant to be quite so frank or belligerent, but—as his father had clearly recognised—Patrick did have a sympathetic ear. Into which Leslie had often longed to speak about the work he'd done during the war.

"Whatever you were doing, it was as valuable as anything I or my colleagues did."

That reassurance felt like the first real touch of reconnection. Such a shame, though, that he couldn't accomplish one of the things he most wanted—to discuss with Patrick what had made his father leave. Mr. Cadmore had effectively closed that door.

"Leslie, I'm not going to go all Gloria Swanson and pretend that keeping this secret has been an unbearable burden, but it's not been easy hiding it from the man I'd always thought was my bosom friend." Patrick's mouth snapped shut.

Should Leslie say, *We could still be bosom friends—more than that, to be honest—if I ever get the nerve to open up and clear the air*, or was it too soon to take such a step? He settled for, "I've never forgotten we were the best of friends and, on the basis of that, I'll confess I've long wished I had the guts to ask my father why he walked out. I guess I'm too scared of the answer. That somehow Mother or I drove him to it."

"No, it was never that, I promise. Good God, is that why you think he swore me to secrecy?" Patrick ran a hand over his brow. "You never drove him to anything. He believed that in going, he'd be protecting you. He was a deeply troubled man, with those troubles lodged deeper than we probably realised, unless your mother had a better grasp of him than either of us."

"That's possible." Leslie had admired the stoic way his mother had handled his father's departure, and this new information could explain why she'd coped as she had. Yet, if she, too, was privy to whatever this great secret was, she'd never let on to Leslie. "I should go and see him, shouldn't I?"

"That's up to you. It's your life and nobody else can live it for you." Patrick drained his pint. "Except Marianne, in getting us together again. She can't understand why we've taken so long to get back in touch. I've not told her what happened—regarded keeping that to myself as an unspoken promise to *you*. She knows we argued. Not what about."

Leslie wasn't sure himself what it had really been about, the words themselves perhaps not matching the meaning behind them.

Patrick continued. "People can get over rows, of course, but I guess it all got a bit complicated. It wasn't long after we'd argued that your father came to see me, and then I assumed you thought I'd been involved in his departure and that had made things worse between us because. So, if you knew nothing about that, why the hell didn't you try to get back in touch?"

"Why the hell didn't *you*?" Leslie raised his hands. "No, let's not go throwing accusations at each other or we'll end up like we were at Waterloo. *Our* Waterloo, I suppose." He started to laugh, less because of the pun than the state of his nerves. Maybe if their stress had turned to laughter back then, they wouldn't have said things they regretted now.

Patrick joined in, to the point that it left him breathless. "Your jokes don't improve."

"I'm too old to change."

Leslie waggled his glass. "Want another? I think this is going to be thirsty work."

Patrick pushed his glass across. "Same again, please."

At the bar, a waitress was placing a complicated drinks order for a group in a side room, meaning Leslie had a bit of thinking time, although he struggled to drag his mind away from that terrible argument they'd had in the train station concourse, an event he'd tried so hard to forget. He should have realised at the time that his father was tied up in it, given some of Patrick's behaviour, which could now be seen in the new light of that letter having arrived.

Leslie remembered saying something about his father acting out of character and wanting to discuss the matter with someone who knew the man, but Patrick had been dismissive, simply suggesting that the family should try talking to each other. That had got Leslie's back up, because the last thing his father had wanted to do at the time was be open with his nearest and dearest. Leslie had made some sarcastic remark about never having thought of that strategy, at which Patrick had told him to grow up. Events had gone rapidly downhill from then.

The arrival of another barman cut the painful reminiscing short.

When Leslie returned to the table with their beers, he decided to turn the topic away from his father. "Funnily enough, Marianne was right to ring you yesterday, but I'm sure it's coincidence rather than anything else. After she and Geraldine left, Mother and I had an interesting conversation, prompted by some of the reminiscences we'd all been sharing over tea. Your birthday party got mentioned: Mother seemed to have got the measure of Eric's little clique when she met them there." Using Eric's name to tag them would keep things neutral for the moment. "She'd been asking about them, their war exploits, what they were doing now—you can imagine—although Marianne hadn't been that forthcoming. That continued when the pair of us were on our own, particularly regarding James. Have you heard from him recently?"

"We exchange letters every few months. He says he gets a card from you at Christmas." Patrick would have had every right to add that was more contact than *he'd* been getting. "If you ever see him, don't mention those days. I don't think he wants to be reminded of them. He was never very happy back then, irrespective of the face he wore."

"That's what my mother said. It's been a bit of an eye-opener, discovering how perceptive she is. Whether that extends to having an insight into our sex lives, I couldn't say."

"I'm pretty sure Marianne's guessed. About us and possibly about the five men in that little gang. She's dropped the odd hint, but I haven't picked them up." Patrick drew leisurely on his pint. "James used to like being around you, and I think he was happy around me, so long as it was only us—as a trio or perming any two from the three."

Another possible cue, although Leslie—like Patrick with Marianne's hints—didn't take it. To have said, *I was happy with you*, would have risked sending them off-track. "Not long after my father went off to start his new life, James went to visit my mother. He'd been having lunch with you at The Gadfly."

"Did he? I remember eating with him—the trout were rising like mad and kept distracting me—but he never mentioned his intention to do that."

"My view is he was probably trying to find some way to offer her sympathy without overtly offering her sympathy, if that makes sense. Respecting her dignity."

"That would be like him." Patrick nodded slowly. "I recollect him asking about your father, and when I told him what had gone on, he seemed rather shocked. A greater degree of shock than I'd have expected from a person who'd had an intention to take up holy orders, but he always was a sensitive soul. Fondness for lost lambs and all that. Perhaps he thought of your mother as one or felt her ill-used."

"Whatever his motive, she appreciated him calling. Apparently, they discussed Fergus Jackson's death."

"What?" Patrick started in his chair. "I'd have thought that was a touchy subject. Did she broach the subject or t'other way round?"

"I don't know for certain, but it wouldn't surprise me if she'd started with asking about Dougal and Donald and then threw in the subject of Fergus on the sly. I didn't get the impression James had been too reluctant to discuss him."

"Perhaps it's like your father seeking me out. Easier to talk to someone who doesn't have a horse in the race. Why the particular interest in my favourite person?" Patrick's voice dripped sarcasm.

"I'm not sure. She's an older woman, with plenty of experience of life, both intelligent and having time on her hands, so perhaps she's simply unleashing her inner Miss Marple. I had no idea until yesterday that she'd been puzzling over it and has a bee in her bonnet about what actually happened when he had his accident." It was so much easier to talk about Fergus through the filter of his mother's interest. Maybe Leslie should have used this strategy years ago, although he hadn't known back then that there was another family bloodhound sniffing along the Jackson trail. "As a result, she grilled me about whether his death might have been due to a self-inflicted wound. I believe James mentioned rumours flying around to that effect. She's not at all convinced it was an accident, plain and simple."

"Are you?"

"To be honest, Patrick, I'm not. Never have been since I first heard about it. I know I wasn't there and you were, so I'm trusting you to put me right." *Maybe I should say, for you to give me a fuller account to my face.* "On the surface of it, there's no explanation other than a tragic accident, because Fergus wasn't the kind to ever have deliberately done that to himself. But it doesn't add up. If anybody had set himself up to get killed, or at the very least given a thumping, it was him."

"He was certainly a man who accumulated enemies." Patrick rubbed his chin. "Do you suspect foul play too?"

"Maybe. Although from what I've heard, that seems impossible. Mother's doubts may come from reading too many mystery novels, but that can't be levelled at me."

"I didn't realise you knew so much about it. You're also the only person ever to mention such suspicions to me. If James thought Fergus's death was deliberately engineered, he never said." Patrick aimed his piercing glance directly into Leslie's face, perhaps trying to read it in the way he used to when they'd been treading the hazardous path from friendship to love. "I've long believed I was the only person to harbour such thoughts. Maybe I should have guessed you'd think the same, although your Mrs. Marple-Cadmore comes as a surprise."

Patrick having his doubts suggested that something had happened that fateful day to argue against an accident and perhaps supported his being innocent. He was the main witness, so why not continue to keep shtum if he'd been involved? Although, if they were going down the Agatha Christie line, guilty folk did create smokescreens. Leslie couldn't let Patrick's allure cloud his judgement.

"As I said, she surprised me. I thought she'd have had no interest in how or why he died." Leslie sipped his beer and waited.

"It appears we've all made a habit of misunderstanding each other. Too many assumptions." Patrick stared into his drink for a moment, then pulled himself upright, straightening those broad shoulders. "Right, what can I tell you?"

"Exactly what happened that day. I've had a garbled version of it from Eric, whom I thought got it from a pal, although I guess he may have heard it from you."

"Not from me direct, but he had other connections to draw on. Eric having been one of the many Fergus got his leg over with, he would no doubt have wanted to know what had happened."

"Which was what? Other than an exercise in the woods and Fergus falling on a knife he shouldn't have been carrying. Bad luck intervened and he managed to slash a major artery in the process. That's the official line."

"I can tell you slightly more than that, although some of the context has to remain hazy. The training was to do with what they were up to behind enemy lines. I didn't know much about these special operations at the time, but it was no surprise Fergus was caught up in them. One of the chaps whose horses I tend was doing something similar, and the tales he's told me . . ." Patrick shivered. "I was present the day Fergus died because I was helping with the dogs, as I'd done before. The exercise, training course, call it what you will, was about defending yourself against guard dogs and avoiding being tracked. While the exact detail concerning who was being trained and why is one of the hazy bits. I don't think it's relevant to Fergus's death except that he was one of the trainees. I didn't know anyone else among his cohort but, Fergus being Fergus, it's quite possible that he and one of the other men were lovers."

"I'd have a guinea on that being the case." So far, so good. Leslie would try to be objective, taking everything Patrick told him at face value; there'd be plenty of time to mull it over, afterwards.

"I was acting as observer, not so much of the men but the dogs. I didn't want them playing up or getting hurt. Some were a bit unpredictable, no doubt because of how *they'd* been trained. I was watching everything through my binoculars, and around half nine in the morning, I spotted Fergus and another man. They hopped over a stile, then split up, Fergus heading towards the woods, maybe for the stream to try and break up his scent. He'd got himself amongst some low-lying bushes when he pitched forward and gave a cry." Patrick raised his glass, although he didn't take a drink. "In any other circumstances, I might have thought he was playing silly buggers. You know what he was like. But I'd swear he would never have arsed around in the circumstances. When it came to the role he'd taken on, he was apparently the consummate professional. Totally different to his dilettante style."

"Could somebody have tripped him? Maybe not intending to kill him, only to give him a fright?"

"If they did, they'd have had to crawl into position. I could see Fergus clearly from about the thighs up. There *was* a slight ridge in the ground preventing me seeing his feet, so I suppose it's possible somebody had crawled into the low-lying shrubs, hidden there, and then stuck out an arm or leg as Fergus went past." Every time Patrick mentioned the dead man's name, the muscles of his left eye twitched. Leslie remembered that tic from years ago—a clear sign of deep emotion. It happened again as Patrick carried on. "Said person would have needed a thick coat or a thicker skin, because there were a lot of old brambles growing there. He'd then have had to hide again and maybe take advantage of the general hubbub that formed around the dead man, in order to escape. Or to blend in with the crowd, if the killer was supposed to be present anyway. That need to disassociate himself could have applied equally in the case of a prank gone wrong."

Leslie nodded. "A simple trip with murder in mind couldn't have worked, could it? The killer couldn't have relied on Fergus falling in such a disastrous way."

"Quite. I also think the notion of someone lying in wait doesn't work. Unless they knew Fergus would take that particular route."

"Let's say the culprit tracked Fergus and took advantage of him going sprawling, irrespective of what caused him to trip. The killer would have had to get hold of his knife and do the deed, which raises two questions. Why didn't Fergus put up a fight and how did the killer know he had the knife on him?" How odd to be putting these questions to the man he'd imagined doing these very things.

"I've got a possible answer to the second part. That Fergus told him. You remember what he was like." A note of disdain in Patrick's voice.

"Could any of us forget?"

"Strangely enough, I saw Frank the other day. Striding down Banstead High Street, looking hardly any older than he was in 1939, although he lost the sight in one eye at Dunkirk. Small beer compared to what he could have lost at that level crossing." The disdain was clearly turning to anger as Patrick, face increasingly ashen, wrung his hands together. "Frank still remembers nothing about that night, but he has recurrent nightmares where he's being run down by a train. By God, I wish Fergus had lived to hear him say that, although I don't suppose the bastard would have felt any remorse. Maybe somebody should have made *him* stand on the tracks and—"

Leslie leaned forward. "Steady on, old man."

"I'm sorry." Patrick passed his hand across his brow. "I've tried so hard not to speak ill of the dead, but I can't help it at times."

"Give yourself a minute. Then go back to why Fergus didn't put up a fight. We'll forget this last bit happened." At least in terms of the conversation; Leslie wouldn't easily shrug off the look in Patrick's eyes.

After a pause, Patrick said, "What I meant to expound on was this. If he'd had some act of bravado planned he'd have been tempted to boast about it, especially if he had a bedfellow in the group."

The use of that particular word, as opposed to *lover*, immediately took Leslie away from the tension of the present and back to happier days. The expression had been peculiar to Patrick, and he'd used it to describe Leslie in some of their most intimate moments.

It could have been used to put you off guard.

Patrick evidently hadn't noticed his disquiet. "I've got another idea, but I'm not going to hog the conversation. What do *you* think about the knife?"

"That it didn't have to have been Fergus's. As I understand it, carrying the things wasn't allowed under your rules for the day, so if a knife turned up with the body, people would assume—as they did—that he'd had it on him secretly. It could easily have been the killer's own, pressed into Fergus's hand. Did anybody bother with fingerprints or the like?"

"No. Not unreasonable in the circumstances because it seemed to have been a clear-cut accident. Fergus was wearing gloves—I think everyone would have been, because it was damned cold—so fingerprints wouldn't have got us far, anyway."

Leslie nodded, then slowly took a drink. He'd been able to imagine a man as clever as Patrick arranging something that appeared accidental despite being pre-planned. Hadn't he run across something similar in the past? Could he have remembered it and been inspired to try his luck?

Near to where Patrick had lived when studying, a woman had been killed when her husband reversed his car into her. The driver had been allegedly distraught, blaming a terrible stroke of fate, his having been distracted by a bird that flew into his windscreen at the very moment his wife had happened to walk behind the vehicle. The inquest had ruled it an accident.

Patrick hadn't believed a word of that verdict, especially when the man married his secretary six months later. He'd aired his concerns with the local police at the time, but they'd had no witnesses or evidence to contradict the husband's story and a dead blackbird to support it.

"Anyone can pick up a dead bird and use it. The detail would have made the story believable." The words sounded in Leslie's mind as clearly as if Patrick were speaking them now. *"Nobody would think of doing a postmortem to see if its time of death coincided with hers. And anyway, people had other things on their minds in 1939."*

In Fergus's case, had the knife somehow been the detail that gave the account of his death credibility?

"Did anyone ever mention if he carried the knife with him when he was doing whatever-it-was out in France? Could it have become so habitual that he'd have put it in his pocket without thinking?"

"That's certainly what the officer in charge of the trainees believed. It was standard issue. Although for me, who owned the knife is less of an issue than how it was deployed and particularly the lack of defence from the victim." Patrick's brow creased in thought—or dissembling. There hadn't been so many wrinkles on that face back in their happier days, but they'd all experienced a lot over the past few years. "I didn't see Fergus flail about or hear him shout or anything else you might expect if he was fighting for his life, even if his assailant was on the ground. Which brings us to the point over which I kick myself, every time I think of it. What you may not know is there was a delay between him falling and anyone reaching the body. Immediately after Fergus tumbled over, one of the handlers came up to me with his dog, which had picked up a thorn in its paw. I prized the thing out, because that seemed to be the priority; given that I'd simply seen Fergus go arse over tip, there'd been nothing to make me suspect he'd hurt himself. He seemed a consummate professional in the field, as I said, so I'd assumed he'd get up and carry on into the woods. Anyway, observers weren't supposed to get involved with what was going on, giving help or the like unless it was specifically asked for because someone had got injured."

Leslie nodded. The dog handler was presumably the person who'd had Patrick in full view during the time of the accident. "Could the dog smell the blood?"

"With the benefit of hindsight, I'd say that's likely. He seemed agitated, but we put it down to the thorn. It had got deeply into his pad, to the extent I suggested that he and his handler step down from their duties, go to get the paw properly dressed and give the lad some rest. Then we heard a terrible shout. Another of the trainees was waving from Fergus's direction and saying there'd been a terrible accident. One of us had to go and get help right away. Jefferies—the dog handler—had his charge to manage and the poor hound wouldn't have been able to get up much speed, so

I set off. We didn't have two-way radios or anything useful like that to get messages back, so it was Shank's pony. I must have run a mile to our mobile unit, got hold of the medic we had on stand-by, and set off back to the scene. When we found Fergus, it was too late." Patrick drummed on his chair arm. "If only I'd thought clearly at the time, I could have volunteered to tend the dog and send Jefferies back, because then I might have been able to help him. Fergus. I know I'm only a vet, but the basic mammalian anatomy has enough that applies across species."

"And as a vet, you should be well aware that if you'd got to him only seconds after he fell, there was very little you could have done to stem the bleeding. Even a medical duffer like me knows that." Leslie reached over to tap his friend's arm. If events had played out as Patrick had related, then he'd be innocent of the crime, the specific threat he'd made about stabbing Fergus notwithstanding. In Leslie's reconstruction of the incident, he'd imagined Patrick being straight on the scene, knifing Fergus where he'd fallen, and then excusing any blood spatter by saying it had come from where he'd been helping the casualty. He'd seen Patrick in the role of killer as an explanation for why there'd been no defence from Fergus—he'd be less likely to expect an attack from a friend and colleague and likelier to be taken unawares.

But, Leslie reminded himself with a shudder, Patrick's account might still have some holes in it, especially if he'd been in cahoots with one of the others. The man who struck the blow.

Back to that account. "So, considering the interval between the fall and the other chap finding Fergus and shouting, would there have been time for somebody to have done the deed? If they were part of your group, they'd have needed to change their clothes too, because the blood would have spurted everywhere."

"There'd have been time to crawl away, although I didn't see any evidence, when the medic and I got back, that anyone had done such a thing. It would have been bloody obvious, the amount of gore about. I suppose someone could have taken advantage of Jefferies and I having our attention on the dog in order to get up and run before Dawson came and discovered the body."

"What did you notice when you returned?"

"That Fergus was dead as a doornail and the other two looked like they were in shock. Jefferies had a bit of blood spattered on his trousers but nothing on the rest of him. He told me afterwards he'd felt like a spare part, because it took all his effort to restrain the dog, rather than be able to help. That's apparently why he had the blood on him, because his dog kept trying to get to the body. The other bloke—Dawson, the one who'd alerted us to the accident—had more on his jacket, although that was easily explained by him having tried to perform first aid, despite the effort being futile. Jefferies had had to persuade him to give up." Patrick shrugged. "Not that I'm any expert on the Sir Bernard Spilsbury type of stuff. All I can say is that none of us had any suspicions at the time."

"Then why have you had any doubts since? Mine are easily explained, because I've been bumbling along in possession of only half the story. Mother had something like a quarter." Leslie snorted, still unsure he had anything like the half he'd boasted of. As he and Marianne knew, Patrick wasn't a great liar, so if he'd really been in collusion, he must have been salting his account with as much truth as he could, leaving significant gaps instead of attempting a lie. "It strikes me that the chaps who appear to be the obvious candidates, Dawson and Jefferies, seem to have been ruled out by the lack of a larger amount of blood on them. Unless either or both had time to go and change their clothes."

"Agreed. Dawson didn't have blood on his jacket when he alerted us to what he'd found. I know I was standing at a distance, but I'm not short-sighted."

And he'd had his binoculars. "Highly unlikely either of them would have a motive, too."

"Everything seems *highly* unlikely. But there are connections, you see. Between the clique of five and some of those present that day." Patrick had always avoided using the name *The Retainers* for Fergus and his gang, thinking it stupid. He'd never approved of the club they'd been members of, either. "Eric would have been able to tell you much of what happened to Fergus because he was big pals with one of the chaps involved with running the course. When I say they were pals, I mean nothing other than that.

Then you have the rumour going round that James had a variety of cousin there that day, although I'm not sure which individual that was or if he was a true cousin or a second once removed. That could be why *James* knew enough to come up with the self-inflicted wound theory he spoke to your mother about. Any of us would have heard the gossip to that effect going round, although we should have ignored it. Still, stories spread like wildfire."

Leslie stifled a yawn, brain tiring from the volume of information he'd had to take in.

"Am I that boring?" Patrick asked, grinning.

"Stop flirting, you." *Did I really say that?* Leslie could feel himself blushing. "I've come off the back of a terrible night's sleep, and while I'd love to carry on chatting, my brain feels like scrambled eggs. Any chance we can continue the discussion another time?"

Patrick smiled. "I don't see why not. Can't be this week, though, because I'm off to a conference in a couple of days. Next Monday? Seven o'clock, here?"

"I can make that." Those interim days would give Leslie time not only to think but to have some other important conversations.

They finished their drinks, then strolled out of the hotel, sharing a handshake as they stood on the pavement. A steady drizzle had started, which meant any chance of dawdling would be thwarted, although Patrick seemed reluctant to go. "If I ask something, will you promise not to bite my head off?"

"Scout's honour."

"If you didn't give me the cold shoulder because of my meeting your father, what was behind it? Did you suspect I had a hand in Fergus's death?" Patrick stepped back. "Was that what you meant at Waterloo when you referred to putting animals out of their misery?"

That stung. There'd need to be a quick reply, because while it must be obvious to Patrick he'd hit the bull's-eye, Leslie wanted to think over everything he'd learned tonight before he entered into that discussion. Best to use an approximation of the truth. "Honestly, I didn't know what to think."

"Hm. Okay, keep your counsel." With a sigh, Patrick stepped forward again and laid his hand on Leslie's arm. "It was so good to see you again. I should thank Marianne for setting us up, although I won't. She'll get a swollen head. Give your mother my best wishes and tell her that if she has any Miss Marple revelations—that Fergus's death reminds her of the affair between The Gadfly's landlord and the Wherwell postmistress—I'd like to hear them."

Leslie chuckled, despite his emotional turmoil. Such a contrast to their last parting. "I will."

Patrick drew his fingers down Leslie's sleeve, briefly stroked his hand, and then turned on his heels, leaving an intense sensation behind him, as though the touch would remain until dawn.

As Leslie headed home, he still couldn't shake off that lingering touch of hand on hand, nor could he entirely lose his doubts. And while the upcoming meeting between Patrick and his father cast a different light on some of what had been said during the great argument, it couldn't explain everything that had happened at Waterloo.

Leslie winced in remembering two soldiers who had walked past them at the time, and Patrick observing that there were men serving their country with proper gallantry, before giving Leslie a sideways look. The perceived slur on Leslie's war service—or lack of it—had cut as deeply as the fatal knife blow to Fergus. Leslie had been horrified. How could the Patrick he thought he knew so well have stooped so low? Leslie had previously told Patrick as much as he could about his work, which had been practically nothing, and had believed that Patrick understood how his lips had to remain sealed. Nerves taut, Leslie had responded viciously.

"Well, you should know, Patrick. Your cows and horses must be vital to the meat supply."

It had been a cheap shot, one that had received a similarly cheap reply.

"At least I know what a man must do for the cause. And I get off my arse and do it."

Leslie, wounded to the core, had flicked his hand so strongly it had caught Patrick's jaw. *"Like putting sick animals out of their misery? They should give you a medal."*

That had apparently been the final straw. With the jibe about hell freezing over, Patrick had turned, gone and they'd not spoken until this evening.

What now, though? Of one thing only was Leslie still certain: Patrick knew plenty that he wasn't telling and not just about Mr. Cadmore. While Patrick's words broadly accorded with what Leslie had heard about Fergus's death, the exact sequence of events was on his say-so alone. Albeit Jefferies must have been in a position to know if the vet already bore blood spatter on him—as would the medic—so no doubt they would have refuted Patrick's account in any official enquiry, unless they'd been in cahoots.

So, had Leslie really spent this evening talking to someone who was as concerned as he was to get to the truth behind Fergus's death or was Patrick the man who, despite all he'd said, was somehow responsible for it? Leslie couldn't forget the threat he'd made to Fergus and the fact he clearly still hated the man, despite him being long gone. Yet, if Patrick was guilty, whether directly or as an accessory, why didn't he stick to the accident theory rather than muddy the waters with speculation? Such a paradox felt worthy of Mrs. Christie herself.

Leslie stared down at his hand, as though it might bear physical evidence of Patrick's touch. Matters had changed, this evening. While he didn't know if Patrick had truly loved him, a spark of attraction persisted. Still, the vital question remained unanswered. Was the man he was falling for again a cold-blooded killer?

CHAPTER FIVE

The next morning, Leslie woke knowing he'd have to summon up his courage to go and see his father. Would that meeting result in the same mixture of relief, frustration, and bafflement that the meeting with Patrick had left him with? Perhaps Leslie should ditch his preconceptions and not spend too much time preparing what he wanted to say, but he was a natural planner and that tendency had to find an outlet somewhere.

He focussed on the logistics. Mrs. Gray—his housekeeper—would no doubt be happy to have Max, on whom she and her sister doted. Leslie could go by train and spend the night in the West Country rather than steaming down and back again in a rush. Anyway, train journeys gave him time to think, which meant he could try to defer all his fretting over the visit until then.

Before that he'd need to talk to his mother. Ostensibly, the conversation would be to update her about what he'd learned from Patrick, because she'd be furious if she wasn't privy to the details. He'd bowdlerise them a touch, naturally, and any references to James and Eric knowing folk who were present on the day of death could keep until he'd seen Patrick again.

Patrick.

Although Leslie had experienced a much better night's sleep, initially he'd wrestled to get off, unsettled by the recollection of Patrick's hand touching his, a touch that remained palpable. On one level it had all been so easy, this meeting he'd so dreaded, but having overcome the hurdle of simply speaking to each other again, a new obstacle came into view. Hope.

He'd assumed he'd discarded any prospect that he and Patrick could resume being lovers, but the previous evening's meeting had changed that view. Not only had they been able to have a civil conversation, they'd started to explore deep areas. While they'd not aired everything that needed airing between them, a start had been made, and it had been a damn sight less painful than Leslie had anticipated, at least on the personal front. Wasn't that always the way, that the worry turned out to be worse than the reality?

Since they'd parted, Leslie had wondered what might have happened if he'd shown a positive response to Patrick's contact, perhaps making a reference to one of the private words they'd used as lovers. Would he have woken with Patrick's head beside his or was that a hope too far, too soon? He'd lulled himself to sleep with memories of the happy days they'd spent together. And woken to the reminder that he still didn't know the extent of Patrick's involvement in Fergus's death.

Now, getting dressed and preparing to tackle breakfast, he focussed on the other issue. Best not to worry about the telephone call to his mother and how he could manoeuvre it into discussing his father or why he would have turned to Patrick for guidance. Though the fact of that visit was odd. No matter the depth of worldly wisdom he possessed, Patrick was hardly the man to provide anyone with a spiritual viewpoint.

Leslie added having a word with Marianne to his list of jobs, because he wanted to know if she'd had an ulterior motive for arranging the meeting, other than simply getting two old friends on speaking terms again. Had she been thinking of Fergus Jackson's death as well, wanting to encourage Leslie to get on the trail, knowing that Patrick would have told him things he'd have never told her? Or was Leslie now assuming that everyone around him harboured suspicions? Whichever applied, he'd grasp the nettle and ring her at her office, assuming he could find the number without too much fuss. Then he'd ring his mother, after which he could draft a letter to his father. In the meantime, he'd have to focus on his job and stop fretting.

One of the secretaries at Leslie's firm, a priceless employee who could always conjure information out of nothing, came up with the number for Marianne's place of work, so he rang her during his luncheon break. However, when he was put through, her brusque tones caught him on the hop.

"Please don't ring me here, because it isn't easy to talk. You're lucky that I'm alone in my office at the moment, because the woman I share with picks up everything." The roll of Marianne's eyes was almost audible.

"I'm sorry. Didn't mean to put you in an awkward situation." *Despite you doing that to me yesterday.*

"I'll call you back this evening if you've got a phone at home."

"We're not *that* rusticated at the far end of the Piccadilly line." Leslie gave her his number and promised to be ready for her call at seven o'clock.

Both were as good as their word, the call coming on the stroke of the hour. Leslie had settled himself in a chair next to the sideboard, Max at his feet, so he could easily pick up the receiver. Not for him standing around in draughty hallways to take a call that could last a while.

"Thanks for ringing. I apologise again for any inconvenience at the office," he said when he answered.

Marianne gave a snort. "They're very old-fashioned, our lot. Hate any private business done on the firm's time, even in an emergency. Thanks for using your company's name with the receptionist."

"She didn't sound like she suspected it was anything other than a business call." Time to get down to things. "Has Patrick spoken to you today?"

"No. Should he have done?"

"You tell me. I saw him last evening, and we soon exploded your story about him wanting to see me because, naturally, *he* was convinced it was the other way round."

She chuckled. "I had to use subterfuge, didn't I? I've felt for ages that the pair of you needed the equivalent of your heads knocking together, and seeing you on Sunday prompted me into action. There's no reason you two should have let it go so long."

Leslie took a deep breath, the desire to tell Marianne that she had no idea what had been in his—or Patrick's—thoughts vying with the no small degree of gratitude. "Did you assume that there were matters we had to discuss?"

"I guessed there might be, although I didn't know for sure." That sounded like the truth. "You were always so close. Did you get the air cleared, by the way?"

"In part. You have no idea, Marianne, how smog laden that air is. Sorry to sound overdramatic, but I think we both got a bit of a shock. I suspect your brother was having to work extra hard not to spill his drink."

"He's much less clumsy now he's grown. Probably at last gained control of his limbs. Still has a propensity for bumping into things or being attacked by inanimate objects, unless he's at work. Where he's a master of dexterity, I'm told." She laughed again.

Patrick had been a master of dexterity in other areas, well away from work. That reputation, though—had he somehow drawn on it as a cover for whatever happened to Fergus? *It couldn't have been me. I'm more likely to have fallen on the knife.* Could it genuinely have been a terrible accident, caused somehow by that clumsiness coming into play, in a way that Patrick could never admit to? No. An accident would surely have left him covered in blood.

"Leslie? Are you still there?"

"Sorry, Marianne. Lost in my own thoughts again. You know what I'm like for wool-gathering. Incidentally, after you'd gone, Mother told me that she'd seen James and they'd discussed Fergus's accident. I was rather surprised."

"So am I. About James, that is. I did think your mother was asking a lot of questions about The Retainers over tea. I suppose she was laying the groundwork for your chat."

"Probably. I'm amazed at how many people appear to be speculating that it wasn't an accident."

"Well, isn't that a bit of an open secret?"

"I'm sorry?"

"Oh, come on, don't tell me that you haven't heard people saying he killed himself? If you had the story from Eric, he'd surely have given you that tidbit."

Tuesday evening was proving as full of surprises as the last few days had been. "I had and he didn't. James aired the theory with my mother, but I've never believed a word of it. Fergus was too fond of life."

"He may have been, but according to Eric—who was in the know because he was connected to one of the big wigs running the course—he may have seen it as the lesser of two evils. Fergus was on the verge of being court-martialled for unnatural practices or whatever the forces call it. Making the beast with two backs with some chap." Marianne paused. "Did you know he was like that?"

No wonder Marianne hadn't wanted to discuss this at work. "Did you?"

"Yes, I did. Dougal told me all about it not long after war broke out. A group of us met in London for something like a last hoorah. Patrick was supposed to be there, but a colt with a broken leg took precedence."

"That sounds typical." Although if that night was the one Leslie thought it was, there'd been no colt to take up Patrick's attention, only *him* and an understanding hotelier.

"He'd probably not have enjoyed himself if he'd come along. Fergus led a group of them off to some night of debauchery, while Dougal was in a particularly sombre mood. He'd had a few but didn't want to go off. He said it would act as the start of breaking ties with the others—he'd met a nice girl and wanted to live a different type of life. That was before the Luftwaffe scuppered his plans. Anyway, as Dougal couldn't spend the evening with his new sweetheart, he asked if I would mind being a sympathetic ear? He didn't make a pass, by the way." Marianne snorted.

"I wouldn't have expected him to. Not that type." Usually the receiver of passes, rather than the initiator. "Very gentlemanly. Marianne, can I ask you something personal?"

"That sounds ominous."

"It isn't really. I wondered what you thought of Fergus's . . . inclinations."

Marianne chuckled softly. "Oh, Leslie. Are you really asking if I mind that Patrick's like that?"

If Leslie hadn't been sitting, his legs might have failed him. "How long have you known?"

"I guessed years ago, although he doesn't know I did. I'd never tell a soul, because he means the world to me and I'd never want to hurt him. Box his ears at times, but never hurt him." Given that she was telling Leslie, she might also have guessed about *them*. "We were talking about Fergus, though."

"We were." Leslie was grateful to get back to the topic. "And what Dougal told you in his heart-to-heart."

"About The Retainers and what they usually got up to, yes. Funnily enough, he wasn't ashamed of having been part of that particular type of men-only club. The sort where one would never entertain one's uncle." She laughed again. "Dougal simply regarded membership of The Retainers as a stage in his life he'd had to go through to become the man he was. I think he found it cathartic having a woman he could tell all this to. He even had to be wary when he wrote to his mother because she kept all his letters—right back to school days—and he was always worried he might let something slip, like mentioning one of the boys in his dorm too often or in not quite the right words. Anyway, after he'd met his girl, he wanted to slough those days off, like a small creature moving into a larger skin. I could see why: she was a delightful creature."

Was that Marianne dropping a hint about her own nature, on the principle that Leslie would be sympathetic? "I never had the pleasure of meeting her."

"I ran across the pair of them shortly before he went on his last sortie. That wasn't long after Donald bought it, so not a great time all round for the old gang. I wish I'd had her address to send my condolences, although that might have been a touch awkward."

"Did she think you were an old flame of his?"

"Something like that, especially when he started going on about people I knew and she didn't, and then names neither of us seemed to recognise. The girlfriend was getting restless, so I cut the conversation short and left them to it, of which I'm very glad, given that he was killed so soon afterwards. Anyway, I'm getting off the original point. It *wasn't* a shock to hear that Fergus had been caught at it with a chap. Perhaps the only surprise was that he hadn't been caught before."

"I agree whole-heartedly with that last part. But if Fergus wanted to take his life, why not hang or shoot himself, rather than do what he did?" Unless he was simply making his end as showy as he'd made his life.

"Because whatever else Fergus was, he was a patriot and wanted to serve his king and country in its darkest hour." Marianne was no doubt rolling her eyes. "Yes, I know I sound like an article from a boys' magazine, but it's true. Eric reckoned Fergus staged the accident because that would cause less embarrassment than a court-martial or a hanging might."

"If you hear stories of me falling on my sword . . ." hadn't Fergus said something along those lines to James? Did that support Marianne's story? "I'll have to think carefully about how much of this I report back to Mother."

"Quite."

"I do appreciate having someone I can speak frankly with. I wish Eric had told me the full story." Leslie rubbed his brow. "Why were you privy to it all and not me?"

"To put it bluntly, I think he was trying to get into my knickers. He'd been attempting that on and off for years and I suppose he thought sharing secrets might gain him some ground. It didn't. Perhaps he didn't tell you all because he didn't want to get into yours."

Leslie resisted telling her that Eric had gone through a phase of trying it on with everybody and, in his case, had no doubt given up after suffering several firm rebuffs. He wondered if Eric had taken Marianne's rejections as he'd taken Leslie's, in the spirit of a sporting defeat by a respected opponent. "What would his prospective constituents make of that?"

"Depends if they believe he'd turned over a new leaf. They'd not be impressed if they knew that the attempted seductions have happened twice since the war ended."

"Really?" Word of that hadn't spread.

"Oh, yes. Although at last he seems to have realised he's got no chance. Or he's run out of half secrets about parliament or other stuff to tempt me with. Coinage of very low value to me, although he knows I'll keep my mouth shut." She snorted. "All the negative stories are small beer when played off against him saving the lives of three children, of course."

"True. He was a bloody hero then." Eric had been based in London during the war, working as part of Churchill's staff and doing whatever he was called on to do in some secret rooms in London, whose fuller history Leslie knew about although not many others did. The role had hardly been one awash with chances of glory, until a raid on London had provided an opportunity. Eric had risked his life going—against the advice of the ARP warden but at the behest of a hysterical mother—into a badly hit building to bring out the three children, one of whom was barely more than a baby. The fact he'd ended up needing stitches had added to the story, with his wounded face all over the newspapers in a timely bit of good news. "Why didn't you tell me about the court-martial before?"

"Because I thought you knew."

"And does Patrick know or have you assumed the same on his part?"

"We've never spoken of it. Patrick and I have never indulged in gossip about other people. Not since our childhood chatter."

"Then if you only talk to him about serious matters, did he ever mention seeing my father before he went off for his life of prayer?" Leslie hadn't meant to sound so waspish.

"He mentioned he'd seen him, but not what they discussed. I know he'd always had a bit of a soft spot for your dad and perhaps the feeling was mutual." Marianne paused. "I'm glad you and Patrick are back on speaking terms, or am I making another assumption that the situation prevails?"

"We're still finding our way." Time to regroup his thoughts before his next telephone call. "I'm afraid I'll have to say goodbye now, as I need to catch Mother. I want to make my first visit to see Father *in situ*, and I won't do it behind her back."

"Give her my best wishes. It was lovely to see her again. And you."

"I will."

Leslie didn't call his mother straight away, taking a moment to sit stroking Max's ear. Marianne's knowing her brother preferred men—and seemingly being unbothered by the fact—would add layers of nuance and interpretation to what she'd been saying on Sunday, although he didn't want to ponder those now.

He focussed on the court-martial she'd said had been hanging over Fergus. Surely it couldn't have been put into motion, or why would he have been free to take part in the training? Since Leslie hadn't been involved in active service, especially the kind where agents were employed to operate behind enemy lines, he would need to find out the form for these things. He'd also have to check with Patrick whether he knew about the hot water Fergus had supposedly got into.

Could Patrick have not only known but been the one to put pressure on Fergus to take an apparently honourable way out? The Fergus whom Leslie had known hadn't struck him as the type of man to decide on such a course of action for his own sake, and while other men might have taken that road in order to protect a lover, that wouldn't have been in keeping with his character, either. If the other man involved had also been in the military, *he'd* surely have been facing his own disciplinary procedures, while a civilian would have found himself up in front of a judge.

The dog still staring at him, wearing a puzzled expression, suggested Leslie might have been unwittingly airing some of his thoughts aloud.

"Sorry to confuse you, boy. Just thinking. And you'll have to wait for your evening walk as I've another telephone call to make. I promise I'll leave writing that letter until we get back, though, or your bladder will never cope." He picked up the handpiece again to ask for the call to go through.

"Hello, dear," his mother said, when she answered. "Did you leave something here?"

"No. I'm a bearer of information. I saw Patrick yesterday, and he's given me his eyewitness account of what happened to Fergus. I thought you'd be interested."

"Oh, I am. Let me get myself comfortable and you can tell me all."

Leslie didn't quite do that, keeping the matter of the court-martial under wraps and avoiding anything that could allude to the shadier parts of Fergus's character. He concluded the account with, "It's a bit of an eye-opener."

"It is. Although that delay between Fergus stumbling and him being found sounds highly suspicious. Somebody could have tripped him, stabbed him, and got clean away."

"Patrick and I had an identical conversation. I need to warn you that we're faced with the little matter of blood. Anyone doing the stabbing would have been covered in it. Or at least badly spattered."

"Well, that's no great obstacle to overcome. The answer strikes me as being rather obvious." She paused, clearly enjoying having thought of something Leslie hadn't.

"Enlighten me."

"I'd have said the assailant would be naked. Then he could simply go and wash himself in some nearby stream—didn't you mention one?—before putting his clothes back on. They'd be clean as a whistle."

Leslie whistled himself. "I never realised you had such a devious mind, Mother. And thinking about naked men wandering about the woods, to boot. Wouldn't such a person stick out like a sore thumb?"

"In any other circumstances, perhaps. But if this was about avoiding dogs, one of the trainees could easily say he was trying to evade them. The likely outcome would be that he'd appear a fool and get ribbed by his comrades."

"I doff my hat to your superior reasoning, Sherlock." He didn't necessarily agree with the conclusion, although a naked man might prove an explanation not only for the absence of bloodstained clothing but for the lack of fight from the victim. Could, however, Patrick and Jefferies really have been so distracted by the dog that they hadn't seen someone moving near where Fergus had fallen? Still, Fergus would surely have appreciated the unclothed form and that momentary lack of guard might have done for him. "There's something else I wanted to discuss, although this is going to be rather painful. I'm going to drop Father a line as I want to go and talk to him."

"You're free to act as you wish. I appreciate being kept informed, though."

"Patrick told me that Father had been to see him in the lead up to his going away. I have no idea what about as Patrick's being very mysterious about it."

"I can't tell you either." Her tones implied she'd known about the meeting, though.

"Would it be painful to talk about him? I've got some questions to ask that may seem strange." So strange that he wasn't sure how to justify them.

"You can ask what you like, on the understanding that I don't have to answer if I don't want to." She sighed. "It's been five years, Leslie, and I think I've got beyond the point of wanting to rant about him or of trying to puzzle out why he did what he did. In effect, your father's dead to me, so it will be like talking about someone who's long gone."

Leslie would pretend he believed all that. "The twins' birthday party. The one we discussed with Marianne. You've mentioned what *you* thought of Fergus and his little gang but what did Father make of them? He was a man who enjoyed observing people." *Now* you're *using the past tense as though he's dead to you as well.* "You must surely have mulled over your impressions between you."

"We did." She gave a chuckle. "He thought the one who's about to stand for election could have done with a jolly good haircut. Said he looked like Oscar Wilde."

"That was Eric's style back then. Very different now, obviously. Much more suited to a move into parliament. What about the others?"

"He liked James, although who wouldn't? I'm glad he didn't become a vicar. He'd have been swamped in cakes and mufflers from the spinsters of the parish vying for his attention."

Some of the bachelors too, no doubt. "Sounds like that curate we had at St. John's. I remember two women almost coming to blows over him."

"He's on his way to a bishopric, they say. What hope can other mere priests have when up against a Ramon Novarro profile?" The wistful note suggested his mother had appreciated that as much as Leslie had. "James doesn't quite come into that category, but your father thought him most polite and was extremely grateful he'd taken care of me at the party. He'd been cornered by some terrible old bore he couldn't get away from, which is why I'd been on my own. Maybe I should have realised that was the shape of things to come."

With the benefit of hindsight, Leslie could see she'd been increasingly left on her own in the final years of her marriage. It had never been in a nasty way, his father always being courteous and apparently caring when he was in her company, but the number of times he'd left her side at social occasions had slowly mounted. As had his fishing trips. Should Leslie have spotted that and taken it as a sign that things weren't well?

"Neither of us realised, Mother."

"No, but perhaps we could have read the clues. Which brings us back to Fergus and his friends," she added, quite brightly. "Your father thought Fergus flash and untrustworthy."

"He got that right."

"The others he either didn't have much of an opinion on, or he never shared it. Now he *did* tell James that if he was in the area, he should drop in and see us—I suppose that's another reason why he visited me after lunching at The Gadfly. He might have thought it would have looked rude if he hadn't passed the time of day."

"James must have made quite an impression, given that Father was hardly profligate with his invitations to people he didn't know well." That reclusive streak—and his love for solitary activities such as fishing—might have been another clue to the life his father had decided to take up, but not every man who enjoyed his own company took it to such extremes.

"Yes. He was very fond of the twins, naturally. I think he preferred having you three knocking around here than entertaining his work colleagues. I miss those days too, helping you make a den at the drop of a hat and then being quartermaster for it. It was like supplying an army." His mother's voice caught, the sob unmistakable despite the crackles on the line.

"I'm sorry I've upset you. I shouldn't have asked about him."

"No, it's not that. I'm being a sentimental old woman, mooning over the past. I did hope at one point that I'd get to re-create those days, with Marianne bringing her children here, but there seems to be no prospect of such a thing. I'll have to be patient and make do with Clare's."

Clare, Mrs. Cadmore's goddaughter, was expecting twins of her own in a couple of months' time. Living at the other end of the Piccadilly line from Leslie, she already took advantage of the open invitation to spend time at Larkspur House to enjoy country life. This arrangement had helped save Leslie's conscience that he hadn't—and would likely never—produce grandchildren for his mother to fuss over. Interesting, and typical of his mother's sensitive nature, that she'd referred to Marianne's prospects of parenthood rather than his.

"They can't be that far off making an appearance," Leslie said, easing the conversation into baby matters and the progress his mother was making on bootees and bonnets. When he felt he could bring the call to a close, Leslie pleaded that Max was bursting to go for a walk and made his goodbyes.

The evening was cool but dry, not an unpleasant time to be abroad with one's thoughts. As they walked, Max showed his usual interest in every lamppost and must have enjoyed the rare opportunity to linger beside them, Leslie being too wrapped up in his thoughts to hurry the dog along.

That bit about James was bothering him. As they'd discussed, it wasn't like his father to be so free with an invitation, so why had he made it? *Perhaps we could have read the clues.* Leslie had taken that as his mother referring to his father's antisocial tendencies but had it referred to a different part of the conversation, maybe the next thing she'd mentioned? *"Which brings us back to Fergus and his friends."*

A horrible thought came to Leslie's mind, as various threads drew together and reminded him of an old Bletchley colleague. Clive had shared Leslie's inclinations, although they'd never been lovers. Clive's father had been surprisingly understanding when he'd learned of his son's preference for men, the reason being that *he'd* had a passionate affair with another man when he was barely twenty. He'd said he put such things away when he met and married the woman of his dreams. Clive hadn't been sure he'd been convinced by that description of his mother, much as he loved her, thinking it more likely that his father had succumbed to the usual pressure to conform. But the story had opened his eyes, as it had Leslie's when he'd heard it.

Had his father been in a similar situation, and had he still felt an attraction to charming young men? It would explain why he'd been so taken with James and had extended the unwarranted invitation to him. It could also explain why he'd sought out Patrick, if he'd suspected the man's nature was the same as his own, and why he'd have insisted on secrecy. It would give a credible reason for why Mr. Cadmore had taken himself off to a cloister, if he felt the need to put himself out of the temptation that James or any other man might have presented. And if he believed that other men who'd taken the cowl would also have eschewed their earthly desires.

CHAPTER SIX

The train sped down into the West Country, over elegant yet functional Brunel-designed bridges, through cuttings and tunnels, across an expanse of glorious countryside. Yet Leslie registered little of it.

If he'd felt his thoughts had been tumultuous the last few years, that was nothing compared to the past few days. He'd been forced to reassess so many things he'd worried over, realising his assumptions—and those of people dearest to him—had created a situation that seemed better suited to an overblown romance from the silver screen than to real life. If only his mother had mentioned James's visit previously or Marianne had been quicker getting into her peacemaker role. Or better still, he'd had the sense to ask Patrick what was wrong at Waterloo, rather than taking umbrage.

If "ifs" and "ans" were pots and pans, there'd be no need for tinkers. Whoever had first used that old saw had known what they were talking about. As did old Will Shakespeare when he'd depicted Hamlet being driven slowly mad by his thoughts. Leslie picked up the newspaper from the seat beside him and set about the crossword, hoping it would provide a distraction from his brooding.

By the time he'd completed it and browsed a few interesting articles, he'd almost reached the station where he'd have to change to the branch line. From there, a smaller train would meander down to the village where he'd booked a room at a pub called The Bear and Ragged Staff. It would only be a half an hour's walk from there to the abbey and, hopefully, some enlightenment. Although of a temporal rather than spiritual nature.

The connecting train was on time, the pub proved to be both clean and welcoming, and the weather seemed set fair for the rest of the day. As Leslie made his way out of the village and along the road, he could only hope those would prove auspicious signs for the interview ahead. When the abbey first came into view, its roofline dominating the little valley in which it was set, he had to fight the impulse to turn on his heels and go home. It was by forcing himself to remember childhood days, him and Patrick and Mr. Cadmore discussing the best strategy for fishing one of the nearby streams or collapsing in laughter at their first attempts to pass a rugby ball—*"Run forwards, pass back!"*—that he was able to proceed.

Like most people, Leslie had a vague expectation of what a monk's life involved and had seen monochrome photographs of Combe Abbey in a guide to the local area, so had built up a clear picture of how the place would both look and feel. Quiet, sombre, other-worldly, downright depressing if seen in the pouring rain, similar to other closed institutions and distinguished from them merely by the presence of a cross and other symbols of faith.

He couldn't have been more wrong.

Perhaps it was the effect of sunlight shining on the old mellow stonework of the buildings or the expansive and open grounds with their pleasant vistas, redolent of some country estate. Maybe it was the presence of children—a group of Boy Scouts given the uniforms, perhaps come for an educational visit—who were being addressed by a handsome and enthusiastic brother who had reduced them all to laughter. This abbey was clearly not an organisation stuck in medieval times, and there was some nebulous quality in the atmosphere: a calm, friendly air that spoke of life and goodness.

The monk who greeted him at the lodge was as welcoming as the landlady at the pub had been, although she'd not been blessed with such a well-cut sandy yet greying beard. A good choice for a porter—if that was his role—should any trouble loom, this man being a good six inches taller than Leslie and brawny with it. He'd no doubt been briefed about the visit.

"Welcome to Combe Abbey, Leslie," he said, with a smile and a nod of his grizzled, tonsured head. "Please feel free to wander our grounds and chapel while you're here. We only ask that you're quiet during our daily offices, which will be less of a challenge for you than for those scouts Brother Mark is shepherding. Brother Andrew will be waiting for you."

After hiding a wince at his father being called by the name he'd adopted, Leslie thanked the porter and asked where he needed to go, feeling rather disoriented and not only by the unfamiliar surroundings. But the porter's directions were clear, so Leslie made his way fairly confidently from the lodge to the main building, where he found a second equally friendly monk awaiting him in a doorway.

"Ah, you must be Leslie. I'm Brother Francis." The monk extended his hand. "You're Brother Andrew's son?"

"I am." Why had his father chosen the name Andrew? Presumably he couldn't use the one he'd been baptised with, Ralph, because he'd have put that away as he'd put off the outside world, but why the name of that noteworthy disciple? Unless it was a piece of whimsy—Andrew had been a fisherman too, if for business rather than leisure. Leslie wasn't sure he'd ever get used to the new name.

Brother Francis extended an arm towards a smaller building, located near the chapel. "I'll take you along to him. He's sorry he couldn't be here to meet you himself, but he's in the infirmary."

"Is he all right?" Visions of his father having had a stroke or heart attack—explaining why everybody was being so kind—threw Leslie into a panic.

"*He* is but his leg's not. He came a cropper on one of our stone staircases yesterday. They're very unforgiving. It's likely a simple fracture of the femur, according to the doctor, although we won't know for sure until he's been to the hospital. Which he insisted on not doing until he'd seen you, so you'd better come on and inspect the patient for yourself. The leg's bandaged and splinted to within an inch of its life so he can't escape us." The monk led the way, telling Leslie about how well supplied their small sick bay was and how *he*, having been a nurse previously, was in charge. "My little earthly kingdom, although rarely do we have anything so spectacular to deal with," he said, as he ushered Leslie in. "Usually it's an outbreak of the flu."

There were four beds in the ward, with Mr. Cadmore lying in the farthest one from the door. He turned, giving Leslie a tentative smile and a wave. His face seemed drawn, although maybe that was merely due to the pain from his leg.

"What have you been doing?" Leslie asked, as he neared the bed. He shook his father's hand and sat on the chair alongside, provided by brother Francis, no doubt.

"Not taking care of myself. I used to warn you not to run on the stairs, though I'm not sure you ever took the lesson to heart. I was simply walking down them and this happened."

"I think he *was* running." Francis patted Leslie's shoulder. "I'll leave you to it."

When he'd gone, Mr Cadmore said, "It's been a long time, Leslie. Too long. My fault, I know. It will sound trite when I say that I've missed you, but it's the truth. I don't get many letters and yours I'll cherish."

"I thought you were supposed to put all earthly attachments behind you. Isn't the spiritual life satisfying all your needs?" Leslie had never intended to be so tetchy. He'd told himself to take a measured approach, to achieve the kind of objective conversation he'd managed to reach with Patrick, but now he was in his father's presence, all his old resentment had come to the fore.

His father had flinched at Leslie's aggressive tone. "You're right to be angry. I left you and your mother in the lurch. How is she?"

"Bearing up as well as can be expected considering the situation. Regards herself as a widow." That was a slightly less harsh way of saying he was dead to her. "She knows I'm here, although not quite what I want to talk to you about. Why did you choose the name Andrew, by the way?"

"It felt appropriate. I had thought of calling myself Brother Peter, the man who left behind him his family and profession to follow the lord, but it felt pretentious. Then I contemplated using his original name, Simon. That would have hurt too much. Hurt both you and me." With a grimace, he moved his injured leg, maybe inflicting physical hurt on himself to match the emotional pain he'd referred to. Yes, using Leslie's middle name would have felt like a low blow.

"I always understood that after the resurrection, Peter took his family with him to go preaching." Wasn't that in the Book of Acts? Some of the apostles had travelled with their wives, anyway, because Paul had been sarcastic about the fact. Still, the part about the hurt spreading two ways had stuck out. "Couldn't you have found a way to serve God at home? You could have got ordained and picked up a curacy somewhere or become a lay preacher. Anything that would have meant you didn't abandon us."

His father flinched again, as if he'd been struck across the face. "That wouldn't have worked. I don't believe I have that particular vocation, for one thing. I contemplated my options and decided the only choice I had was to leave the world behind and come here, you see. I felt nothing else would work."

"The call of Combe was so strong? Your 'particular vocation' here overrode your family ties?"

"No. It wasn't only that. I don't think you'd understand my reasoning, even if I felt I could tell you everything that was in my mind back then. It wasn't a rushed decision, believe me. I'd wrestled with it for years."

That accorded with the theory Leslie had formed, although he'd leave discussing that—and the meeting with Patrick—for the moment. "Did Mother know about this 'wrestling' you'd been doing? The long dark night of your soul that you say must have led you here."

"To some extent. She knew that I was deeply troubled, although I dare say she wouldn't have told you that. She wouldn't have wanted you upset. And now you've ended up distressed, but that's not her fault. It's all mine." The self-flagellation sounded genuine. "I didn't simply up sticks without warning, Leslie. I tried my best to help her understand that I felt the need to devote myself to this very different life but the deepest details—no, we never discussed them. I rather had the feeling she didn't wish to."

That last part might have been factual, despite his mother's interest in solving mysteries. The one surrounding Fergus's death was safe to delve into because it didn't cut close to home. Yet the equivocation in his father's words—he'd *rather felt* she didn't wish to discuss these details—suggested he'd not tried that hard to get her to listen. However, the fact that such a conversation had been attempted was news to Leslie. Perhaps talking to Patrick had spurred Mr. Cadmore into action.

"I saw Patrick last Monday," Leslie said, keenly observing his father's face for any reaction. "We'd not spoken in a long time, and he was under the mistaken impression that I'd given him the cold shoulder because of that meeting you had with him, not long before you left home. The meeting that I had to confess I knew nothing about."

Mr. Cadmore's face had turned deathly pale. "He promised me he wouldn't mention that to anyone."

"Oh, whatever you discussed with him is perfectly safe. He merely said you'd met, not what you'd spoken about. Patrick's a man of his word." *Does he always carry out what he promises?* Best for the moment not to get distracted by Patrick's threat to Fergus. "It was one coincidence after another, last weekend. I was down at Larkspur, so I went to walk my dog on the common. I bumped into Marianne. When I related this to Mother, she naturally invited her around for tea, and somehow the talk turned to The Retainers. Patrick's little clique of acquaintances."

"We met them at the twins' party." His father's clipped tones were in keeping with his constrained face.

"You'll remember them, then. Once met, never forgotten, irrespective of your being here."

Leslie's words were no doubt continuing to hit home, making his father uncomfortable. "It's not like that, Leslie. We don't leave our memories—good or bad—at the porters' lodge."

"I'm glad to hear it. Can you recall the youngest of the pack, James? He came to see Mother not long after you'd relocated here." Given the surprised, troubled expression in his father's eyes, that news also bothered him. "She suspects James's visit was mainly to offer his condolences, although he was too well bred to actually use those terms. She appreciated his concern, though. I hadn't realised that you'd encouraged him to call at Larkspur whenever he was in the locality. It sounded out of character, but Mother was sure it had happened."

"I was no more a hermit back then than I am now." His father evidently didn't like the way the conversation was going. A certain sign that Leslie was approaching the heart of the matter. "What did James have to say to her?"

"Oh, gossip, mainly. Nothing of any great importance, I believe." Leslie didn't want to risk a diversion into discussing Fergus's death, not when he felt so close to finding out the truth. "She was very taken with him, as she'd been at the party. It's to be expected, given his schoolboy looks and innocent air. He's broken plenty of hearts, that lad."

"I can believe that." Mr. Cadmore's face remained inexpressive, as he evidently fought not to let any feelings show. If he took his vows seriously, he'd balk at telling an outright lie, so he'd no doubt be choosing his words as carefully as possible.

"But I'd still like to know why you chose *him* to extend an open invitation to. I don't recall anybody else—apart from the twins—being in that situation, and you'd known them since we were all barely out of nappies."

"I found him interesting to talk to. His strong sense of vocation, for one thing."

"James told you all about that at the twins' party?"

"No. I happened to run across him in London, shortly before the war, when he was up there visiting someone for spiritual advice. He seemed rather upset, so we went for a pint and a chat. I'd have done the same had it been Patrick or Marianne in such a state." Mr. Cadmore smoothed the bedclothes, gaze fixed on his hands.

Run across. Accidentally-on-purpose or by prior arrangement? Presumably, Leslie was being told as much of the truth as his father could cram into the tale—James's godfather *was* a vicar, living in London, and James used to visit him regularly to discuss matters divine. Yet Leslie had seen James not long after Mr. Cadmore had renounced the world, and he'd never mentioned the meeting. Why was that? "What did you chat about over your beer?"

"He was having doubts. Not concerning his belief in God, which remained strong, but about entering the church. He was on the path to abandoning that idea." He raised his head to face Leslie again. "I think that decision was for the best, one way and another. Parish priests need a touch of iron within them, and I'm not certain James possessed that quality."

"No." And his personal life would have made it difficult for him to adhere to the church's rules, unless he'd opted for celibacy, and James hadn't appeared to be that type. "Did you see him, afterwards? I don't think Mother said he'd been to Larkspur, apart from when he'd been with Patrick at The Gadfly and went on to visit her."

"He never took up the invitation to call on us when I was still at home, no." Eyes back on the cover again and the question was basically left unanswered.

"Ah, well, another mystery to add to the pile." Leslie crossed his arms. Was there any point in continuing, given that every time they were making progress, his father played a straight bat and blocked his enquiries? "I'll get to the bottom of them all one day, I suppose."

It was odd—and highly suggestive—that Mr. Cadmore hadn't asked any of the obvious questions that should have peppered this conversation. *Why are you so interested in whether I met James? What other mysteries make up this pile you're talking about?*

"Tell me about yourself, Leslie." His father gave him a smile. "You've not said anything about what you've been doing these five years."

"I assumed you wouldn't be interested." That dangerous word. *Assumed.*

"Why shouldn't I be interested? I didn't entirely leave you and your mother behind. It was parts of *me* I was trying to get away from."

"I think I understand." If Leslie was right about his father's nature, then his departure made some sense. Whether he dared confront him outright about it was another matter. Leslie began his potted history, skimming around his war service by saying he still wasn't allowed to talk about it, but relaying a few innocent anecdotes about people where he could. His current work was a safer topic, given that his personal life needed a sidestep or two. If he was wrong about why his father had come to the abbey and if he reacted like most people to the notion of men who loved men, then Leslie would risk further estrangement.

His father asked pertinent, kind, and unobtrusive questions about Leslie's news, especially when they got to the part concerning Towser. He'd a soft spot for the dog, having helped nurse him after he'd suffered an adder bite on the common, and gave his condolences that the hound had gone the way of all flesh. They were discussing whether Max would be allowed to visit Combe, given his villainous tendencies, when a gentle tap came on the ward door and Brother Francis appeared and offered them a cup of tea.

"Yes, please." Leslie's throat was becoming parched, both from talking and strain. Although that had eased in the last few minutes while they'd been focussed on him.

Mr. Cadmore nodded. "That would be most kind. Rustle up a biscuit for Leslie, if you can. He's always been fond of them."

The simple statement, redolent of childhood days and packets of biscuits sneaked from the larder to take out on father-son fishing expeditions, almost unmanned Leslie. He and his father had been so close back then. Should he not make another effort to put aside the hurt and attempt to understand, on Mr. Cadmore's terms, exactly why the man had felt no option but to take this drastic step in his life?

Once Brother Francis had gone, Leslie said, "He seems a nice chap." That sounded banal, compared to what he really needed to discuss, but he didn't want to risk entering tricky waters only to be interrupted by the arrival of refreshments. "He says he used to work as a nurse."

"Yes. Saw a lot of action in the war, he tells me. He was up most of last night, keeping an eye on me and, when I couldn't sleep, he told me a few tales of field hospitals that would make your hair stand on end." Mr. Cadmore launched into an anecdote that Francis had told him about some poor casualty who'd kept being dropped off his stretcher by a pair of newly arrived and totally useless orderlies.

Francis arrived halfway through the account, chuckling at his patient's rendition of the tale. "Neither use nor ornament, that pair, not when they arrived or after we'd had them a couple of weeks. They were sent off somewhere else where they could do no harm." He swung a bed tray in front of Mr. Cadmore, then unloaded the steaming cups and a plate of biscuits. The latter he left with the instruction that he didn't want to see any left when he returned.

"He treats his charges like they're no older than seven," Mr. Cadmore said, when Francis had gone. "It seems to work, though. Thank you." He took a biscuit from the plate that Leslie had edged towards him.

"Combe isn't at all as I envisaged it would be," Leslie confessed. "Nor are the monks what I expected."

"Ah, no. That's Abbot Barnabas's influence, you see. He's firm in his belief that while we exist partly within the world and out of it, that balance should reflect the present day, not the age of the crusades." His father shot Leslie a curious glance. "Were you met at the lodge by a monk with a magnificently maintained beard? One that must have been flaming red in its pomp?"

"I was."

"That was him, then. The abbot. Acting the part of porter. Quite disarming when visitors later meet him in his office and realise they'd mistaken him for one of the brothers. He tells them not to worry, as there's good precedent and if they'd mistaken him for the gardener, he'd have been thrilled."

"He sounds like a breath of fresh air. Perhaps the church would be better if he was actually out in the world, leading the organisation. It could damn well do with it." Leslie sipped his tea, which was hot, strong, and perfectly brewed.

"He'd hate that. Says he can't play politics, which is what the job would involve. He's found his niche and does his best within it. As you can imagine, he's very well respected locally, especially when he drops into The Bear and Ragged Staff for a pint."

"That's where I'm staying. I must ask the landlady about him. Barnabas sounds an appropriate name, because wasn't he some big, hearty chap, colleague of Paul's?"

"That's the impression I get from Acts." Mr. Cadmore picked up another biscuit. "When the abbot was a mere novice— although I suspect he's never been a *mere* anything—he toyed with adopting the name Judas. He feels that chap has had his name thoroughly besmirched over the centuries and would love to know the truth of what went on two thousand years ago. You should hear his doubts over the accuracy of some of the reports, like Judas being a thief. The abbot reckons the man was trying to force Jesus's hand, to make him perform a huge miracle and chuck the Romans out of the country, and then when Judas realised how wrong he'd been, he took his own life. If he'd had the guts to face up to what he'd done, he might have been forgiven and had fish for breakfast on the shore like Peter did."

"The story is always edited to suit the people who came out the other end smiling."

"Exactly. Anyway, the abbot decided that the choice of the name Judas would be too scandalous."

"He'd never have made abbot if he had gone with it, I guess." Leslie sat back, nursing his cup. He and his father hadn't talked so easily in ages. Albeit things had been made tricky when Leslie hadn't been able to discuss the details of how he was serving his country with his family, but coming to Combe had evidently worked a change in the man. Or perhaps the intervening years had caused a transformation in Leslie. Or both. "There was also another chap, showing round a group of scouts, I think. Brother Mark? He seems the sort who'd be better suited to life in a scrum than a chapel."

His father's face clouded over. "Mark arrived at Combe when he was barely out of his boyhood. He thought he'd find peace here. He has now."

That was clearly a veiled reference to serious matters. Maybe, given his age, Mark had avoided the draft by taking the cowl. "Perhaps I should ask to talk to the abbot. He might give me a better understanding of what makes men come here."

"I'm sure he'd be pleased to chat with you if he's free." Mr. Cadmore's shoulders had eased into his propped-up pillows, evidence perhaps that he thought he'd weathered the worst of an anticipated interrogation.

He hadn't. "Maybe he can help with the one thing we can't get away from, although I don't expect he'll break any confidences. I wish you would tell me yourself why you came here. I'd swear on all that's holy that I wouldn't report back to Mother, but I don't suppose that's going to persuade you. If you wouldn't let my best friend tell me . . ."

Mr. Cadmore slowly shook his head. "I was wrong to put Patrick in such an intolerable position. I was getting desperate, and he was the only person I could think of to talk to. Patrick was always such a sensible person, from when he was very young. If it's any consolation, he doesn't know the full details, either. I told him only as much as I needed to tell him."

"He knows more than I do." Leslie raised his hand. "I don't want to get into a fight. Not now when I've remembered how much I used to enjoy simply chatting with you. The last few minutes have felt like old times."

"I've valued them too." His father smiled, as tenderly as he would have done if they'd been down on the river, trying to tempt the fish to bite. "Your visit has been like a blessing; one I don't deserve."

"Isn't that what grace is about? I could do with a touch of it myself, so here's a final plea. Whatever made you come here, my not knowing your motivation makes the situation worse. I've ended up imagining all kinds of dreadful things, none of which may turn out to be the real reason."

Mr. Cadmore closed his eyes. "You wouldn't want to know, believe me. While you might hate me for having kept my own counsel, I doubt you'd want to speak to me again if I told you the full story."

Leslie desperately wanted to say, *But I would. Of all the people you could confess to, I'd likely be the most sympathetic. Didn't you recognise in me what you loathed in yourself?* Instead, he said, "Then I have to tell you where my thoughts are. I've been putting two and two together and don't know if I've made four, five, or fifty-three." The attempt at levity eased the tension for a moment, both men giving a snort of amusement. "I think your coming to Combe was connected to James."

Leslie waited, desperately trying to read his father's face, but no emotions were playing out on it, apart from a flinch when James had been mentioned. He continued, "I believe something happened involving James, something you're deeply ashamed of, perhaps without good reason to be. If I'm correct, then I can assure you I completely understand why you wouldn't have wanted to tell Mother the whole story and why she wouldn't have wanted to hear it."

He waited again, for what felt like hours but which, from the steady ticking of the clock on the wall, could have been barely a minute.

"And what do you want me to do, Leslie?" Mr. Cadmore asked, eventually. "I'm not leaving here and returning to the outside world. I daren't. This is my sanctuary, and now I'm safe in the hands of the abbot and God."

Leslie nodded. It appeared he'd guessed correctly but was unlikely to get any confirmation of the fact. Time for another effort, and this really would be the final one. "I'm not asking you to leave. All I want is to stop being tormented by my thoughts. If I've worked out the motive that brought you here, that would be enough for me. I swear."

"I can't confirm or deny it, Leslie." His father, pale and face racked with conflict, appeared to be having a Gethsemane moment. "Please don't share those thoughts, because if you tell me where this trail has led you, I'm scared my face will give me away. Whatever you think my motivation was, the reality is much worse, believe me. If I say it verges on breaking the law, can we leave the rest unsaid?"

Another knock on the door, heralding the arrival of Brother Francis, seemed to be a miracle of timing. The angels must have been watching over his patient. Francis came to the bedside, contemplated his charge for a moment, and said, "I think that's enough for today. I'm accompanying Brother Andrew to hospital tomorrow, and he's going to need all his strength for the poking and prodding ahead."

"I was about to go, anyway." Leslie rose, made to shake his father's hand but then changed his mind. He leaned down and kissed his father's brow. "I'll be back for another visit, when I've had time to think and my head's clearer."

"Please do. It's been lovely to see you." Mr. Cadmore clasped Leslie's hand with great affection. "God bless you, my son."

Leslie gave him a watery smile, then turned, unable for the moment to find any words. As he reached the ward door, his father gave a final, "I still won't be able to answer your question, though."

Leslie sat on a bench in the sunshine, waiting. As they'd left the ward, he'd asked Francis if there was any chance the abbot would be free to talk to him, and the nurse had promised to go immediately and find out.

"I'm sure he'll spare a few minutes for you if he can. If he can't, it will merely be pressure of other commitments. You'll find a rather comfy seat with a view over the river valley if you head down this path and around the corner. One of us will be along shortly."

Leslie followed the path to the bench as instructed, grateful of the time to gather his thoughts and choose his words. However, the swift reappearance of Brother Francis brought his planning to an abrupt close. "Abbot Barnabas says he'll be delighted to see you. He won't be long."

"Thank you." Leslie wasn't sure if it was appropriate to shake hands—did monks expect to do such things?—so settled for a friendly thumbs-up, which Francis returned, grinning, before departing.

The abbot arrived a few minutes later, apologising if Leslie had found the wait interminable. "I never cease to be amazed at the variety of business I get drawn into. It's not all prayer and piety."

"I can well imagine." Leslie had got to his feet, unsure if they'd be staying or going elsewhere.

"Shall we walk?" Barnabas gestured broadly with his hand, taking in the grounds.

"Why not?" Leslie fell into a measured step beside the abbot, as he was led towards a path that eased its way down to the river.

"I find it's always easier to talk when side by side, especially when on the move," Barnabas said. "Less intimidatory, I suspect."

Leslie shot the abbot a sidelong glance, but the man of God was grinning. "Which of us do you think is likely to feel intimidated?"

"Not you, I hope. I try not to be too scary." Barnabas lightly cuffed Leslie's arm. "You wanted to talk to me, and I guess you'll have questions that I may not wish to answer or indeed be able to."

"Then I must try not to bully you. I've plenty of things to ask that you'd readily answer, for example about the life here, but I think in the circumstances that would be a waste of time for both of us. I feel confident I can already report back to those at home about the special qualities of Combe, the atmosphere and the like. It's an impressive place."

"Thank you."

"It's my father I want to discuss, as you'd no doubt already deduced."

"I had indeed." They'd come to a fork in the path—how symbolic was that—and Barnabas steered them to the left. "I wasn't abbot here when your father arrived as a potential novice, although I took him under my wing and he's been there ever since. He's a good man but a troubled one as *you've* no doubt already deduced. I'm aware he's not told you or your mother much about what drew him here."

"Barely anything. He talks about Combe being his sanctuary, although he won't tell me what from. I've made an educated guess, although I can't be sure if I'm right." Unlikely that the abbot would reveal what Mr. Cadmore hadn't, but Leslie would hang on every word, searching for a clue.

"Is it so important to know? I appreciate it's difficult having that great chasm of uncertainty looming close to you, but if you could somehow find a way to accept his decision, that may be the best you can hope for. Best not just for him and you but for all concerned." The abbot, who'd been walking with his hands mainly tucked into the sleeves of his robe, pulled them out to spread them, as though weighing options. "Yes, it's easier said than done, yet no harder than living with a vain hope. I doubt he'll ever tell you more of his own volition."

A pragmatic answer, suggestive of the men whose names Barnabas had favoured when he'd become a monk. "He *did* tell me about your original choice of adopted name."

"Ah yes. Poor Judas." The abbot shook his head. "My heart has always bled for him. I'm quite convinced he couldn't have been half as bad as he's made out to be. Our Lord wouldn't have had much truck with him if he was, surely?"

"My father said something rather interesting about Judas. That if he'd had the guts to face up to what he'd done, rather like Peter did in facing up to having denied knowing Jesus, then he might have been forgiven. As Peter was clearly forgiven, afterwards."

"Plenty of food for thought on that point, isn't there?"

"I agree. Not least because it could apply to my father too. Why can't he face up to us and admit whatever it is he's done, or thinks he's done? If I'm right in my 'educated guess,' then I'd forgive him like a shot."

Abbot Barnabas stopped, turned to Leslie, and studied his face for a moment. "Would you?"

"Of course I would."

Barnabas laid his hand on Leslie's head, as if in benediction. "Then, my son, either you're a true Christian or your educated guess has hit far from the mark."

CHAPTER SEVEN

*L*eslie ambled slowly back to the village, Abbot Barnabas's final words to him ringing in his ears as loudly as the abbey bell summoning the faithful. *Had* his guess about his father been wrong or was it simply that the abbot wasn't worldly enough to have figured out where Leslie's thoughts had led? Did Barnabas think he'd deduced his father had committed adultery or some other great offence to his mother?

Yet, there'd been no implication in the bedside conversation about another woman being involved, only the strong reaction every time James was mentioned. Whatever the truth of the matter, James was somewhere in the heart of it.

When Leslie arrived at The Bear and Ragged Staff, the landlady was tending a bright patch of flowers by the front door.

"What did you think of Combe, then?" she asked, rising from her labours.

"It's not at all how I imagined it. Quite beautiful and rather jolly, if that's the right word. I can see the appeal of spending some time there."

"That's Mr. Barnabas's influence, that is." Interesting that she didn't use his official title, although perhaps he preferred that when he was away from the abbey. "He comes in here once a week for a pint or two and a chat. Says that's how he keeps abreast of all the local affairs."

"Not what you'd expect."

"No. Mind you, he always says he doesn't want to be so full of heavenly stuff he's no earthly use. He always has a sympathetic ear and a wise word, with a bigger dollop of the first than the second."

"That's rare in itself. Most folk want to give advice rather than merely sit back and listen." Further evidence of how skilled the abbot was at handling people. "Any idea what he did in civvy street, if I can call it that? Or is he one of these types that's spent most of his life as a monk?"

"Mr. Barnabas was a policeman." The landlady smiled, clearly delighted at Leslie's gasp of surprise. "A sergeant in the detective branch, he tells us, until he saw the light back in the thirties."

"Never. It looks like today's going to be one long surprise."

"I thought I was having my leg pulled when *I* first heard, but every word's true. We had somebody staying here last year who got the shock of their life when Mr. Barnabas walked into the bar. They'd known him back when he was a bobby on the beat."

No wonder the abbot was so astute, having seen such a different side of life. How many villains or potential villains had he taken for a bit of a walk *so as not to be too intimidating*? Or had that been a skill he'd developed only in his cloistered life, dealing with novices and hearing their confessions?

"Have you any idea why he turned his back on the force and came to Combe?"

The landlady grinned. "Ah. Now that depends on who you ask. Rector says you don't need no reason other than hearing the voice of God whispering in your ear. Dr. Snellgrove, he reckons it's less to do with God than ordinary ambition. There's no guarantee you'll get your deserved promotion in the police force and not everybody gets to be commissioner or whatever they call the bigwigs who run the show. Doctor says that at Combe, an ambitious man can make his way."

That wasn't a bad assessment. The abbot would be king of all he surveyed at Combe rather than a cog—no matter how big a one—in a huge machine.

"I'm glad he chose us, though," the landlady said, "or we had him chosen *for* us. I didn't know the old abbot—John—except by reputation, but he was a right tartar by all accounts. A bit nasty with the novices, although I don't know exactly what's meant by that. My old dad said I wouldn't want to know. John broke his neck slipping and falling down one of those big old staircases they have at the abbey. I always wondered if there was a chance he'd been pushed."

Leslie raised an eyebrow. "Really? Any idea who would have done such a thing?"

She shook her head, tapping her gardening gloves against her palm. "As far as I know, there was nothing to suggest it was anything but an accident. The obvious man to have done it was Mr. Barnabas himself, given that he was in line to get the job, but you can count him out. He wouldn't harm a fly and anyway, he wasn't here at the time because he was off at some meeting with other church folk. If somebody gave the miserable old codger a push, it wasn't Mr. Barnabas."

"When did all this happen?"

The landlady wrinkled her brow. "Middle of the war, forty-two or forty-three maybe, although I wouldn't swear to that. Seems like a hundred years ago, now."

"Doesn't it just?" Discussing the previous abbot's demise might have been a strategy he could have employed with his father, to get them talking companionably again, because the fall had likely happened after Mr. Cadmore entered the abbey. Although maybe that was for the best, as one mysterious accident that might have been murder was enough for anyone to be getting on with. "I won't interrupt your gardening any further. It's a shame to come here and then waste a lovely day like this, so I think I'll take the air before dinner."

"That'll work you up a decent appetite." She bent to her work again. "I've a nice bit of beef stewing up a treat, mind, and a new keg of beer on tap, so don't you be too late for your meal."

Leslie found himself smiling, as relaxed as he'd felt in a long time. "I promise I won't. Not with those as an incentive."

After he'd had a wash and changed his shirt, Leslie set out for his stroll with no particular destination in mind. It didn't take long for him to explore the village and decide that, pleasant as it was, there was nowhere suitable for sitting and thinking. Instead, he'd try to find a place where he could survey the countryside. While views he encountered aplenty, there was also a severe lack of convenient benches like Combe had boasted, although Leslie did find a wall he perched on. There he could not only bask in the late-afternoon sunshine but look out over the fields, down to the river and the woods. After a few moments with his eyes closed, taking in the sun's rays and trying to order his thoughts, he decided he should take a break from thinking about the meeting with his father. Perhaps if he turned his thoughts to the other mystery in his life, with all the emotional complications that entailed, his subconscious could work out the next step in the family matter.

As he opened his eyes, he realised that the undulating terrain in front of him, with the nearby edges of woodland and the twinkling water, wasn't dissimilar to how he'd pictured the place where Fergus had died. This area was on a larger scale, no doubt, but maybe it would help him picture the scene from the observer's point of view.

Scanning the countryside, he imagined Fergus running furtively across the field, tripping, then falling out of sight. Patrick—standing where Leslie was sitting—being distracted by the arrival of an animal needing his attention. That part of the story had the ring of authenticity, because he'd always have regarded the dog as his priority. Leslie turned to one side, imitating the action Patrick could have made, then tried to guess how long Patrick's attention might have been away from Fergus. When Leslie turned back, probably sooner than Patrick would have done, there was a deer—a roe buck, he thought—right in the middle of the field, as if it had been dropped there from a plane. Presumably the deer had come bounding from the woods and must have been visible for at least part of the time, yet he'd not seen it. If Patrick and Jefferies had been fully occupied with the dog, a man could definitely have been in Fergus's vicinity and escaped undetected. As, Leslie reminded himself in a sudden stroke of the bloody obvious, the other chap—what was his name, Dawson?—had gone unnoticed when he'd approached the dead man. Unless Dawson had been there much earlier, although in that case wouldn't Patrick have seen him?

If only Leslie had known about Abbot Barnabas's surprising past when they'd met. It would have been interesting to put the puzzle of Fergus's death to him, especially in view of what had happened to his predecessor and how the local rumours had flown around. Would he have been able to offer, from his experience—which must have included dealing with unexpected and potentially suspicious deaths—an explanation of how somebody could have so skilfully engineered a man's demise that they'd evaded arrest? No doubt he'd have come up with a better explanation than Mrs. Cadmore's theoretically naked attacker.

Funny how the landlady of The Bear and Ragged Staff had been convinced that Abbot John's death had been murder. Was there an equivalent of a pending court-martial hanging over the previous abbot's head, so he'd thrown himself down the flight of steps rather than face the consequences? Or were all of them—the landlady, Leslie's mother, Leslie himself—being deluded into seeing what wasn't there? Telling themselves that when a highly unpleasant man met his death, surely there was something suspicious in it?

Leslie eased himself off the wall, although not before realising the roe buck was now far off in the distance, and while he'd had his eyes on the fields all the time, he hadn't registered its movement. Maybe the seemingly impossible murder of Fergus could be solved. And maybe Leslie would find that Patrick couldn't have been responsible.

Pleasantly tired from the day and fed with beef that had lived up to its advertisement, Leslie made his way into the lounge bar to tackle his second pint of the equally excellent beer. He'd barely taken a sip when the landlady's cry of "Good evening, Mr. Barnabas" made him turn toward the door.

"A pint of your best, Mrs. Elsie," the abbot said, "and one for yourself." Clearly he hadn't given all his worldly wealth to the abbey, either. Unless a couple of drinks could be counted as legitimate expenses for keeping up good relations with the local community.

"Let me get those, if I may." Leslie leaped up. "This gentleman has been extremely helpful."

"Thank you." The abbot inclined his head. "Actually, I was hoping you'd not upped sticks and gone home."

"I'm enjoying the break. And my woman-who-does would be mortified if I came home too early and reclaimed the dog she's babysitting."

"Ah. You mustn't get on her bad side, then." The abbot took his pint, then steered Leslie to a different table, one no doubt better suited to a quiet chat. "You've been much on my mind today, since we talked, so I've had a quiet word with the Guv'nor. He reminded me how your father swearing himself to silence and making others take the same promise is all very well, but it's not fair to those who get left behind and in the dark. Life *isn't* always fair and good people are made to suffer through no fault of their own—the war's shown us that if nothing else has—but I got the feeling I was supposed to be helping you a bit more than I had. In a way that doesn't compromise my promise to your father. Which isn't going to be easy but the Guv'nor does like to set people a challenge. Keeps us out of mischief, I suppose." The abbot chuckled, his face breaking into wrinkles of amusement.

"If you could do that, I'd appreciate it greatly." Leslie sipped his beer. This was an answer to prayer, although he wasn't aware of having made one.

"You're an intelligent man, and from what I've heard you've done well for yourself. Your father's proud of you, you know, especially with what you did in the war. Not that he knows the details, but he reckons it had to be something incredibly clever." Barnabas nodded briskly. "Now, I guess that if I give you some clues, you're quite capable of going off and working things out."

"Clues?" Leslie grinned. "That sounds like Sergeant Barnabas talking. Only Barnabas wouldn't have been your name when you were on the force."

"You've heard about my past? I bet Elsie told you." He jerked his thumb towards the bar.

"She did, although she was nothing but complimentary about the fact. It seems the locals are pleased to have you here and your previous career adds to your distinction."

The abbot smiled shyly. "Well, well. Still, we're not here to talk about me or else you'd be bored stiff with all the doings of my old patch. Did you notice how worried your father is about going to hospital? No insult to you if you didn't, because he's good at hiding stuff."

"I didn't register that he was particularly worried about that, although he did seem on edge most of the time. I thought it was because of my visit and what I was talking about, but it might have been the hospital playing on his mind."

"Aye, well, he hates being out of Combe now."

"Which is why he calls it his sanctuary."

"Exactly." Barnabas took a drink. "He'll be praying—and I mean that literally—he doesn't have to stay overnight at the hospital and that he'll be in, out, and back into Brother Francis's care in two shakes."

As he listened to the easy, common-sensical voice, Leslie could vividly picture the abbot as a beat bobby, chatting to all of those under his care, making them feel both special and reassured. Perhaps the skills needed to nurture the monks weren't dissimilar to what he'd used in his previous job. "I'll pray for that too, and for an easing of my father's mind, because something weighs heavily on it."

"You're right. It's not breaking a confidence to tell you that he bears a burden of guilt and part of it was a long-time forming. He wrestled with his conscience for years before making the decision to change his life. Unlike me, because my vocation came as a total surprise. I woke up one day and I knew." Barnabas broke into another wrinkly smile. "Although your father did have a similar occurrence happen to him. An incident, if I can call it that, which tipped the scales."

So far, all the hints were in line with Leslie's conclusion. "Earlier today, you said that if I forgave my father, I was either a true Christian or I'd hit wide of the mark in my guesses. Nothing you've said now changes what I've been thinking."

"Then maybe you need to think further." The abbot took a long, slow drink. "We're on dangerous ground, Leslie. As dangerous as that flight of steps your father fell down."

"The Combe staircases sound a positive death trap." Maybe he could get some further clues to his father if he approached the subject roundabout. "Didn't Abbot John fall foul of them?"

"He did indeed, although the official verdict was an accident, no matter what folks like young Elsie think. Now"—the abbot raised his hand—"I'm not saying it doesn't happen the other way round, where murder's covered over to make a death appear accidental or due to natural causes. I know that from when I was a copper on the beat." He'd turned pale, those friendly eyes now bleak. "I can remember one woman—widow she was and face like an angel—who had three lovely little children. They were beautifully cared for, no doubt about that. The eldest got dysentery and died of it. All her neighbours were distraught for her. Still, she bucked up and carried on for the sake of the other two. Everyone admired her for that. Then, about a year later, the second child was taken ill and, despite the doctor's best efforts, she died too. Heartbroken the mother was—or appeared to be— and the neighbours were rallying round her and cursing God that He'd brought such tragedy on an innocent woman."

The abbot paused, staring into his glass, although not drinking from it.

"Which is when people became suspicious?" Leslie asked.

Barnabas nodded. "I said you were an intelligent chap. Yes. One child dying is a tragedy. Two *might* be tragic, but it might also be deliberate. That sort of stuff has happened before. I started to watch the woman and child like a hawk—asked the local vicar to, as well, given she went to his church regular as clockwork. Nice chap, good as they make them, although not without an understanding of how wicked people can be. So, while he was shocked when I first suggested anything untoward could have happened to those two children, the more he thought about it, the more he came to share my point of view that things weren't right. He was the one who found out she'd had them both insured. With different companies."

"Ah. She hastened their ends to speed up paying out the policies?" Leslie shivered. That story put matters into perspective: while every murder was sinful, in the pantheon of wickedness, killing one's own child had to rank at the top.

"That's certainly what we suspected. After I heard about the insurance, I went to visit her. Didn't say anything directly about how I thought she'd murdered her little 'uns, because we could have been wrong, but I laid all the caring cards on the table. Made it absolutely plain that the vicar and I had been praying for the welfare of the youngest—which we had—and how we were confident that the angels would be watching over her. Said how we'd be doing all we could down here on earth to keep her safe too. Must have scared the mother into behaving herself for a while."

"'For a while'? What happened after that, to the other child?"

"He's fine. The vicar got wind that the mother was planning to move, no doubt to somewhere she could get a third policy paid out on without anyone being suspicious. After that, I guess she'd have gone to ground altogether. We knew a sympathetic judge who sped up having the child made a ward of court because of parental neglect so we could take him into care. The mother kicked up a fuss, as did some of the neighbours, accusing us of picking on a poor, innocent woman who'd had enough sorrow in her life." Barnabas raised an eyebrow. "She had them all deceived, as we expected. The vicar helped soothe the situation, which took a level of diplomacy I couldn't have managed. He couldn't accuse her of murder outright, until we got an order for an exhumation on the other two. Dear God, that was a horrible business."

"What did it show?"

"One of them showed signs of poisoning, while in the other that was debatable. Both had enough fibres in their noses and throats to suggest they'd been smothered. The insurance companies picked up on things at that point and jointly employed an agent who worked with us. Lo and behold, her husband had also died of so-called natural causes and she'd had him insured with yet another company. She'd changed her name, in case anyone got suspicious, and she might have carried on with her nasty little game with no end of men—brides in the bath in reverse, if you like."

"What happened to her? And the child?"

"When she was confronted with the fact that we had evidence she'd killed her children, she confessed. Showed us what she'd given them to make the mites ill in the first place, the very pillow she'd used to smother them, and gave us a full explanation of how she'd drugged them so they wouldn't put up a struggle. Almost boasted about it: mad as a hatter, behind that angelic face, so I doubt it was simply a case of greed. She was unfit for trial and got committed, never to be released, I hope." The abbot drained his glass. "Her little boy's fine, though. The vicar knew a couple who were desperate for a child, and they adopted him. His family came to Combe, a few years back, because they wanted to say thank you to me for saving his life and make a donation to the abbey to show their gratitude. I told them not to be so daft because the only repayment I'd ever want was for him to advise me on my aches and pains when he's qualified to do so. He's at Winchester College now, with a view to going up to Cambridge to read medicine."

"Bright lad, then? Shame the other two didn't get their chance to shine." Funny how Leslie felt such a sense of loss for two children he had never known and yet had experienced not a jot of grief at Fergus's death. How many people *did* regret his passing? There might have been parents alive at the time, or an ex-lover who'd mourned him.

"You're right there. Wicked shame. Still, out of all that evil came a bit of good. That case was at the heart of my big revelation about my true vocation. I'm not saying God made it happen to nudge me towards the cloistered life and then to Combe, because

I don't believe He'd do terrible things to further some end of His own. But He used it to tell me what He thought I should do."

Leslie nodded. Was Barnabas using this story to tell *him* something related to his father's choosing this vocation? If so, he wasn't sure of the connection. Not yet. "Would you like another?" he asked, pointing at the abbot's empty glass.

"Yes, but it's my turn to get them in." Barnabas rose and headed to the bar, leaving Leslie to mull over the awful tale he'd been told and applying it to Fergus.

Who benefitted from his death?

The question, so obvious and so stupidly overlooked, came careering into his mind, cutting through all his other thoughts. He—and maybe others also—had been focussed on the victim and his character. The ill will he'd generated and the threats made to him, both personal and martial. Leslie couldn't recall anybody who'd profit from Fergus's death, apart from the world as a whole being better off now that any potential victims of his schemes, financial or personal, were protected. Somebody might have had the man's life insured, although it was doubtful such a policy could apply to somebody on active service, but there might have been another financial benefit, for example through an inheritance. Fergus had never seemed to be short of a bob or two, so where had that money gone after his death?

"You're miles away."

Leslie, blinking, found the abbot laying two pints on the table. "Sorry, I *was*. Thanks for this." He raised his glass. "What you've just told me about brought to mind a chap I knew—not a great mate but a friend of friends—who was killed during the war. An accident in training that some folk think was self-inflicted and others are sure was deliberately engineered. A bit like what was said to have happened with the previous abbot, so that's twice I've been reminded of it."

"Tricky waters, these type of cases. You don't want to get into them if you can avoid it." Barnabas, sipping his beer, nodded slowly, perhaps thinking of his experience of dealing with irate neighbours when they'd taken the boy into care. "Any evidence to support the death not being accidental?"

"Not much. The victim had plenty of enemies and he was possibly about to face a court-martial. It sounds thin, I know, but it's a pricking of my thumbs, like *you* must have started to feel about that woman. Even a chap who was there when the accident happened says he has his suspicions although he can't quite work out how it could have been done. The victim apparently fell on his knife, you see, one he wasn't supposed to be carrying."

"Ah. That and the court-martial would add fuel to the self-inflicted-wound camp's fire. They may have a point." Barnabas tipped his head towards the bar. "No doubt my friend there told you about the rumours going round that the previous abbot may have been pushed down those stairs. She may not know about the camp who say he chucked himself down them because there'd recently been complaints made about how he treated novices. Some of the complaints related to years ago, although the grievances had only recently surfaced. Thing is, from what I knew of the man's character, I bet he'd have wanted to stay on and fight his corner out of sheer bloody-mindedness."

Fergus had been bloody-minded too. More likely to be killed in a lover's jealous rage than kill himself. "Murder's definitely ruled out in the abbot's case? One of the novices that complained about him couldn't have returned to give him a nudge down the stairs and into the next world?"

"I confess the sergeant part of my brain considered that, and I did mention the idea in passing to the chief constable although he dismissed it. Oh yes, he was there at the funeral, believe it or not, supposedly to pay his respects to an old friend. Abbot John had important connections, you see and, to be honest, nobody at Combe was among the complainants. And while anyone could have got into the grounds from outside—it's not as if we've got the place fenced off—they'd not have been able to get into the abbot's lodgings, which is where it happened, because the old s—" He paused, grinning. "That was nearly the sergeant speaking. The old man was obsessed with locking the door to his rooms, which was near the bottom of the staircase up to his bedroom. I don't bother with that, although I've had a handrail installed for those stairs, because I don't want to come a cropper myself if I can't sleep and need to wander down."

Similar to Fergus's case, then. Not so much *who* might have done it but how could it have been done. "I've two other questions to bother you with, one spiritual and one civvy street. First of all, is murder ever justified? I'm not thinking of your old abbot, but he brought the matter to mind. Hitler, say. If somebody had got hold of him in 1936 and quietly disposed of the menace, thereby likely saving millions of lives in the process, would that have been defensible?"

The abbot glanced at him sideways. A troubled look. "Now, that's something I've wrestled with too. Jesus tells us that if somebody strikes us on one cheek, we're to turn the other, which is all well and good when it's only us involved, but when it comes to protecting someone else . . ." Barnabas shrugged. "All those people in the concentration camps—men, women, and little children—wouldn't have appreciated everyone turning the other cheek back in 1939, would they? So, I'm afraid I can't give you a definitive answer. Too complex for us mere humans to work out. Is your second question as tough?"

"I hope not." Leslie fortified himself with another mouthful of the excellent beer. "In your professional—or should I say erstwhile professional—opinion, how could you stab a man through an artery and not get yourself covered in blood?"

"Hm. That's the easiest thing you've asked me. I can't guarantee this would work, but I reckon you'd lessen your chances by coming on him from behind and then you'd do this." The abbot glanced around bar, probably to check they weren't being observed, then mimed grabbing someone, perhaps by the head, jerking him backwards, and stabbing viciously. "I remember something like it from the East End. Get your hand away quickly enough and you might avoid much of the spatter. Now, promise me you're not thinking of using such a method."

That was certainly a way Fergus's killer could have done the deed. Leslie raised his hand. "I solemnly swear."

Someone hailed the abbot from the other side of the bar, at which Barnabas said he'd have to go and chat. They shook hands and he went, carrying the remains of his pint, leaving Leslie to ponder how the man had so neatly sidestepped parts of the conversation and to wonder why exactly he'd had the story of the murderous mother outlined so clearly. To demonstrate that Barnabas was nobody's fool or to encourage Leslie to remember that the most innocent face could mask a killer?

James had a face that had been compared to an angel. Did Barnabas know about him from his private discussions with Leslie's father? And could James, like the murderous mother, be hiding a dark secret?

CHAPTER EIGHT

As the train headed north and east towards London and home, Leslie could appreciate the scenery in a way he'd not been able to on the journey south and west. England was certainly a magnificent country, one whose freedom it had been worth fighting for.

It was turning into another glorious day and if the weather held, he and Max could enjoyably stretch their legs later.

His subconscious must have been working overtime, because twenty miles from London he suddenly saw—as clearly as if it been written across the green and pleasant land—something he should have realised the day before.

The clues had been not only in Abbot Barnabas's words but in his father's. *Sanctuary.* Leslie had taken that in its broadest sense, a place where the man could feel safe from the world and its temptations, but what if it had been meant in the old way? A place where Mr. Cadmore was safe from prosecution, as long as he remained there? In Leslie's mind that would be a church, although the grounds of Combe might fulfil the same purpose. To be honest, he didn't know that much about the subject, except for being pretty sure it no longer had a legal application, although the Benedictine order might see things differently. Church authorities didn't always go along with secular law, and maybe Mr. Cadmore had turned on his persuasive skills to nudge them in what he felt was the right direction.

The idea of sanctuary would also explain why Leslie's father had been so reluctant to go to hospital and why he didn't want to stay there overnight. Brother Francis accompanying him could be significant too, ensuring the man wasn't left alone, although Leslie doubted his father could run away. Perhaps Francis's main role was to stop anyone else laying hands on his charge. Still, if Leslie was right about what had prompted his father to become a monk, it seemed a far stretch that a policeman would be so officious as to follow his father all the way to Devon simply to arrest him on an indecency charge. Treason or some other major crime might warrant that, although the former surely had to be ruled out because Mr. Cadmore had always been a true supporter of king and country.

If he'd confessed—or partly confessed—such a thing to Patrick, Leslie could imagine the advice he'd received. *Give yourself up to the police or take yourself off where you can't bring disgrace on your son and wife.* There'd be plenty to discuss when he and Patrick met tomorrow evening. What the hell could Leslie's father have been seeking sanctuary for?

Monday evening, Leslie entered the bar, rather fraught at having been delayed on the underground, to find Patrick already waiting for him. While the initial atmosphere wasn't as constrained as at their previous meeting, some of the tension had understandably returned. They still had much to discuss and plenty of reconciliation to go through before their relationship could be anything like it had been.

As they ordered their beers, Leslie asked about the conference and listened with growing amusement to Patrick's account of a belligerent delegate trying to disrupt one of the sessions and finding himself thrown out.

"All in all, it was worthwhile going, though. I hope your week's been as profitable," Patrick concluded.

"Workwise, yes. The rest . . ." Leslie shook his head. "Do I start with my mother's bizarre theory about how Fergus was killed, Marianne's tale about the court-martial, my father seeking sanctuary, or the abbot who used to be a copper and whose predecessor may have been pushed down the stairs?"

Patrick had been listening to the list with increasingly wide-eyed amazement, and he'd certainly raised an eyebrow at the word *sanctuary*. "I think you'd better start with Combe. It sounds like something out of a book."

"It was." Leslie gave a brief description of the abbey and its remarkable leader. "Before I went down there, I spoke to my mother, both so she'd know what I was doing and to get further information. As a result, I built up a little theory about why Father went and left us. Nothing I heard at Combe contradicted it, not that he mentioned anything outright. I'm going primarily by how he reacted to what *I* said."

"What's this theory?"

"It's about him and James." No reaction to that, although Patrick might have steeled himself not to give the game away, whatever Leslie told him. "Mother said he'd been very taken with James, which wasn't suspicious in itself, although issuing an open invitation for him to call was totally out of character. When I saw Father—which was in the Combe sick bay as he's got a suspected broken leg, so that was rather bizarre in itself—he flinched every time James got mentioned. Then it turned out they'd met up a couple of times in London, supposedly by chance. To discuss James's doubts about his vocation. That might have formed part of their conversation, but I doubt it was all. And then he kept saying he was better off at Combe, as were we with him being there." Leslie wet his whistle. "Which is a round-the-houses way of getting to my theory. That my father was—perhaps still is—attracted to men in general and James in particular. As a result of which, he felt he had to take off and leave us behind in case he brought disgrace on the family. After he'd spoken to you, of course, because he thought you might be a sympathetic ear, either because you were an old friend or because he'd recognised a kindred spirit."

Patrick took a slow draught. Eventually, he said, "You're getting closer. I know your father didn't tell me everything behind his choice, and that includes the exact nature of his relationship with James. He confessed he was perhaps overly fond of him, and I interpreted that in the same way as you have."

"But other things caused him to go? You're not breaking any confidences if you simply say yes, because I've deduced that myself, after some hefty hints from Abbot Barnabas, who feels a responsibility to Mother and me."

"Then, yes, there *was* more. What do you think it was?"

"Something particularly serious. Something he felt he needed to have sanctuary for. In the old meaning of the word—a place he was immune from facing justice."

Patrick's eyes narrowed. "He never used the word 'sanctuary' with me, and he didn't talk about facing justice, either, or I'd have told him to report to the police. He didn't tell me all the details, however, so you could be on the right track. I'm probably going to break his confidence, but what you've said puts another perspective on me keeping shtum. He believed he might have inadvertently caused a man's death. I have no idea who the victim was or the exact circumstances. I asked if he'd done something like striking an object when driving in the blackout, failing to stop, and subsequently thinking he might have hit a pedestrian. All your father would say was that accorded with the general principle, although the details weren't correct."

Leslie nodded. That fitted in with what he'd learned at Combe. "Whatever it is, surely he can't be actively under suspicion? As far as I know, nobody's tracked him down about it, and if Mother's had the police round on his trail, she's not mentioned it. She wouldn't have kept that to herself. Hold on." He drummed the table. "Could it have been the tramp in the churchyard?"

"Eh?"

"Take your mind back to playing hide and seek at Larkspur. *That* particular game."

"Ah." Patrick smiled, his cheeks flushing. "The one when Marianne got so annoyed at us."

They'd been twelve, and the game had changed their lives in a stroke. He and Patrick had, by accident—at least Leslie had assumed it was accident at the time although hindsight had made him revise that opinion—tried to hide in the same small, dark cupboard under a flight of stairs, which was one of Patrick's favourite hiding places. He'd started a play fight on the grounds of his territory being usurped. They'd indulged in such a thing often before, what his mother would have called boys being boys, but never had the fight ended in such a way.

Until that time.

Whispers, giggles, an intense awareness of the other boy's presence and proximity; Leslie could relive them now, as vividly as the day itself. Bodies touching, a brief "Do be quiet, or she'll find us," and then that first kiss. It had never been established who'd initiated it, each insisting it was the other when they discussed it later, but both had participated willingly. Perhaps it had been inevitable, the result of years of friendship being re-shaped by their beginning the change from man to boy. They'd always been special to each other and, given the wakening of their natures, the result was predictable. If it hadn't been in that cupboard, it would have been somewhere else, not far down the timeline. They'd certainly repeated the experiment often.

All adolescent stuff, nothing other than a few snogs and the odd exploratory fumble until they were older and had spent a glorious week together one summer camping in Devon. A holiday that had seen them experience one of the rites of manhood. Once they'd discovered what to do, they'd not stopped. Until the great argument.

"What are you grinning about?" Patrick lowered his voice. "What we did in the cupboard?"

"And what we did in that tent in Devon."

"Ah, yes. Funny where an innocent game of hide and seek can eventually lead. I've often wondered why Marianne became so irritated at us that day. At first, I'd supposed it was simply because she'd been left unfound for too long and felt she was being edged out of our games. Later I concluded she'd got wind that some line had been crossed, although I've never spoken to her about it or about us."

"Neither have I. Although I'm always left with the feeling that she knows what we were to each other. She probably read our faces too well either when she finally found us, or since. Guilt would have been written large." Especially if she'd already begun to understand her brother's nature.

"I suspect she'd have only understood in retrospect and her refusal to play again was initially instinctive, rather than calculated."

"You mean the world to her, you know."

"The feeling's mutual. We understand each other, you see. Not the details, perhaps, but the big picture." Patrick took another drink. "Have you found anyone else to play hide and seek with? Since we met our Waterloo at Waterloo?" Trust him to leaven an important question with that quip.

"Nobody serious. You?"

"Been too busy even for much of the *nothing serious.*" Unlikely as that seemed, it was no doubt true given Patrick wasn't great at telling lies. "You mentioned the tramp in the churchyard?"

"Oh, yes." Leslie dragged his thoughts from matters romantic to murderous. Whatever had prompted Patrick to ask about Leslie's love life, he clearly didn't want to pursue the topic at present. "I'm pretty sure the poor chap died of a combination of hypothermia and malnourishment. I overheard a conversation between Father and Mother about how he'd been round to our house begging the day previously and had been sent off with a flea in his ear. That lack of charity had certainly grown on my father's conscience, with the knowledge that if we'd given the tramp a bite to eat or the money to buy it, then things might have turned out differently."

"Did he take it so badly?"

"Absolutely. It got to the point he was agonising over it, so Mother had to give him a stiff talking to. The notion of a wider implication to our actions was something he was bothered about during the early years of the war, as well. I was home for a few days, and I recall us all discussing bombing raids and whether the death of innocent civilians would prey on the mind of the air crew."

"I never thought of anything along those lines. I can imagine your dad discussing it with James, though. The tramp's death might have preyed on him much more after an encounter with he of the bleeding heart." The soft spot Patrick had for James evidently hadn't prevented him seeing those feet of clay.

"I'm sorry you've been burdened with all this. My father had no right to impose his confessions on you."

"I can't deny it gave me some sleepless nights at first, wondering if I should talk to the police, but I've long concluded that if it had been a serious offence, then the chickens would have come home to roost. I did try to persuade him to tell you all this at the time—he could have left out any mention of James—but he was in too much of a lather to think straight." He paused, then said, "I'd forgotten how easy you are to talk to. How things never seem as bad after we've discussed them."

"I've missed you too." Leslie raised his beer. "Here's to us being able to have a civil conversation again."

"I thought we never would." Patrick, with a wan smile, chinked his glass against Leslie's. "We need to talk, seriously. About why your jibe about putting sick animals out of their misery hurt me so much."

Damn. Leslie had resisted one cue—the Waterloo quip—to discuss their argument but now it looked unavoidable. Would this be about Fergus? "Go on."

"Two things happened earlier that day that put me out of sorts. Your father's letter I've told you about. You may or may not know that I'd also had to shoot a filly who'd broken her leg panicking during an air raid." Patrick sighed. "Lovely little horse, the one I took you to see. At Briggs' place. I'd been hoping that having a pint and a chinwag with you might help me see the brighter side of a world that had become very dark."

"Dear God. I genuinely had no idea." If true, that explained Patrick's apparent overreaction. But the whole tale could still be a clever cover story for what Patrick had really reacted to at the time—the implication that Fergus had been the one put out of his misery. A story only produced now when it was needed. Leslie remembered the horse, though. She'd been barely more than a foal, all long-legged awkwardness, and Patrick had spoken of buying her once the war was done. The breeder was an old pal who'd moved from Kinebridge and would have charged an honest price.

"For a while I thought you might have heard about it from Briggs, since your firm handles his business, which is why it felt such a low blow. After seeing you last week, I knew I'd been wrong." Patrick took a long draught. "Back to the present. You mentioned a court-martial."

"Right." Leslie felt slightly punch-drunk at the change of focus, especially as—in the moment that had just passed— Fergus's death had seemed less important than Patrick's dark eyes and his lopsided smile. Eyes and smile that could still hide a killer or a conspirator. "Marianne had it from Dougal— No, I've got that wrong. You've distracted me. Dougal was the one who opened her eyes to what The Retainers were really about and that was before the so-called accident. *Afterwards*, Eric told her that had Fergus survived, he'd likely have had to face a court-martial for indecency with another bloke."

Patrick whistled. "I had no idea. I wasn't part of his company, or whatever you'd call them. Operational group? I was merely there to help deliver part of the training, so I'd not have been briefed on any disciplinary matters. I had a short conversation with Fergus when he arrived with the others—typical of when you catch up with old acquaintances. He said nothing about being under a cloud, but then I guess he'd be unlikely to open the conversation with, 'I think I'm about to be put on the fizzer of all fizzers.' Hm. Does it strike you as odd that they continued training him if he had the sword of Damocles hanging over him?"

"I wouldn't know the process. Is it *innocent until proven guilty* or vice versa?" Leslie shrugged.

"Not sure I can say, either. I suspect they operated within their own rules. Suffice to say, Eric never mentioned any of this to me, but then I've not seen much of him since. I suppose he may have got his story from his pal, Chappell. The man who had all the agents under his wing."

"He sounds rather a high hat to be overseeing a training course."

"He was there on the liaison side, along with another chap whose name I couldn't tell you. The actual bloke in overall charge of the course—our man, if you like—would have wanted to make a show for them, although not quite in the way it turned out." Patrick gave a rueful grin. "I wonder if *he* found himself on a fizzer."

"Well, wherever the story came from, it's most likely the origin of the self-inflicted-wound theories. Fergus committing suicide rather than risking disgrace to himself and whatever branch of the services his mob were aligned with." Leslie shook his head. "Doesn't sound like his style, though. The Fergus I knew—not that I knew him very well—would have braved it out. Despite the fact he'd made some quip to James a couple of weeks before he died that reports of him falling on his sword would be exaggerations."

"James didn't mention that." Patrick frowned. "Still, I'm with you on the court-martial bit. Fergus would surely have gone through it and worn the fact almost as a badge of honour. And if he'd chosen that strange method of suicide, he'd have needed the knowledge of exactly where to stab himself, although he may have learned that as part of his training. In order to kill an enemy quickly."

Patrick would probably have such specialist knowledge, Leslie reminded himself, with a tingle of his spine. Another weight tipping the scales towards the guilty side of the equation. He forced himself to focus on facts, not speculation. "Abbot Barnabas said something similar, while we were having a pint. I thought it was an ideal opportunity to get some 'professional' advice without making any degree of hoo-hah, so I asked how someone could stab a victim through an artery without covering themselves in blood."

"Didn't he think you were a maniac, asking that?"

"Not at all, because we'd been discussing the rumours that the previous abbot had been pushed down the stairs, which led into some of Barnabas's old cases. My question followed on logically." Although if the abbot *had* thought Leslie a touch unhinged, he'd have been too polite to mention it. "He not only had a suggestion, he mimed the whole thing. Grab someone from behind, stab them or slash their throat quickly, then get your arm clear."

"That could work. We should have thought of it, Leslie Lad." The nickname again. Used deliberately to remind him of happier days or a simple slip of the tongue? "Typical commando type of tactic, as well. Very in keeping with the typical men we had for training and what they'd have been taught to do."

"It's better than my mother's theory. Which sheds a whole new light on the maternal mind." Leslie snorted. "She thinks the reason the killer didn't get covered with blood is that they took all their clothes off before the attack."

Patrick snickered so hard he almost spilled his beer. "That's novel. We didn't think of that, either."

"I'm pleased we didn't. Would it work?"

"Hm." Patrick gave a shrug. "I've heard of folk stripping naked on survival courses, when it starts peeing down with rain. They stuff everything in a bag with a towel, then sit on it. When the rain stops, they can towel down and put on their dry clothes while other folk are walking around dripping wet and getting cold. I don't recall it coming up on the dogs program, though. A person has a scent as well as their clothing, although it might help when you're crossing water if you can strip and carry your clothes rather than get them wet as well. I don't recall anyone employing such a tactic on that day."

"I didn't mention this bit to Mother, but could a naked attacker explain why Fergus doesn't seem to have put up a fight?"

"Knowing him, he might have thought it was his lucky day, especially if the man was well-endowed. Perhaps he thought he could set off into the woods for a quick one—you know how he quite liked an element of danger in his encounters."

"Not personally I don't." *Do you?* That was another question which had gone unasked throughout their relationship, despite the frankness with which they'd discussed Eric's frequent passes and consequent rebuffs. Probably it had never been needed: Leslie and Patrick had shown an old-fashioned, almost staid, loyalty to each other, from hide and seek through to Waterloo.

"I never did, either, although I've heard all about it. It's one of the reasons James—" He cut off abruptly.

"Yes? One of the reasons James did what?"

"Had begun to loathe him." Patrick paused again, before asking, "Exactly how much do you know about James and Fergus? I mean specifically around their relationship?"

"Hardly anything. I avoided that crowd whenever I could, remember?" Leslie smoothed a non-existent wrinkle in his trousers while racking his brains. "At opposite ends of the spectrum, I'd have said. Hedonistic Fergus who really didn't give a shit about other people's feelings and—what did you call him?—bleeding-heart James. I didn't know if they'd slept together but I assumed so. All the other Retainers did."

"'Retainers'?" Patrick snorted derisively. "I'm not sure anything they retained was worth having."

"Quite. Refusing to get embroiled with them was one of the best things I did in my life." Patrick must feel the same. The fluidity of sexual liaisons within that group wasn't his or Leslie's style. It had earned them plenty of digs from the clique—and some downright insults from Fergus—but they'd decided to put up with that, rather than conform.

"You always were sensible."

"I tried to be, although I can see how easy it would have been to get drawn into the clique. When I first knew them, I didn't get the impression they were as sybaritic as they later became, although maybe they were hiding it."

"No, I think you're right. They got worse. Fergus's influence, probably, aided and abetted by Eric. How *he's* changed, eh?" Patrick's wry smile suggested he wasn't entirely convinced by the transformation.

"True colours coming out or false ones?" Leslie snorted. "What I still don't see is quite how James started hanging around with the other men in the first place, let alone getting dragged into their less savoury activities."

"He knew Dougal, through being at school with his younger brother. He probably saw the older sibling swanning about in his cricket whites and fell hopelessly in love. Where Dougal led, James followed."

"I never knew that. James certainly seemed to hero-worship the others, although I'd always felt it was Fergus who was his idol." No doubt the other four men would have taken advantage of that hero-worship to satisfy their desires. "James's rose-coloured spectacles must have grown darker with time or something specific happened to change his opinion. Exposure of Fergus's feet of clay maybe?"

"I guess so. I asked James a couple of times why he didn't simply cut loose from the rest of them, but he seemed like a snake, transfixed by a mongoose. Only snakes don't have that air of innocence James gave off."

Leslie nodded. James had always given off the air of being a fish-out-of-water when he'd been with The Retainers. It had been that quality, rather than his schoolboy face, which had made both Leslie and Patrick pity him back then and which would no doubt have appealed to Mr. Cadmore. Perhaps that was another reason why Leslie's father had decided to confide in Patrick: if James was tied up in his motivation for leaving the world behind, then talking to a mutual friend would be logical.

"How did he feel about Fergus at the point he died?" Leslie asked.

"Ambivalent." Patrick shook his head. "When I saw him at The Gadfly, that day he must have gone to see your mother, he got quite upset talking about him. That while he couldn't feel about Fergus the way he once had, the man would always have a special meaning in James's life. He was the one to deflower him."

"He always took a delight in debauching the innocent. The naiver the better."

"Yes, he was a right bastard. Whatever James saw in him beats me."

Leslie gave him a sympathetic smile. "Their relationship hurt you, didn't it?"

"Well, I was a fool, thinking I could nestle James under my wing and protect him from the worst excesses. He did tend to kick against it." Patrick sighed. "I know rites of passage are all very well, and I'm not one to decry the delights of the Turkish bath or an occasional overindulgence in grape or grain, but there are places where you have to draw the line. The old seven percent solution for a start."

Stuff to keep you going, stuff to help you wind down—they both knew people who used the things, especially during the war. Whether for fun or with the intention of getting themselves through the next mission or getting some sleep afterwards when their bodies were awash with too many chemicals—sheer adrenaline or artificial stimulant—to allow them to drop off. Patrick didn't approve of any of them.

"Your birthday party. The one at Kinebridge, where *they* came along. I've been wondering whether Fergus was on something then."

"He was. He tried to persuade James to take some, but I managed to convince him not to. I told him I'd seen a woman jump in front of a train when she was under the influence of drugs, and it shocked him into compliance. I'd based it on what happened with Frank, of course, although he didn't know that. James never liked the man, so it would have had no effect." Patrick grinned and wrinkled his nose. He'd always been handsome, but when he pulled that particular face, he was magnificent in a goes-straight-to-the-trousers way. "Don't tell your mother this, but that pressurising from Fergus was, I believe, why James spent all that time fetching her food and chatting. She was his sanctuary from the coercion."

"It'll stay our secret." Leslie was about to wink but stopped in time. *Flirting again and with the man you keep thinking was behind Fergus's death.* And whose possible motive for the killing they were discussing right now. "Did James ever succumb to the temptation to use drugs?"

"Not that he admitted to me. You know about his heart condition?"

"Yes. I guess that's one of the reasons we wanted to protect him from the worst excesses." There'd been something wrong with James's heart since childhood, perhaps as a result of a bout of rheumatic fever.

"Exactly." Patrick's eyes narrowed. "Do you know otherwise about his taking whatever Fergus was touting?"

"No, but James told Mother that when he'd last seen Fergus—the 'fall on my sword' remark meeting—they'd both been unwell afterwards. She suspected they'd drunk too much. On reflection, it might have been a bad reaction to another stimulant or Fergus having got his hands on a contaminated batch."

Patrick stroked his chin. "Fergus would have regarded that as a feather in his cap. You know, when I first saw him arrive for that training, he gave me such a smug grin that I wanted to punch it right off his supercilious face. I guess it's easy with hindsight to assume he was gloating over some event or other, like successfully initiating James in yet another vice, although it might have been simply that he knew something I didn't. He was like that."

"It amazes me he wasn't punched more often."

Patrick snorted. "Too right. Did you know it was Fergus's influence that made James initially doubt and then reject his vocation?"

"I had no idea." Leslie shivered. If that malign power had continued to be exercised over the younger man, James might have ended up completely broken. Had Patrick decided to take the ultimate step to protect him, concocting a plausible account of the so-called accident with the help of Jefferies and Dawson?

Patrick lifted his pint and drained it. "Another? Or would you prefer whisky?"

"I'll stick with a pint of mild. It's my round, though." As he went to get the drinks in, Leslie reminded himself not to let his guard down. Only a fortnight ago he hadn't imagined seeing Patrick again, let alone chatting to him on such terms, friendly to the point of flirtation. It would be so easy to let the past speak too loudly, to extend the offer for Patrick to come back for coffee, with the inherent, coded significance they'd both understand. But that couldn't be allowed to happen while Leslie still had his doubts. Patrick could have learned to tell lies effectively in the intervening years.

When Leslie got back to the table, he said, "Talking to the abbot made me realise we'd missed an obvious question about

Fergus. I had, anyway. Who benefitted from his death? In a tangible, inheriting-a-fortune type of way."

"I *had* thought of that but drew a blank. I've got screeds of stuff I wrote in a notebook at home—doing my Poirot bit helped fill some cold and boring nights." Patrick didn't indicate if that remark was supposed to be sarcastic, pathetic, or factual. "He was an only child. His father died leading his men across the Sambre-Oise canal back in eighteen and his mother didn't remarry until Fergus had almost finished school. Surprisingly, he got on well with his stepfather."

"Not the usual story."

"Quite. They wrote to me, a couple of months after he died, to see what I could tell them about what happened that day. The letter had come all around the houses, so it may have been written sooner after the event."

"Did they have suspicions it wasn't the accident it was said to be?"

"I don't think so. She was quite pragmatic about casualties of war, having been widowed that way. I think she merely wanted to talk to someone who'd known her son and had been there at the end. I played a straight bat on it all." Patrick took a draught of beer. "They both seemed genuinely grief-stricken. As for inheritance, he wouldn't have had that much to leave—you remember how he liked to flash his money around."

Leslie nodded. So, they were back to the motive being personal rather than financial. "What else is in this notebook of yours?"

"A list of anyone else who knew Fergus who also had a connection to those present that day, for a start. Eric's mate you know about, although he was back at the base and had been for at least the previous half hour before I arrived there to get help."

"You made sure of that, then?"

"Naturally I did. For all the apparent camaraderie, Eric never really trusted Fergus." Patrick leaned forward. The bar, while not crowded, was busier than earlier and they were on delicate conversational ground. "If it was murder, I don't think it happened on the spur of the moment. The thing had to have been well planned, so, as you asked, who would benefit? Eric did, for a start. If he'd already decided he wanted a career in politics and didn't want to risk the entire truth of his past coming into the public gaze, then Fergus's potentially loose tongue would have needed bridling. His constituents would likely vote for someone who'd been around the paddock with the mares but servicing the stallions—especially if he'd been doped up on occasions too—are another matter."

"Yes. He's standing for the constituency where I work so I've had to keep my mouth shut. Any scandal affecting him might rub off on us." So many dangers for men like them in many aspects of everyday life. "Talking of association, if Eric knew about a court-martial coming up, did he think he'd be in danger of tainting via an old friend? It's the best motive we have so far."

"Except that Eric didn't have the opportunity, even at second hand via his mate, so we need to discount him." Another swig of beer. "This is rather good. Almost pre-war quality. Anyway, connections. Dougal apparently knew one of the other trainees we had there that day. Fergus told me when we had a chat before the training started. I never found out who exactly it was because he bet me a pint I'd never guess and, obviously, the bet never got checked out."

"Didn't Dougal once say he'd swing for Fergus? Or was that Donald? I can never remember which or why."

"It was Dougal, after they'd been on an enormous bender. I never regarded it with any seriousness. Anyone can make these idle remarks."

Time to confront Patrick with his own words and watch the reaction. "Like you saying you'd not be surprised if someone ran Fergus through with a bayonet?"

"And that it might be me? Yes, exactly." The offhand manner in which those words were dismissed appeared genuine, as did the way Patrick's jaw suddenly dropped. "Dear God, you weren't thinking I'd meant that as a real threat?"

"As I've said, I haven't known what to think. I got a hell of a shock when I heard how Fergus had died and then remembered your words. At the time I didn't have all the details to hand so for all I knew *you*—or anyone with sufficient motive—could have done it." If Patrick took umbrage at the words, so be it. It was time for honesty.

As it turned out, Patrick didn't seem perturbed, merely making a reassessment of matters. "You should have told me that ages ago. I'm not stupid: I did try to examine the matter from an outside point of view, as I fall into your motive category."

Were those the words of an innocent or guilty man? "And your conclusion was . . .?"

"That anyone would eliminate me from serious consideration. I couldn't have got near Fergus without being seen by Jefferies, and I couldn't have planned anything in advance as I didn't know who we'd be training until they arrived. So, I chucked myself off the roll call."

Was that list proof of Patrick's innocence, a sign that he—like Leslie—wanted to get to the truth, especially as he'd been present and still doubted the official version? Or was it instead part of elaborate preparations in case he was accused? Laying bricks in the defensive wall he would rely on by pointing out who else might have had motive and opportunity. If some of those involved had been subsequently killed on active service, nobody could call them to give their version of what happened and refute the allegations. *Beyond reasonable doubt* was a broad enough burden of proof that a little muddying of the prosecution's waters might be effective.

"Was I on that list?"

"Only briefly." Patrick flashed him a smile. "And purely because I was making a list of everyone who couldn't stand Fergus. It was a long one, as we'd both expect, although it was easy enough to whittle it down. Once I'd eliminated people who couldn't have been there unless they miraculously appeared and disappeared without being observed, I was only left with those folk who had a connection to people who were definitely present. Including James, with his cousin of a cousin or some other distant relation."

Leslie took another swig of beer. "Doesn't it all strike you as a bit too coincidental? It sounds like it's only Donald out of that clique of five who *didn't* seem to have a link to that day via someone. Add on you being there and it's positively suspicious.

Patrick shrugged. "Coincidences happen. If it wasn't coincidental, then somebody manipulated things to get us all together, and I can't offhand think of anyone official who could or would have done so, although I don't rule out the principle. I can't deny that it's odd, though. I ran several of those training sessions, and Fergus's was the only one whose participants I had any connection to. So, yes, I did consider the matter. Great minds think alike, don't they?"

"It appears so." Not completely in this case, though, unless Patrick was also torn between desire and suspicion. Plenty of evidence of the former—that remark about great minds had been playful—but had he ever seriously suspected Leslie of involvement in Fergus's death, or simply put him on the list for the reason he'd stated? "As for coincidences, I accept that they *do* happen, but they make me uncomfortable. Did you think of a satisfactory explanation that doesn't rely on serendipity?"

"I did, actually, but it only works if you put Eric at the hub of things."

"You think Eric somehow manipulated who was present that day?"

"No. I don't think he'd have been in a position to do so, for a start. What I had in mind was that he accounts for what appears to be deliberate manipulation, but isn't." Patrick chuckled. "I'd forgotten how appealing you look when you've no idea what I'm talking about."

Leslie hissed, "You can stop flirting. Answer the question."

"As you like." Patrick grinned. "I couldn't tell you how agents such as Fergus were recruited, but if this pal of Eric's had said he was keeping an eye out for suitable candidates, the man might have either suggested some names or persuaded people he thought fitting to put themselves forward. Fergus would have leaped at the chance and then Dougal—if approached—probably said something like, 'I want to join the RAF, but I know someone else who might be up your street.' Friend of a friend. Cousin of a cousin. You know how these things happen."

"I do." There'd been a similar process in the early days of recruitment at Bletchley. Somebody knew a suitable chap who knew a suitable chap and so on. All of them persuaded they'd be serving their country better using their brains than their brawn.

Patrick's uncharacteristically cruel remark at Waterloo came back to Leslie's mind, still stinging. Time to clear the air further. "Patrick, you've mentioned my comment about putting animals out of their misery and why it hurt. Your taunt about proper men getting off their arses and serving their country stung me, too. I wasn't a D-day dodger or a conchie. What I did I couldn't tell anyone about. Still can't. I *can* tell you I know about recruiting people with a proven set of skills."

Patrick studied him for a moment. "I've been an idiot. I never thought you were a conscientious objector but when everyone kept asking what you were up to and I couldn't say anything other than 'flying a desk' I began to wonder what the hell you *were* doing and why you'd chosen it, rather than something active, which would have been more in character. I didn't once doubt your work was important . . ."

"But you thought I'd found myself a cushy, safe little corner to see out the war from?" Leslie snorted. "You're not the first to think that."

"I'm sorry. I'd got myself into such a state, what with Fergus dying in the way he did. I may not have liked the man but to think he'd survived in France only to die in a pool of his own blood . . . and then that bay filly, who wouldn't have had to be killed but for Hitler's bloody planes. I couldn't see anything in perspective." Patrick raised his hand. "Please. Let's not get into another row. I want to clear the air, not fog it again."

"Alright, then." Leslie passed his hand across his brow. "Where were we?"

"Calling on people with certain skills." Patrick produced his trademark lop-sided smile.

Leslie nodded slowly. "I was going to say that perhaps our particular type makes for good agents. Or we recognise the skills involved. We're used to keeping secrets and putting on a false face to the rest of the world."

"Exactly. Open to blackmail, admittedly, although that might be the least of your worries behind enemy lines." Patrick took another drink. "The more you consider those involved, the less of a mere coincidence it appears."

"Does it help explain what happened to Fergus? You say the thing had to have been well planned, although surely it could have been a spur-of-the-moment action. A quick look round, the coast is clear and—" Leslie mimed throat cutting again.

"Unless all the gods of good luck were shining down on the attacker—which is possible but seems unlikely—then some degree of thought had to have gone into it. Getting Fergus into a place where he could attack him unseen, ensuring he wasn't covered in blood afterwards . . ." Patrick spread his hands. "I've got screeds of notes about it. Argued myself back and forward to no avail, with nothing to show for my efforts except being convinced it wasn't an accident. At times it's become almost obsessional, especially since the war ended and I could devote proper thought to it. It's the cloister into which I've retreated, if it isn't tasteless to make the analogy. You really need to see these notes of mine. Maybe you'd spot something I've missed."

"I doubt that would be the case, although I might have an attack of the bleeding obvious."

"You could come down now, if you want. I've got the car with me because I had to come here today to advise a couple of civil servants. All too boring, so don't ask about it, but it means the trip gets counted as legitimate mileage."

Leslie wondered if he should be offended by being tagged onto another meeting, but he couldn't blame Patrick for being canny with his petrol and combining his different businesses. Or should that be a case of combining business with pleasure, given the twinkle in the man's eye? There'd been a distinct hint that the invitation wasn't simply to peruse a notebook and might involve being run to the railway station early the next morning to catch the milk train.

"I think I need to refuse, although that's because of the short notice and my dog, Max. There's nobody at hand to let him out, so the poor lad's legs will be crossed into knots." Funny how Leslie could feel himself becoming consumed with worry over that issue, rather than getting exercised about any potential emotional whys or wherefores. Perhaps he'd been subconsciously waiting for the invitation to be made.

"Ah, sorry, I should have thought. Bit of a complication that, having to make sure he's cared for. Worse than children, I'd imagine, for ridding your life of spontaneity." Patrick's brow creased in disappointment. "It's one of the reasons I didn't get a dog when Digger went. That and not wanting to have the heartbreak again."

"It must have been so hard for you. I'm sorry." Leslie's mother had told him the story. Digger had been living with Patrick's parents, because his war service had taken him abroad. While the dog had hardly been in his puppyhood, he'd been healthy enough and should have lived on a fair few years. But he'd been chasing a cat, dashed out in front of an army lorry, then been hit and killed outright. The accident had happened after Leslie's split with Patrick and had preyed on his conscience at the time, making him toy with contacting his ex-lover to offer condolences. But the combination of the still painful dig about, *"What did you do in the war, Leslie?"* and the impossibility of saying what one really felt in services mail had knocked the idea on the head. Maybe that had been for the best, as a meeting then might not have been as effective as this delayed reunion was proving. Water under the bridge had enabled a greater degree of candour.

"As I said, it broke my heart." Patrick flicked Leslie a rueful glance, no doubt thinking of the pain their split had caused. "Stupid, isn't it, considering how many of our pals went west, that Digger's death hit me worse than any of theirs."

"He was part of your life. Like Towser was part of mine." *Like you were part of mine.* Leslie wouldn't say that, though, in case he sounded like Celia Johnson in a tear-jerking romantic movie. "Everyone loved Towser, even my father, and he was no great fan of pets. He used to take him fishing at the times he preferred canine company to human."

"Dogs can be more reliable."

That didn't sound like a dig at Leslie. Whatever else had come between them, unreliability—or indeed faithlessness of any kind—hadn't been an issue.

"Towser was certainly a good judge of character, which my father appreciated. He appeared to have a nose for trout too. Allegedly he once located a huge fish in amongst a bed of watercress, although that story may be apocryphal."

"I seem to remember Towser being everyone's friend, especially if there was a scrap of meat involved. Although I did hear he once caught a burglar, unless that's also nothing but rumour." Patrick chuckled.

"I can vouch for that one being true, although it wasn't quite as the rumour mill had it. He reacted oddly to a man on Kinebridge High Street when my mother and I took him for a walk. The reaction was so odd that I sidled up to the local beat bobby who happened to be outside the baker's shop and said the bloke had to be a wrong un. Towser's strange reaction and all that." Leslie had never known him to be wrong, whereas Max had no sense of whether he was meeting Florence Nightingale or Jack the Ripper. "The man saw me talking to the constable and scarpered, so said officer grabbed the nearest bike—I think it was the baker's boy's, which added to the farcical nature of the scene—and gave chase. Successfully all round, because the bloke had filched some poor old woman's jewellery."

"I wish I'd been there to see it. Did Towser join in the chase?"

"He'd have liked to. I had to keep a tight hold on his lead or he'd have been away. The only other time I heard him growl so viciously was when he met Fergus."

Patrick snorted. "Well, you did say he was a good judge of character."

"Character and actions. I was in The Gadfly having a pint with your father and mine, when Fergus appeared. He'd been visiting someone on business and stopped in for a swift half. He got talking about one of his investment schemes."

"The old man told me about that. Nobody rose to the bait, thank God." Patrick drained his pint, laying down the glass and pushing it away.

"I suspect Towser helped. Fergus didn't want to stay around a growling lump of muscular canine. I don't suppose one can—" Leslie's words came to an abrupt halt. "Sorry. I've just remembered a couple of things about that day. One was my father saying that Fergus was the type of man who if he didn't change his ways would probably find himself getting beaten up in an alley one day. Typical of what people said who weren't taken in by the oily Jackson charm, despite it being unusual for my father to speak so harshly. The second thing was his eyes when Fergus wasn't facing him. A look of sheer hatred."

"Not like you to forget something like that."

"Not normally but I'd have to be forgiven in the circumstances. It was the night Towser was taken badly ill. We had to have the vet to him: he reckoned the lad had picked up some rat poison or something similar when he'd been off the lead. Everything that happened across that day and the next has become a bit of a blur, I was so worried about him. Rightly, as it turned out. He recovered but was never the same healthy dog again. Something to do with his internal organs—your area, not mine." Neither would Leslie ever totally recover from his loss.

"I'm so sorry. Did you discover where he picked the stuff up?"

"Eventually. I went so far as to suspect Fergus, when I was at my wits' end." Leslie raised a hand. "No, I don't think he did it. Another dog, one I'd seen out when walking Towser, was also taken badly ill at a similar time."

Patrick gave him a sympathetic smile. "I know you've got Max now, but it's never the same. Towser was a one-off."

"Yes. Max doesn't have the same ability to gaze into people's souls. Perhaps my father had a similar facility, on the quiet, which is why he trusted you." Leslie leaned forward, struck by how quickly Patrick's smile had disappeared and how white he'd turned. "Are you all right? You look like you've seen a ghost."

"Not quite. I've been struck by a disturbing thought, one that hit with the force of a bullet." Patrick briefly shut his eyes and took a deep breath. "I don't want you to get angry about this, but what you've told me about your father's hatred of Fergus sheds a different light on what he told me. When you saw him, he talked about sanctuary, right?"

"Yes. I . . . Dear God." A disturbing thought hit Leslie. "Are you thinking it's a case of 'sanctuary' as in the thing you'd need if you'd been involved in murdering Fergus? But he couldn't have done it. Not even as a character in the most bizarre mystery story could Father have got himself to wherever you were doing the training, crawled through the undergrowth, tripped Fergus, and done him in."

"I'm not so daft I'd suggest that. Anyway, he has an alibi," Patrick added with a rueful smile.

Leslie's turn to be shocked. "How the hell do you know that? Did he make a point of telling you during this heart-to-heart?" If so, how odd for him to mention it.

"Yes. At the time I put it down to his being upset, what with this great decision he was on the verge of making and whatever was going on with James. Naturally, given how soon it was after the event, we discussed Fergus's death, but that made your father particularly upset. He wasn't terribly coherent." Patrick closed his eyes again, hand to his chin: clearly this was almost as painful for him as it was for Leslie. "Could he have convinced someone else to do the deed?"

Leslie winced, having been moving towards a similar conclusion. "Well, we both know what he was like. A real dab hand at persuading other folk to take on a job or whatever and leaving them oblivious to having been influenced. He could have had a motive if he was in love—for want of a better expression— with James and knew the pressure Fergus had put on the lad. Maybe including making him ill with drugs or even encouraging him into one of those suspect investment schemes."

"Exactly. Your father might have also seen it as part of some crusade. Ridding the world of a menace and protecting others."

Protecting others. Yes, that would chime with the man who'd not only cried at the sermon about the death of children but had subsequently run a choirmaster out of the parish because he didn't trust the man around the choirboys. "Funnily enough, Abbot Barnabas and I discussed whether taking a life could be justified if it led ultimately to the greater good. I had Adolf in mind—thinking back to that conversation *we'd* had—although the abbot gave me a strange look when I raised the matter. Perhaps I'd accidentally hit on something Father had confessed." Leslie slowly drained the last of his beer, taking stock. "I can't imagine him making a concerted effort to arrange someone else's death, not unless there's another side to him which I never knew." Yet hadn't that already been proven, given the departure to Combe? "What I can envisage is him getting upset and making threats. Perhaps saying how the world would be a better place without Fergus in it, in the way he'd made similar remarks about the führer and his generals. Then, when Fergus died, Father would have remembered that conversation with James and been mortified. He'd not really have intended it, any more than I might in saying I'd swing for the bloke, but he could have assumed that James took him at his word."

"In which case, he went to Combe either as an act of penance or to escape a charge of being an accessory before the act or whatever they'd call it. Some variety of agent provocateur."

"Yes. It's like the guilt he felt about that tramp. It wasn't specifically his—or my mother's—lack of charity that led to the man dying of exposure. She was able to come to terms with that fact, but I know it kept gnawing at him. Is this at all in line with whatever he told you?"

"Absolutely. It has to be the conversation with James that he was referring to. Irrespective of coincidences happening, wouldn't it be carrying credulity too far to think your father might have been pally with someone else who was present when Fergus died?"

Leslie nodded. "Exactly. Although he didn't need to have spoken to anyone who could actually have committed the deed, merely someone with connection enough that my father could have believed his words had initiated events that led to Fergus's death. For which James Lyth is the only candidate."

Patrick, with an uncharacteristic scowl, nodded.

James Lyth, of the choirboy looks and the much-vaunted innocence. How deeply was he embroiled in this?

CHAPTER NINE

There had been little else to say. They both knew that the conversation would need to continue, but it was too late—and Max's needs would be verging on the urgent—to carry on. "We'll pick this up next time," Patrick had said, rising and easing his muscles, as though the burden of Mr. Cadmore's secret that he'd been carrying had been a physical weight as well as a psychological one.

"We will," Leslie had replied, leaving the matter of venue to be decided on.

As they left, at almost exactly the same spot where he'd touched Leslie's hand the week previously, Patrick paused and said, "We never did organise you seeing those notes of mine, did we?"

"Bring them to mine." Home turf seemed safer, somehow allowing a greater degree of control, rather than Leslie finding himself stuck at Patrick's, miles from home. "One evening this week could work or next Saturday, if not?"

"Saturday's best for me. Sorry to be an old bore, but my assistant's off the rest of the week—his mother's been taken ill and he needs to get down to Bristol to organise his father, who's completely hopeless by all accounts. It means I'll need to be covering two lots of work unless I can get my paws on a locum at short notice, and I'm not hopeful about that."

"Saturday will be fine. If you want, Mrs. Gray—she's my glorified lady who does—can throw together a lunch for us.

She appreciates any excuse for showing off the magic she can perform with whatever she can get her hands on food wise."

"It's a deal. Only let me bring a decent ham. I have a few farmers—or, to be accurate, farmers' wives—who like to slip me tidbits on the quiet when I've been up tending their livestock. There have to be perks to the job, considering some of the things I do."

Leslie laughed at the thought of where Patrick's strong yet gentle hands sometimes had to go. "Mrs. Gray will be delighted. Twelve noon at mine?"

"Yes. If I knew where *yours* was, which I don't, not being telepathic."

"Sorry, I'm such a numbskull. Let me jot it down." Leslie found paper and pen, writing his address and telephone number, which were both different from when they'd been a couple. "Max will be delighted to meet you."

"The feeling's mutual." Patrick slipped the paper into his wallet, as if it were some secret formula that mustn't fall into the wrong hands.

The parting handshake lingered a touch too long again, as did the smile they shared. As Leslie set off for home, he couldn't help but wonder—given how much clearing of the air had gone on— what Patrick would be offering as dessert and if it would involve a double bed. Although he didn't know as yet if he was ready to accept what was on the menu.

Next morning, Leslie was still mulling things over. The previous evening had raised a lot to take in, on all three fronts. Fergus's death, Mr. Cadmore's entering Combe, Leslie's relationship with Patrick—on the face of it all separate but becoming increasingly intertwined. In particular, the idea that Mr. Cadmore could have believed himself responsible for Fergus's death, while ostensibly nonsensical, had gained traction in Leslie's mind. If the man had been under increasing strain, perhaps because of guilt associated with his attraction to James, then he'd likely not have been thinking clearly. Had Leslie's father made a "Who shall deliver me from this turbulent priest?" type of statement and convinced himself it had been acted on?

As he shaved, washed, got dressed—all the everyday tasks—Leslie reached the conclusion that there was only one logical next step. He had to see James and, if luck was with him, he'd do it before Saturday, even if that meant taking a day's leave. It would feel slightly treacherous seeing James on his own, given that he and Patrick now seemed to be forming a partnership to get to the truth behind Mr. Cadmore's taking the cowl, but logistics had to come into play. Easier by far to get two people together rather than coordinate three busy lives. He'd ignore the consideration that Patrick didn't always see straight where James was concerned and might not be the most objective interviewer. To *him*, James had always been the victim, the wronged innocent with his choirboy looks; had that now changed as a result of their conversation the previous evening?

What he did know was that his own brain had been reconsidering a wealth of information, old and recent, while he slept, because he'd woken with a changed point of view. What if James, far from being the blameless prey, the young man who had admirers drawn to him—both romantic and platonic—had played an active role in making things happen? What if he'd pursued Leslie's father, given his liking for older men, and had noticed a responsiveness in him to male advances that his family hadn't? He could imagine James playing on that mutual attraction to pour tales of woe into Mr. Cadmore's ear, building up sympathy and perhaps egging him on into denouncing Fergus.

The first challenge was the practical one, Leslie not having an up-to-date contact address or phone number and not wanting to befuddle the operator with a request for "James Lyth, believed to be living in Wales." He could contact Eric, though. The man had been in touch with the office when drumming up support for his nomination as candidate and his number was tucked away in Leslie's desk there. If he didn't know where James was now, he might be able to start Leslie on the trail.

However, when Leslie called him at lunchtime, Eric sounded distracted. "Sorry, old bean, long time no talk and all that, but I'm a bit rushed off my feet at present, so if you've rung for a chinwag, can we make it another time?"

"I should apologise for bothering you. I wanted a current telephone number or address for James, if you have it."

"Oh yes. Why's that?" The guarded note in Eric's voice was unmistakable. He'd not want a reminder of his past.

"It's to do with my father." Keeping on that track rather than mentioning Fergus might be less contentious. "I'd be grateful if you could oblige."

"I've got one somewhere. I'm afraid I'm about to go into an important meeting. However, once I've finished, I'll ring you back with it if you can give me your number. I know I have *that* too, but it'll save time if I don't have to root it out."

Leslie gave him it, with no great confidence that he'd be called any time soon. Eric might not think it a priority to do a favour for someone who couldn't—or wouldn't—vote for him. So, it was a pleasant surprise when the telephone call came a couple of hours later, although it wasn't Eric but his secretary on the line. A clipped young man, who introduced himself as Gareth Briggs and who'd evidently been told that this request was somehow tied up with party business given the thanks he passed on to Leslie for "furthering the cause." Leslie didn't disabuse him of the notion, being both indebted for the information and broadly sympathetic to Eric's need to hide the past.

"You needed the telephone number for a Mr. Lyth?"

"Yes." Perhaps Eric had avoided using "James" as it might suggest a personal connection. "I appreciate the help. It's an important matter."

As the young man gave the details, repeating them to ensure the crackly line hadn't led to the number being misheard, Leslie couldn't help wondering if Gareth was the secretary Marianne had made the unpleasant "lame duck" joke about, although he'd likely never find out. He thanked Gareth and returned to the work piled on his desk.

He called James in the evening, half-expecting that the telephone would be answered by the chap he lived with, but James came straight on the line, sounding grateful that he'd been caught on his own.

"*He's* down the allotment association or something madly gay like that," James said. "How's your mother?"

"Doing very well, all things considered." Leslie didn't want to get into chitchat now, though. He had one aim in mind. "Is there any chance you and I can meet up? I've a couple of things I want to discuss and in person's better than on the telephone."

James didn't seem surprised at the request. "Of course we can. I'm actually coming down your way tomorrow. A few days in Oxford with work. I could get the train into Paddington station on Thursday evening, if you like. There must be a bar there or nearby."

"I don't want to put you to any trouble. It would be easy enough for me to come to Oxford instead."

"No, I feel I owe you an explanation, so I should be the one making the journey." The words didn't sound like those of a guilty man trying to hide the fact, but Leslie wasn't sure he should make such a judgement so glibly and without seeing James's face. He wasn't a hundred percent sure that Patrick didn't have a guilty secret still hidden.

"Thursday it is, then. I know a little place near the station. No, not one of *those* kinds of places."

"Pleased to hear it. We're all trying to maintain our veneer of respectability."

They agreed a time and place, then Leslie brought the call to an end. James had sounded chipper, much as he always had, though the point about owing an explanation had been made in darker tones than usual. Would it turn out to be something like, *I'm sorry I seduced your father!* or was Leslie, yet again, barking up the wrong tree?

At first glance, James appeared hardly to have changed. Only when Leslie got closer could he see the fine lines etching the boyish face. In a few years' time, James would appear prematurely aged, as could so often happen when an angelic face had been tempered by dissipation. Admittedly, Leslie could be reading hints of debauchery into James's appearance, his viewpoint being coloured by a change of perspective. One turn of the kaleidoscope might shift James from his traditional status as a hapless victim. Like when you looked at a baby and tried to find a similarity to one or both of its parents: you saw what you wanted to see.

The bar proved blessedly quiet, possibly because the price of drinks kept it exclusive. They went through the usual rigmarole of ordering beer, finding a table where they could talk in relative solitude, and then some sharing of news, professional and social. James spoke warmly about his "special friend" David, the chap twenty years his senior in whose house he'd now become a fixture. All the references to David were salted with that special expression James wore when he knew something others didn't, an expression identical to a mischievous schoolboy's.

"You seem to think you owe me an explanation," Leslie said, when he'd become tired of banalities.

"Ah, yes. It's about your parents. I went to see your mother when I was down Kinebridge way, and I'm afraid we started discussing Fergus Jackson's death, because I'd seen him not long before he died and she was interested in what all the old crew were up to. If she's got a bee in her bonnet about whether his death was accidental, blame me for having wound her up."

"She already had an interest in his death, I believe, so the worst you did was agitate a bee that was in occupation." Leslie couldn't help the sharp edge to his voice. He reminded himself how unfair it was to change his view of a man based on nothing but speculation, but he could no longer regard James in the old light. "You said 'parents,' plural. You've mentioned my mother, so what do you want to say about my father?"

"Simply that we met on a few occasions in the months before he went to Combe. He was very kind, listening to my worries and helping me to wrestle with my vocation. I felt you ought to know."

"I was already aware you'd met and what you supposedly talked about, but only because my father told me when I went to visit him this Saturday just gone. You clearly knew that I was in the dark up to that point and assumed I still was now. Why?"

James suddenly appeared to find the contents of his glass far more interesting than facing Leslie. "Because he asked me to keep quiet about our meetings. Given my past, he felt they could be open to misinterpretation."

"If you don't mind me saying so, that sounds like a load of nonsense. Why should anyone misinterpret a man meeting an old friend of his son's to discuss such an important issue?"

James smiled, a touch of the genuinely nice little boy coming through again. "I don't know why I've been so stupid as to think I could lie to you. You were always too astute."

"I don't feel like I've been particularly astute the last few years." On the contrary, he felt like he'd been in a daze and was only now coming out of it. "However, I'm not here to judge you or my father. All I want is the truth and to know how much of it I can tell my mother. I'm tired of people hiding behind walls of so-called confidentiality."

James took a fortifying drink. "You want the truth? He was attracted to me and I was attracted to him. Par for the course for me, although I really did feel bad about it." Probably not for long, although this time there did appear to be some honesty in what Leslie was being told. "Your father was uncomfortable and embarrassed about his feelings—ashamed of them, really. When he was at school, he'd fancied some of the older boys but assumed that desire was only what many youngsters go through in the circumstances. A crush, soon to be grown out of."

"Did he ever have any suspicions about me? That I'd felt the same about the boys I knew?" Patrick in particular.

"If he did, he didn't mention it. He wouldn't have discussed private matters that concerned other people."

That was in keeping with his character. "This mutual attraction. Did you act on it? A simple yes or no is all I need."

James blew out his cheeks. "A simple yes or no won't cover it. We tried to but it wouldn't work. I don't mean we couldn't find a time or place—that wasn't an issue—only that when it came to the deed, he balked. Made an excuse and left, as they say. We never met up again."

While it was a relief to know that his father had remained faithful to his wedding vows, it raised more questions about his going to Combe. He couldn't have been ashamed at committing what the law saw as indecent acts if the indecent act hadn't happened. Unless this was the specific incident Abbot Barnabas had referred to as creating the final nudge to the abbey. "I'm guessing he experienced a lot of shame about what he felt. And what he was about to do."

"Yes. I mean, it's not so bad for chaps like you and me and David, all fancy-free and whatnot, but he had your mother and you to think about. Your father loves her deeply—loves you both—and didn't want to burden you with his disgrace. I think it was that love which stopped him in his tracks when we were in the bedroom together." James raised his hand. "No further details, I promise."

"For which I'm grateful. I'm also relieved to hear that he still had affection for us. It seemed hard to believe when he upped sticks." Leslie could imagine his father's internal wrangling, although he was angrier than ever that the man had sought to discuss his deepest worries with comparative strangers rather than those closest to him. *And aren't you a chip off the old block, with those questions you don't dare ask?* "You used the word 'loves,' not 'loved.' Are you still in touch with him?"

"Yes. He doesn't want me to go and see him, naturally, but we exchange the occasional letter, mainly on spiritual matters. I think he'd quite like me to take the cowl. Feels I may have been mistaken in chucking up my vocation. I remain unrepentant." James chuckled. "Besides, I'm not sure David would approve of me taking a vow of chastity."

"Quite." The thought of any of The Retainers embracing an abstemious lifestyle was ludicrous. Still, James's assertion didn't ring true. Mr. Cadmore had recognised as clearly as any of them that James wasn't suited to the life of a priest, albeit the life of a monk would probably mean he'd be less at risk of being taken advantage of. Or was Leslie going to doubt the "too soft" part of James's nature too? Best to stick to facts. "You spoke to my mother about Fergus Jackson. Did you discuss him with my father?"

"Not after he died. I didn't see your father in person after that." James studied his glass.

"Haven't you discussed him in your letters?"

"I tried to, on the principle of your father having met Fergus a couple of times so perhaps having an interest in what had happened. I wanted to explain what rumours had been going around, but he told me in no uncertain terms that the subject was closed. I didn't raise it again."

"What about before Fergus died? Did the pair of you discuss him then?"

"Only a bit." James's wide-eyed demeanour might have taken in someone who didn't know him well, but Leslie was sure he wasn't telling the whole truth. "Obviously Fergus—and my relationship with him—was tied up with my doubts about being ordained."

Time to move from facts to a leap of supposition. "You saw Fergus not long before he was killed. Did you see my father after that?"

"Yes. That was the day of failure I spoke about. I was upset about my meeting with Fergus because I'd been sick as a dog afterwards, and I daresay it was that which prompted your father into making an offer that he regretted afterwards." James had now turned to face him, perhaps surprised by how much Leslie already knew—or appeared to know.

"Whatever else my father was or is, he's always been sympathetic to those in need. To the extent of flogging himself afterwards if he felt he'd failed them or made the wrong choice. You'd have been knocking on an open door if you were upset about Fergus, because Father already had no love for the man. What exactly did he say to you about him?"

James seemed to consider for a moment. "I can see there's no point in prevaricating. He was angry with him, particularly when

I told him that Fergus had persuaded me to try some stuff at that last encounter. He'd said it would improve my mood and help me see things clearer. As I said, it only made me ill. I was still feeling rough when I met your father."

"I can imagine Father's reaction to that story." Perhaps Fergus's actions would have been seen in a similar light to Herod's: the innocent made to suffer.

"He was livid. Went into a speech about how the world would be a better place if men like Fergus had been drowned at birth. He wasn't the only person who felt that way, as both of us know."

"True. No wonder so many rumours have flown around about his death." Leslie paused, to drink some beer and see if James responded to the statement, but the only reply he got was a nod. "Did Fergus tell you he was at risk of a court-martial?"

"Yes. Something to do with one of the younger men he'd been working alongside in France. Oh, I shouldn't have mentioned where he was based."

"I won't be telling anyone you did. Go on."

"Well, there's not much to tell. The usual story of Fergus trying his luck: this time with a raw recruit. *He* said his advances got rebuffed, at which point the other man started telling people he'd been coerced into sexual activities—which was a lie—and when Fergus returned for a spot of leave and further training, it all kicked off. Whether the court-martial had actually gone as far as being been set up, I doubt. He was worried about the prospect, though, under the cool veneer. It's why I wondered if he'd staged his accident." James's hand on his glass showed a slight tremor, perhaps betraying deep emotion. "Naturally, I didn't tell your mother every part of this. I felt it would have been unfair to all concerned."

Leslie nodded. "If it had got that far, was Fergus going to fight to prove his innocence?"

"He said so. We both know he never lacked bravery. But when he was telling me the story, he was already under the influence of whatever he'd got us to take, so what he said may not have been an accurate reflection of his state of mind."

And James's memory of the meeting may have been affected in the same way. "Did my father know this was hanging over Fergus?"

"Only after I told him. I wish I hadn't, because it made him angrier still. Although I'm not sure if that was because I'd be tainted somehow by association or that he felt aggrieved at the thought of another young man being led astray."

Leslie held his tongue about which one had been doing the leading when it had been James and Mr. Cadmore together. It seemed likely James had milked his supposed innocence for all it was worth. Was still milking it.

"Just as well that Fergus wasn't present that evening," James continued, "or there'd have been violence done."

"And not long afterwards, Fergus was dead, in horrific circumstances. On an occasion where several of The Retainers had connections to those present. You included."

James raised a hand. "Steady on, there. What are you insinuating?"

"Nothing. I'm merely stating facts. Patrick, some mate of Eric's, a pal of Dougal's. Your second cousin." Leslie smiled, pleased that he'd rattled James. "Who was your relative, by the way? Patrick was interested to know."

"Alec Jefferies," James said, after a significant pause. He'd evidently realised he'd not get away without answering the question.

"The dog handler?"

"Yes. Patrick probably didn't realise, because when I heard they were going to be working together, I asked Alec to keep his relationship to me quiet. I didn't want the past getting in the way, either for bad or good. I know Patrick had a soft spot for me. Not in the same way he had for you, naturally. Shame that's all done with now—I had hoped you'd end up like an old married couple."

Leslie felt his hackles rise. Old married couple? *Mind your own bloody business.*

James, apparently oblivious to the effect his words were having, continued blithely. "Maybe you'll get together again. I always felt you were made for each other."

Maybe he was speaking with the best of intentions and genuine concern, as Leslie's mother might discuss Marianne if she'd broken up with a long-term sweetheart. But as James had played his part in breaking up the Cadmore family, the sentiment didn't quite ring true. "Alec must have been upset about what happened. I hear he was one of the first to see the body."

"Eh?" James blinked. "Oh, yes. Yes, he was. I mean, we all became rather inured to violent death during the war, but Alec wasn't expecting to see so much blood."

James had done his bit during the conflict as an air raid warden, having been unfit for active service because of his heart condition. That could have finished him off in the field but had been unlikely to pose a risk while he flew a desk. He'd surely have seen plenty of dead bodies when dealing with the aftermath of bombings.

"Did Alec have any view on what had happened?"

James shrugged. "Simply that it had been an accident. I know I got rather concerned that Fergus had done it to himself, perhaps in a moment of depression after one of his induced highs if he'd been thinking about the court-martial. Now I think it could have been nothing other than a tragic mishap. A *there but for the grace of God go any of us* type of moment."

"Neither Alec nor you think there could have been a deliberate element to the death? Not on Fergus's part, on somebody else's." Leslie studied James's face as he asked the question, noting the disquiet it caused.

"I'd be a liar if I said that I hadn't considered the possibility. I talked it over with David, knowing how many folk would have been pleased to get rid of him, but neither of us could work out how it could have been done in the circumstances. David's a Conan Doyle fanatic, and while he *will* quote that awful line about eliminating the impossible and having to believe what's left, we couldn't even come up with an improbable solution." James drained his pint, although the way he pushed his glass away suggested he didn't want another.

Leslie could think of an improbable solution, one that might have appealed to Holmes's penchant for the convoluted. What if Jefferies had deliberately inserted a thorn into the dog's paw, knowing that Patrick would always put the dogs' welfare first? If that turned out to be true, Patrick would be angrier about it than at Fergus's death. If Jefferies had then ensured the vet was the one to go off to get help for the injured man, that might have given him the opportunity he needed. Patrick would have been away for ample time to allow Jefferies to finish off Fergus, clean himself up, and be ready to act the part when Patrick returned.

Don't be so bloody stupid.

The timeline didn't work, for a start. Fergus had gone tumbling while Jefferies was approaching Patrick, and it was the other man, Dawson, who had alerted them to his being dead while they had still been fussing over the dog.

"Do you really think Fergus could have been murdered?" James's question cut into Leslie's thoughts.

"I don't know what I think happened. I realise that men who aren't well liked *do* have accidents or die of natural causes, but something about this business doesn't feel right. Didn't Fergus say to you that it would be no surprise if he ended up being stabbed?"

"He said I shouldn't be surprised if I heard about him falling on his sword, or words to that effect. I took it to refer to the threat of court-martial."

That didn't quite agree with what James had said earlier about the man's mood, nor what Marianne had reported, but Leslie would let it pass. "Alec's never dropped any hint about suspicions concerning that day?"

James, frowning, appeared at a loss before wagging his finger. "Do you mean about Patrick? No, *he* couldn't have had anything to do with it. Alec had been trying to find Patrick, to get help after his dog picked up that barb in its paw, so when he spotted him, he kept a close eye on the man. Didn't want him wandering off somewhere so he'd have to chase him farther. That covers the crucial period, I think. Unless . . ."

"Unless what?"

"Well, it's occurred to me that, as far as I know, we only have Patrick's word that Fergus took his fall when he was supposed to have done so. I guess there's a tiny possibility that he might have done the deed, got himself clean, and then resumed his observation position." James produced a sympathetic smile. Leslie would have put money on his not having had the thought just occur to him, that this was a deliberate attempt at either stirring up trouble or deflecting attention from Alec. Yet it chimed with the concerns he'd had. "It would mean the time of death wasn't quite as had been attested, but the body was found a little while after the event, so would a few minutes either way make a difference when it was examined? I'm not clever enough to know all the medical stuff, although someone in the business might be."

Someone in the business like a vet? All Leslie's misgivings, which had been ebbing away since he'd re-established contact with Patrick, came rushing in again. Timing would have been the key to everything, and a heap of luck. Not being seen while committing the act, for a start.

"Have I been indiscreet?" James said waspishly. "Feel free to ignore me being an old gossip."

Leslie rose, pushing away his unfinished drink. "Nothing would give me more pleasure than to ignore you, James, but it appears I must accept that I can't. I don't think there's much point in us meeting again, as you've given me whatever explanation you felt was owing and added plenty on top. Words once spoken can't be unsaid."

He turned on his heels and left, desperate for his home and a good long walk with Max.

The underground journey homewards passed in a blur. Leslie couldn't have told anyone where he'd changed lines or how busy the platforms had been. All he could think of was Patrick and the simple solution that he'd already committed the murder by the time Jefferies arrived with his injured dog. That would mean he could have been telling the truth about everything that happened after the stabbing. Leslie needed to consider this objectively.

Opportunity: that wasn't in doubt, if he shifted the time of death. Motive: plenty. Means: there was the rub and the thing that might argue against his guilt. If the crime had been planned to look like an accident, then where did the blade come in? Patrick would no doubt have been carrying a scalpel or similar item with which to attend to canine casualties, but the presence of such a knife by the casualty, or evidence from the wound that one had been used, would have pointed straight to the culprit. Patrick would never have been so stupid. So, he'd have had to be carrying another knife, one he could pass off as Fergus's and which would never have been linked to *him*, or opportunistically used the weapon the victim had about him. The latter was better in keeping with Patrick's character, being a person who might strike out in anger rather than coldly nursing revenge. Yet, how could he have known about the knife, unless Fergus had shown him it? Had there been an argument, with the weapon brandished? In that case, couldn't Patrick have claimed self-defence, rather than constructing the misdirection about time of death—misdirection that had in part relied on Jefferies and Dawson turning up when they did, the dog with the serendipitous thorn in the paw.

Patrick would never have committed such a deed with dogs around, especially if they were tracker dogs.

That subjective thought gave Leslie more reassurance than any amount of objective thinking had. Yet, if James had actually been deflecting attention from Jefferies, then all the points about means and luck still applied. What if luck had never been a part? Maybe the killer knew about Fergus's knife, decided to make use of it, and engineered all the rest at very short notice. If he went down that route, then Jefferies distracting Patrick at the key time seemed highly suspicious, especially when he'd made a point of not revealing they had a mutual connection. But Jefferies couldn't have killed Fergus prior to approaching Patrick, nor could he have done it afterwards, because Dawson . . .

Dawson. Another attack of the bloody obvious. If he and Jefferies had been acting in concert, then the whole thing was workable. *Jefferies distracts Patrick at the crucial time, moments after Dawson has tripped Fergus, thus allowing him the opportunity to attack the victim with less of a risk of being observed.* Maybe there'd been no need to trip him, as they could simply have taken advantage of a genuine fall, although if Dawson had been involved in similar war work to Fergus, and had undergone the kind of training these agents were rumoured to have undergone, then the assault from behind—exactly as the abbot had demonstrated—became eminently possible.

While Patrick had been away, the pair of them could have done any clearing up that was necessary, perhaps with Jefferies giving Dawson a change of clothes. Coordinating their actions would have been a challenge, but that could have been overcome if they'd planned on a particular time, with a view to carrying out the assault *then* if they could and if not, abandoning the attempt. That dealt with opportunity, so what would have been the pair's motive? Alec Jefferies could have been ostensibly driven by vengeance at Fergus having inveigled James into taking drugs, especially if their effect had been worse than he'd admitted. Leslie knew of folk who'd ended up at death's door because they'd taken too much of the wrong stuff, and if Jefferies had been persuaded that the only way to prevent something like that happening again was getting rid of Fergus, he might have seen this as the ideal occasion. It would be put down as another death in training, the sad but inevitable consequence of preparing people properly for battle conditions.

So, what about the knife? If it was Fergus's, Dawson may or may not have known about it, which in turn led back round to the question of how they'd have killed Fergus otherwise. You had to be damned skilful to be able to break a man's neck and make it appear to be the result of a fall, and any other method would surely have screamed foul play. Did agents have cyanide capsules and could someone make it appear that a man had tragically yet unintentionally bitten into his?

Head beginning to spin, Leslie concluded that he clearly wasn't cut out for amateur sleuthing, although he couldn't wrench his thoughts away from James and the pivotal role he appeared to have played in one significant occurrence and might have played in another. He got out the little jotting pad he habitually carried and attempted to produce a timeline, acutely aware that he didn't have the exact dates for when things had been happening or how long had passed in between.

James and Fergus had met a couple of weeks before his death. They had both been ill afterwards. At some point between then and Fergus's death, James and Mr. Cadmore had shared an encounter that had been turbulent in various ways and seemed to have been the catalyst in making the latter head off to Combe. Hard on the heels of these meetings, Fergus had been killed. Had there been enough time for James to get Jefferies to engineer the crime? Mr. Cadmore had perhaps believed so, unless the pivotal point in his leaving home had simply been his desire for James and the debacle of the bed they'd nearly shared. No, the timescale didn't suggest that. He'd entered the abbey after Fergus's death, with his heart-to-heart with Patrick happening in the interim.

If Leslie had concluded that James was tangled up in the murder and had seen a way in which it might have been done, then it was equally possible his father had done the same and, remembering the rant he'd unleashed against Fergus, felt he'd somehow prompted it. Any information Mr. Cadmore would have had about the death would likely have been obtained at second or third hand so might have been riddled with inaccuracies, and he'd have been capable of misinterpreting it. Unless Patrick had given him more accurate details and those had added to his burden of guilt.

Leslie stared blankly at the train windows. Whatever the truth, his chat with James had left a sour taste in his mouth that might never go away.

When Saturday came, Leslie found himself increasingly contending with bubbling up nerves, and he wasn't sure if they were due to the renewed concern about Patrick's role in the murder or simply the man's imminent presence in his house. The choice of home turf rather than a neutral venue was feeling less and less like a sensible one. Whatever the cause of his anxiety, he felt horribly like a man who was about to embark on his first serious date.

Fed up with moping around and getting under the feet of Mrs. Gray, who was giving the house a spruce up, Leslie decided he needed to stretch his legs, hoping that the exertion would steady him and clear a mind that was becoming worryingly cluttered again. Max—who wagged his tail madly at the sight of his lead, no doubt not believing his luck at all the extra exercise he was getting—would also benefit from being taken on a longer than usual morning walk. The day was fine, the temperature not unpleasant, and the pavements quiet as they strolled towards the local park.

"Get a grip." Leslie didn't realise he'd spoken the instruction aloud until Max turned and stared at him with a bemused expression. "Sorry, boy. Not a new command for you, just an old one for myself."

He really did need to get a grip or he'd find himself wandering down the rocky road into mental strain. Yet why was it that as soon as a thought had some clarity in his mind, it became fuzzy again?

"I wish I had a life that was as easy as yours," he told the dog. "To have nothing else to think about than food, walkies, and cocking your leg up a lamppost."

Max, maybe taking the last part as another new instruction, obliged at the one he was standing next to, which gave Leslie a much-needed laugh. Here was hoping that the rest of the day might throw up some equally unexpected gems.

Luncheon was excellent, Mrs. Gray's salad and homemade rolls proving a magnificent accompaniment to the splendid cooked ham Patrick had brought with him. He'd insisted she take some home to share with her sister, to which Mrs. Gray had demurred, although with such a wistful look in her eye that Leslie had threatened he wouldn't let her babysit Max unless she did as requested and take the treat she deserved.

"She seems like a real diamond," Patrick said, as they drank coffee after their meal.

"I'm lucky to have her and long may that situation prevail. She's clearly taken with you. I noticed her blushing." He'd introduced Patrick to Mrs. Gray as an old friend, and he'd been effusively charming to her. Whether she had any suspicion about what "old friend" represented in reality—and what her reaction would be if she did—he couldn't tell.

Despite the fact Leslie reckoned that Mrs. Gray never listened at doors, they'd made sure that while she was in the offing they'd confined the conversation to catching up on family and work matters, including some amusing things that had happened in Patrick's practice in his assistant's absence.

One of the consultations had involved an overwrought owner of a pampered pooch, at which Leslie had confessed that the only person who spoiled Max was Mrs. Gray. "I forgot to tell you what happened when I told her you were coming over and what you did for a job. She apparently convinced herself that Max had contracted a terrible disease, which is why I'd called you in for specialist advice rather than use the local man."

"Oh, bless her. I suppose me in the role of an old friend appearing out of the blue didn't help."

"Quite. I didn't find out why she seemed so worried until the next day, when her sister rang me to say she'd barely slept for fretting and could I give an answer about Max's health one way or another? Funny how people get things into their heads for the slenderest of reasons."

Patrick shook his head ruefully. "We should know all about that, Leslie Lad. Both got a track record for it. Do you think you've reassured her?"

"Eventually. Max helped by positively leaping all over her when she next came, although that may have been due to the bone she brought him. The treat was no doubt because the tinker wasn't imminently likely to kick the bucket. Anyway, if you could drop something into the conversation about how he's the fittest dog you've ever seen—subtly and convincingly of course, in case she thinks we're trying to cover a crisis up so we can let her down gently later—I'd be grateful."

"I'll make it a priority. If only for the dog's sake, rather than your grey eyes. Mrs. Gray will be ruining him with bits of cake and other stuff he shouldn't have, otherwise."

The last person to mention Leslie's eyes had been Patrick himself, before the argument at Waterloo, when he'd called them *come-to-bed grey eyes*. The memory prompted Leslie into action. "You talked about our track record for making assumptions. Can we clear up another one? Why did you think I'd given you the cold shoulder because you'd had a secret discussion with my father? A meeting I knew nothing about. Simply a guess?"

Patrick grinned. "No pussyfooting for you today, is there? I had good reason, because that's what James told me."

"What?" Leslie pulled his fingers through his hair. "How the hell would he know what I was thinking at any time, let alone around then? I don't think I'd seen the bloke in ages."

"I know that, because I remember asking him if he'd had it direct. He was adamant it was so, and I'd always understood he'd heard it via your parents. That's certainly what he implied. I don't think I merely imagined it."

"I bet you didn't. If you tell me you got it from James, I'll believe you. Whether *he* thought it was a fact I'll reserve judgement on. Begs a load of questions, though, like how he knew you and my father had met. Ah, how stupid of me—" Leslie raised his hand "—it's obvious. He must have heard it from the horse's mouth, since he and my father have kept in touch by letter all this time."

"Have they? James is a real dark horse, isn't he?" Patrick sipped his coffee. "Did your father tell you they'd been corresponding when he saw you at Combe?"

A knock on the door heralded Mrs. Gray saying that she was off home unless she was needed further.

"We'll cope, thank you."

"I'll make him wash up," Patrick said, with a flash of his most charming smile.

Once she'd gone, they returned to the question. "The letters between James and Father. I found out about them a couple of days ago, when I met James for a pint." Leslie couldn't mistake the surprise—and disappointment—on Patrick's face.

"You didn't tell me you were meeting up."

"When I last saw you, I didn't know we would be. Last-minute opportunity came up, and then it was a matter of practicality, you being so busy with your assistant away. I didn't think you'd want to be dragged off to Paddington station at a few days' notice." The explanation didn't seem to be working, perhaps because it was largely being constructed as he spoke, albeit based on fact. Leslie should have anticipated this and would have to expand on what he'd said. Although he'd leave out the detail about calling in a favour from Eric, because that might elicit the question of why he hadn't asked Patrick for one. "After we chatted, I decided to ring James, as we had to get to the truth. He was coming to Oxford for a few days and offered to pop up to London. He reckoned he owed me an explanation and as it turned out, he did."

"Go on." Patrick poured them both another coffee from the pot.

"He confirmed what I'd concluded about my father being attracted to him. They'd met several times."

Patrick's moue of disgust echoed Leslie's thoughts. "If there are sordid details, please spare me them. I don't need to know anything further."

"I know you don't, but airing it clarifies the situation. There's nothing physical coming up. I was amazed about the letters, but James swears my father wants him to take the cowl, as well, although—in view of what I'm about to say—I think that's a lie." Leslie gave a summary of what he'd learned about the two men's dealings, including what had been said between them about the court-martial, Mr. Cadmore's rage concerning Fergus, and the failure of events in the bedroom.

"You'll be relieved at that. The bedroom bit, not him getting angry at Fergus. We can both sympathise with that." Patrick patted Leslie's arm in an affectionate manner, redolent of happier times that had seen plenty of bedroom successes for *them*.

"Yes. The more I think about it, the more it turns my stomach that they could have . . . you know." Leslie winced. "It mightn't have been so bad if he'd got entangled with a total stranger. I have been trying to drum up some sympathy, thinking of what I'd have done if I'd been in a similar position to my father, haunted by desires that I'd either kept buried for ages or hadn't realised I had until James came along to awaken them."

"Many men are in the same position. Happily married, with children or grandchildren, and that family life isn't necessarily solely a matter of maintaining a respectable front. Nothing about your father's behaviour has ever suggested he didn't have a happy marriage. He could have simply struggled to find a means of fulfilling both parts of his life—as some other chaps have managed to—and still square his conscience."

Leslie nodded, appreciating Patrick's objective summary of the situation. "I suspect it was conscience rather than anything else that prevented him going all the way when he and James were in that bedroom together. I bet James gave it his best shot at making things happen, though. Anyway, before my mind starts to haunt me with images of that, let's get onto the other bit of the puzzle. I got out of James that he's related to Alec Jefferies, and before you remind me that you didn't know that, you weren't supposed to. Jefferies had been told to keep his connection on the QT, which may be suspicious in itself."

"James kept it on the QT, as well. When we met at The Gadfly, he made no specific reference other than something like, 'Isn't it a small world? I'm vaguely related to one of the chaps who was there that day, but I don't think you'd have run across him.'" The imitation of James's voice was spot on, if emphasising the habitual air of helplessness. "I asked him who that was but never got an answer. Before he replied, he raised his glass to take a swig of beer and some bloke bumped into the back of him. The beer went flying, there were apologies all round, and we had to get cloths to mop it up. After which he started to reminisce about that time Eric managed to soak himself in Guinness and ended up going home wearing someone else's trousers. In the light of what we've just discussed, that spillage and the subsequent change of conversational direction seems highly suspicious. Although I suppose if you believe you're on the trail of a murderer, everything seems suspicious."

"Certainly, at the moment, I'm re-examining everything I know about James. I really don't think he's the little angel we all thought him."

"I've been having similar thoughts this past fortnight. It's been a bit of the old 'scales falling off the eyes' business." Patrick pointed to his notebook, which lay at the other end of the table. "I don't think you'll find him listed among the main runners and riders in there. I'll need to revise them."

"Well, it all does lead into a possible solution for how Fergus could have been killed, although it's as full of holes as a Swiss cheese. Do you want to discuss it here or repair to what Mrs. Gray calls 'the parlour' and I call my snug?" A cosier place to sit, with a fire nicely laid and a view of the garden.

"Snug it is." Patrick rose, picked up his notebook, and waited to be shown the way.

En route, Leslie stuck his head round the kitchen door to encourage Max to come along and meet their visitor properly. "You don't need to mind your p's and q's in front of him," Leslie said, as they took chairs either side of the hearth. "He's oblivious to anything that doesn't concern food or walks."

"Quite right, eh, boy?" Patrick stroked the dog behind his ears. "You don't want to concern yourself with the stuff that bothers humans."

Leslie nodded for reply, temporarily choked with emotion at seeing the pair together—sitting at *his* fireside—and the instant rapport they'd established. Max was a tart of a dog and liked to be everyone's friend, but the way he snuggled against Patrick's leg, face lifted and observing him with obvious affection, was unusual.

"Your theory?" Patrick's question was probably well-timed, because Leslie had been on the brink of saying something he might have regretted, a rather too sentimental reference to past times they'd shared.

"That James, knowingly or unknowingly—and I'd suspect the former—persuaded Jefferies to get rid of Fergus. He and Dawson could have been working together, with Dawson committing the deed, while Jefferies's primary role was to distract you at the key moment and ensure you had to go off and get help. Creating time and opportunity for them to clean up what needed cleaning and do any staging of the scene to make it appear an accident."

"Sorry to steal your thunder, but I'd actually considered a scenario like that and rejected it." Patrick, with an apologetic smile, leaned forward and handed Leslie the notebook. "Read this, with as open a mind as you can manage at such a remove of time and so much speculation in between. I started these notes not long after that training course, when I wanted to get everything down while it was still fresh in my mind. They've been added to subsequently, so may not read logically."

"I'm not expecting the standard set by Mesdames Allingham or Christie." Leslie opened the notebook's cover, to find Patrick's familiar, neat handwriting. "There's today's paper on the table, if you want to browse that while I'm occupied with this. Or there's plenty of books if you'd rather read one of those."

"Am I allowed to do the crossword in the newspaper? I won't be treading on your toes?"

"Feel free." Leslie hadn't been able to concentrate on it that morning, anyway.

The notebook began with an objective, highly detailed account of what had happened on the day Fergus had been killed, including annotated maps of who had been where and when, alongside some description of the topography. Everything confirmed Leslie's mental image of the scene, as did the timeline of events that came on the next pages. He didn't really learn anything new, Patrick having been accurate in his recollection and retelling of the story, although the details became clearer. Dawson, for example, had been smeared with blood on the sleeves and chest of his jacket, ostensibly from where he'd tried to help the victim.

If the account wasn't true, if it was part of a guilty man covering his tracks, it was an impressive work of fiction. Surely Patrick couldn't possess such low cunning?

Leslie needed to find out how much of this account had been noted contemporaneously with the incidents it described. "Did you write all of this part at the time?"

"Eh?" Patrick's head shot up. "Sorry. Struggling with a nasty little play on words among the across clues."

"How long after Fergus died did you make these notes?" Leslie showed the pages concerned.

"Over the next couple of days, whenever I had time. I needed everything jotted down while it was clear in my mind and before other folk's versions of events started to cloud mine." Patrick stroked the dog's head, which was positioned on his knee vying with the newspaper for attention. "My primary aim wasn't investigation, but to ensure I could give an accurate account to any enquiry that ensued. Mulling over whether his death had been murder came later."

"And was there an enquiry?"

Patrick shrugged. "If they held one, it was all done internally. I was never called to answer questions, although the chap in charge did send someone to take a statement. Chappell—Eric's pal—wanted to make sure the right thing was done by his men, or so this officer said."

"Thanks." Leslie got his head down over the notebook again. The next entries came in a different pen, evidently made later. Pen portraits of all the main characters involved, again serving to flesh out Leslie's knowledge, although nothing he learned appeared significant to his eyes, apart from the fact that Jefferies had been on Patrick's team for a month and had clearly never mentioned his relationship to James. Although, to grant the man the benefit of the doubt, he might have felt it unwise mentioning as a mutual connection someone whose proclivities were illegal.

The list of people had been annotated in red pen, probably as Patrick thought over the mystery, because the notes concerned what involvement they could each have had with Fergus's death—the old pair of means and opportunity again—and any reason they might possess to have killed him. The only person who had anything of real note against his name in that category was Patrick himself.

Time to air James's hinted accusation.

Leslie glanced up, only to be struck again by how like old times the scene in the room was. Both together by the fire, not needing to speak, simply comfortable in each other's company while occupied with their own business. Should he say something to that effect?

A knock on the front door, the postman with a gardening catalogue too thick to go through the letterbox, and the moment was gone.

"Mrs. Gray will enjoy going through this on my behalf," Leslie said as he re-entered the room, flourishing the catalogue to gain Patrick's attention. "Less interesting than your notebook. I notice you've included yourself on the list of *dramatis personae*, by the way."

"I have, given that I was there." Patrick smiled—a smile that soon disappeared when Leslie continued.

"You also appear to have included yourself amongst the suspects. When I saw James, he rather made a point of saying how you'd have been in prime position to do the deed. Or to have already done it and cleared away the evidence before Jefferies came up with the dog that needed help."

"The little sod." Patrick appeared angrier at James than either affronted at the accusation or determined to plead his innocence. "I suppose he thought I'd then pretended to see Fergus fall, long after he actually went down."

"Something like that. You'd be feeling safe, given your veterinary knowledge, that the time of death couldn't be pinned down exactly. Especially if there was a delay before the body was found."

"I hope you didn't believe him."

"I can't help but admit that the idea did shake me, although I've managed to persuade myself you'd never have done anything with so much blood involved while there were dogs about."

Patrick, evidently choosing his words with care, stroked the now sleeping Max on the head. "Because they'd have smelled the residue of Fergus's blood on me?"

"I was less thinking that than the fact you wouldn't have wanted them to get upset." It seemed so daft now, accusing Patrick, when he gave off such a convincingly innocent air. Yet James's idea was a valid one. and Patrick's own notes pointed out his status as suspect. "I know less than nothing about tracker dogs, because they're clearly trained to react differently to the average hound, but Towser hated the smell of blood. He'd have gone mad if he'd seen that body."

"Too bloody right. It sounds callous, given that Fergus died, but I keep thinking about the dogs, especially the one with the thorn in his paw. I'd dismissed the idea of Jefferies's involvement for a couple of reasons—you'll get to them later in the notes—but if I thought he'd deliberately hurt his charge as part of a plan I'd—" Patrick stopped. "No, I'd better not make any further threats. They can come back to bite you."

As the bayonet remark had. Leslie smoothed the notebook. "Was that why you listed yourself here? If so, it's honesty of the highest order."

"Less honesty than objectivity." Patrick looked him straight in the eye. "I didn't do it, Leslie. I can't deny I was pleased to see the back of Fergus and from that day, there have been times I'd have gladly shaken the hand of whoever did it. But I swear, on all that's holy, it wasn't *my* hand that did the deed."

They paused, eyes fixed on each other. While the dreaded question hadn't been asked, an answer had been given. If Patrick could make that assertion and be lying, then he wasn't the man whom Leslie had known so well and loved so deeply. Nor was he anyone he'd want to love again.

"I believe you." At last Leslie could say those words and mean them. "It's the detail of the dogs that seals the deal."

"Not my trustworthy nature?" Patrick snorted and went back to reading the newspaper.

The next set of notes Leslie read detailed various ideas in no particularly rational order. These were all similar to ones Leslie had considered himself or discussed already. He soon reached the theory about Jefferies and Dawson being in partnership, noted the bit about any decent dog handler being unlikely to hurt his own charge, then read that the pair were said not to know each other.

"How can you be sure?" Leslie asked.

"How can I be sure about what?" Patrick rolled his eyes. "Even after all these years, I can't read your mind."

Leslie grinned. "You'd try the patience of Job. How can you be sure Dawson and Jefferies didn't know each other prior to the day Fergus was killed?"

"Because Jefferies asked me who the idiot with the long hair was—meaning Dawson, only I didn't know he was called Dawson at the time. He did have long hair, but I think it was part of the image he was cultivating as part of his persona in France." Patrick tapped the arm of his chair, waking Max and then having to apologise for interrupting his slumbers. "I've literally this minute remembered Fergus making some remark about that. Some quip along the lines of, 'With legs like those, cross-dressing's an obvious ploy for him,' although I have no idea if there was anything behind it or whether he simply fancied him."

"Dawson wasn't the young man Fergus had allegedly seduced, was he? It might give him a motive, if so."

Patrick shrugged. "No idea. If he was, I didn't register any tension—or indeed attraction—between them. Anyway, regarding Jefferies, he could have been dissembling when he appeared not to recognise Dawson, but his reaction seemed genuine enough. Some people are better actors than either of us, though, especially if they come prepared for their role. Hey, Max, had enough of me?"

The dog, whining, had got up and walked towards the door. Leslie eased out of his chair. "The silly sod needs to visit the garden, and he's left it to the last moment."

Patrick gestured for Leslie to sit down. "I'll take him while you carry on reading. You're probably about to reach the old *cui bono* bit."

As predicted, he soon did, this section being much as expected. It consisted of a simple list of people, not all of whom had been present on the day, as Leslie discovered when he saw both himself and James on the roll call. Each person had at least one reason written against them, some being annotated with *highly unlikely* or—in his case—*don't be stupid*. The persons reckoned to have some of the strongest motives, objectively speaking, were also among those who hadn't been present.

"Reached the part about his financial beneficiaries?" Patrick said, re-entering the room with a much happier Max in tow.

"Yes. This whole part fills in a few blanks for me. Fergus always played the family issue close to his chest, and I didn't care enough to press him on it."

"I had most of the information from Eric and James, who also told me Fergus had left a decent amount. Hadn't yet run through it all on riotous living." Patrick, settled in his chair again with Max taking up position at his feet, had taken a volume from the bookshelves as he'd returned. The crossword must have been completed or abandoned.

"This older sister who got everything in Fergus's will. She was living in Canada at the time?"

"As I understand it, she emigrated there with her husband and children in 1939, which is interesting timing, although not in relation to her brother." Patrick's frown showed what he thought of the move, although the family wouldn't have been alone in having left Britain with the prospect of war looming. Protecting one's nearest and dearest or deserting the country in its hour of need, depending on how one viewed it.

"And his mother went with them?"

"Yes. She and his stepfather, which was a sore point. Fergus felt both he and Britain had been abandoned, a viewpoint I can sympathise with."

Leslie nodded. With his real father having died when Fergus was still young, he'd have felt the apparent abandonment deeply. "His family upping sticks probably didn't help in terms of keeping him in line."

"Quite. But all in all, I think we can eliminate financial gain as a motive."

"I'm glad to see you discounted my motive, as well." Leslie pointed to the relevant part of the page. "His having tried to tap into my father, financially."

"I told you I'd been thorough and objective. Those grey eyes of yours weren't enough on their own to make me eliminate you from consideration."

The second mention of his eyes. "Would you please stop flirting? And you can stop pouting, while you're at it. For one thing, it makes you too distractingly attractive. It always did."

Patrick replaced the pout with a rueful smile. "You used to like me flirting. How did it get to this, eh?"

"Because we're a stubborn pair of buggers who made assumptions and didn't bother to check whether they were correct before we ripped each other to shreds."

"Thank God we've cleared things up, then." Patrick leaned forward, hands clasped between his knees, a pose he only took when he was being deadly serious. "I've missed you, Leslie. I confess I'd have cheerfully punched you on occasions, as I'm sure there were times you wanted to belt me. But I have to admit it's been a bit miserable without you."

Leslie suppressed a grin at the British male's capacity for making understated yet profound romantic pronouncements, answering in kind. "I've missed you too, you silly sod. No." He raised his hand to discourage Patrick from leaving his seat. "If you come over here, we both know where it'll lead."

"Really?" Patrick, eyes wide, was a picture of mock innocence. "Care to enlighten me, or will that sully the dog's ears?"

"No and yes." Leslie shook his head. "Patrick, I've been thinking about this moment for a very long time. Thinking it would never happen too, so it's come a bit too soon for me to get my head around. Especially as I'm trying to figure out all the other stuff. I feel like there should be nothing romantic on the menu until we get to the bottom of this business."

Suddenly, Patrick bridled. "Because you still think I might be guilty of Fergus's murder?"

"No, as I've already told you. I believe what you've said, and if you're acting like the doctor out of *The Murder of Roger Ackroyd* to distract me from the truth, it's an Oscar-worthy performance."

"You're mixing books and films there, Leslie Lad." The use of the nickname suggested Patrick's umbrage was receding as quickly as it had arisen. "Why, then? I mean, I know the change has come around quickly, compared to how we were when we met a fortnight ago, but it's not like we're going anywhere we haven't already been."

"I know, I know. I simply don't want to be distracted now I feel I'm closer to the truth, particularly about Father. As you said, I've made too many assumptions over the past few years and I've fallen into the trap of too much sloppy thinking. The boss would have had my guts for garters during the war if I'd demonstrated so little logic." That would leave Patrick to ponder over why Leslie had needed to employ logic. He produced the most encouraging smile he could muster. "Once I've got some of the answers I need, I'll let myself think about you, me, and a big bed. In the meantime, I'm going back to this." He raised the notebook, with a pleading look.

Patrick seemed to consider this for a moment, slowly nodded, and then raised his novel, in return. "I'll console myself with Biggles, then. I've not read one of his adventures since Larkspur days, so it'll raise memories of past times, soon to be repeated. I hope."

"As long as you take the stories with a pinch of salt, they're still good fun, especially the earlier ones." Leslie had found them strangely consoling in his darkest moments, reminding him of happier times—as Patrick had just said—and always speaking of good triumphing over evil. But the sight of Patrick making himself comfortable, book in hand and Max still glued to his side, threatened immediately to tear up his resolution about eschewing romance until the mysteries were solved. Time to concentrate solely on the notebook, rather than the hands that had written in it.

Working through the last few pages—which had clearly been updated after their recent meetings—Leslie didn't encounter any great revelation, although he was steadily refining the theory he'd presented earlier. By the time he'd reached the end, and after a moment or two's contemplation, he was left with the feeling they might both have been blind.

"Paddy Boy . . ."

"You've not called me that in years. I'll take it as a good omen."

"As long as it's a deferred omen, then yes. I think we might be missing the obvious, on a couple of counts." Leslie tapped the palm of his left hand with his right index finger. "The knife. We've never really considered why Fergus was carrying it, apart from him either being bloody-minded regarding the rules or so used to stuffing it in his pocket he was carrying it unwittingly. What if he'd put it there intentionally for the purpose of self-defence? Because he thought he was in real danger from someone who was going to be present that day."

Patrick, whistling, laid Biggles aside. "I knew if you read my notes, you'd think of something I hadn't. It *is* bloody obvious, isn't it?" His face began to drain of colour. "Hell's teeth. What if he was worried about the wrong man? Me, I mean, rather than the person who killed him. Because he knew I always stuck up for James and would have gone mad if I heard about Fergus making him ill with dope."

"It wouldn't surprise me if that had crossed his mind. We both know he never really liked you, and that dislike could have become twisted into a paranoiac belief that you'd take the opportunity to attack him. Especially if James had been doing some shit-stirring." A cold sensation tingled through Leslie's spine. "Thank God you didn't end up having a confrontation with him, either as part of the training or because he'd wound you up."

"I know. I might have been the one 'accidentally' falling and stabbing myself."

Leslie shivered. "Was there any indication he was worried about you? He didn't give any hint, like keeping his distance?"

Patrick shook his head. "No. There was nothing in his demeanour or behaviour to give me any suspicions, but as I've said, I didn't have much to do with him and we only passed a few words. Including the comment about Dawson. I don't recall Fergus showing signs of nerves or whatever around any of the others, either. I tried to remember at the time whether anyone had been aggressive towards him and I couldn't think of a single instance."

"How did he sound when he made the cross-dressing remark? Jovial? Bitchy? Hostile?"

"You're thinking it might have been Dawson he was afraid of?" Patrick shrugged. "Nothing I remember supports that but, as we've said, they'd have been good at dissembling. Have you ever read the Christie story *The Idol House of Astarte*?"

"If I have, I don't remember it. Why?"

"The victim accidentally tripped and the killer—under the pretence of going to help—stabbed him. Complete spur-of-the-moment thing. It could have applied here, especially if Fergus had been knocked out when he went down and the knife had fallen from his pocket." Patrick stroked Max's head seemingly automatically. "It means there doesn't have to be collusion or a great plan. This could be exactly the instant decision that an effective operative would have to be good at making because their lives behind enemy lines might depend on it. For all I know, Dawson may have had experience of carrying out a similar attack."

"That would take out the need for Jefferies to be involved." Strangely, that felt a relief, because it further reduced the—admittedly small—chance that Leslie's father bore some responsibility. "Dawson might have spotted Jefferies talking to you and counted it in his assessment of the situation. Abbot Barnabas could have been spot on with his theory of a surprise attack from behind."

"Yes. And the blood on Dawson we assumed was due to him 'helping' Fergus and a futile attempt at first aid."

Leslie drummed the chair arm. "I've thought of something else, although it contradicts the theory about Fergus carrying a weapon for protection. You said the knives were standard issue. Dawson could have been carrying one for protection if *he* was the scared party. Easy enough to pretend it was Fergus's. As for motive, it doesn't need to have been Dawson himself involved with the court-martial. His close friend or colleague having been led astray could be enough incentive for taking revenge or making a pre-emptive strike."

"Like my potential motive?" Patrick snorted. "You could be right. The comrades-in-arms loyalty can be a fierce thing. Although, to flip it back again, did Dawson—or anyone—need a motive if Fergus made the first move in a fight?"

Oh, to have been a fly on the wall—or on a blade of grass—that fatal afternoon. "Where's Dawson now? That's not a question I'm expecting you to have an answer for, by the way."

"I might be able to get you one, though. So, that's something we can pursue when we can. What's next today?" Patrick raised his hands, as though signalling surrender. "That's not meant to be a pass, I promise."

"It had better not be, because I mean what I said. Result first, bed afterwards." Leslie gave him a grin, though. That felt like a binding commitment made now, and the idea of the reward for a successful solution was becoming increasingly appealing, the previous awkwardness gradually on the wane. The simple domesticity of the afternoon had worked as well in terms of their reconciliation as any previous clearing of the air had done.

Patrick, sombre-faced again, said, "What if we don't get a result to either problem? Your father keeps playing a dead bat on all questions, Dawson turns out to have died at the hands of the Germans, and anyone who knows what really went on continues to keep mum. Do we end up in thirty years' time grey-haired, arthritic and still refusing to share a bed because we didn't achieve the impossible?"

"I hadn't thought of that." The prospect seemed awful. "Let's remember that a month ago it seemed impossible we'd even be talking to each other civilly again, so maybe the incredible can happen. But that sounds terribly like a bad pep talk."

"I'm glad you admitted that, because I'd have had to point it out, otherwise." Patrick grinned. "Do we set a point of review, then? A time by which, if we haven't reached a conclusion or a point where we've got a reasonable chance of achieving one, we say, 'Sod this for a lark'?"

"Three months," Leslie said, for some reason sure that was the right timescale.

"Did you choose that deliberately?"

"No. It came to mind as being neither too long nor too short. Why?"

"It'll be around the anniversary of when we played hide and seek. *That* day. Seems appropriate, doesn't it?"

"Yes. I suppose it does." Their eyes met, lingering so long it threatened to unman Leslie. It would be so easy at this point to say, *To hell with waiting for a solution, let's do it right now*, but that would be a mistake. There was also a chance that the commitment he'd made, three months or not, would itself seem like a huge blunder come morning, but he'd have to cross that bridge when he came to it. He broke the eye contact. "Three months it is, then. We still don't have our plan of campaign, though. Should we try to find out about the young man Fergus had got ensnared with?"

"Seems logical. I'll get on the case because I may have the right contact. Same bloke who could put us on Dawson's trail. One of my customers, again, so my job does come in useful."

"Quite the spy network. Better use than the connections I build up in the office."

Patrick snorted again, rousing Max from a doze he'd just got into. "Sorry, lad. Cover your ears while I point out to your master that *he* doesn't have to spend his day with his hands in unmentionable places, so there must be some recompense, whether it's people giving me ham or information. Oh, you recognized the word 'ham' did you?"

"I think he'd recognise the name of any food in any language. It's a gift he has. Shame he can't use it to help us."

"Well, I'm not promising anything on the secret operatives' front, so don't hold me to account if I draw a blank. Still, if this chap doesn't know, he might be able to point me at someone who can help. Hey, none of that." The dog, having been disturbed, had clearly decided he needed to put his paws in Patrick's lap.

"Max! Stop being a tart." But if Leslie was working hard to keep his hands to himself, the dog held no such inhibitions. "I'll write to Combe. Not to my father—I'm not ready for that yet—but to Abbot Barnabas. We'll see if he'll be more forthcoming if I specify what we think and he only has the matter of saying a yes or 'No, you're still a long way off.'" He'd slipped naturally into using *we* as opposed to *I*. "I don't think his tongue will be as simple to loosen as James's was, although what he says is likely to be more reliable."

"How detailed will you be when you ask him to verify why your father went to Combe?"

Leslie shrugged. "While I doubt he's easily shocked, I'll avoid getting too deeply into what happened in that room with James. Or what didn't happen. I'll take my time to compose the right text. That *is* something I've learned in the office." He yawned, stretching and easing his limbs.

"Boring you?"

"Pfft. Been sitting here too long and utilising too many brain cells. Fancy us taking your new friend for a walk?"

At Leslie's words, Max leaped up, bounded towards the door and sat waiting.

"I think he's insisting. Where's his favourite place?"

"It varies. Typical dog, I guess. Sometimes it's the park, other times he seems to turn his nose up at that. Drags me past the gates and down to a bit of open ground near a stream, the kind of place we'd have loved when we were little—lots of areas where you can make dens or play hide and seek."

Patrick, grinning, raised an eyebrow. "Better not do that today. We both know what it can lead to."

"We'll stick to the park."

It was a good choice. Plenty of families taking an afternoon stroll and some nursemaids with their charges with whom some idle flirting—good camouflage—could take place. Max was on his best behaviour, especially where the women were concerned, and the presence of people to watch gave plenty to talk about. Quite like old times with Towser on the end of the lead.

Once they'd all had enough exercise, they headed back to Leslie's, pace slowing as they neared his front door and the time when they had to say goodbye. At last, it became obvious to both men exactly what they'd been doing subconsciously with the dawdling and lingering, shared glances.

"We're acting like a pair of young lovers," Patrick said, with a snort and a toss of his head. "I'll take the plunge and go, on the principal that we'll be standing here until midnight if I don't. Then we'll end up having to take him for another walk."

"And so on, ad infinitum." Leslie grinned, then stuck out his hand. "Good luck with your spy network."

"Same to you. Report back next weekend, Captain Cadmore." Patrick gave a mock salute and backed off.

"Silly sod. You'll find yourself on a fizzer if you give me any additional lip. Come on, boy." Leslie took the dog back inside, returning to his sitting room to find that Patrick had left the notebook behind. He picked it up, savouring the feel of the binding and breathing in the aroma of old paper, infused with a subtle hint of Patrick himself. An unmistakable note that he'd borne since childhood and that took Leslie's thoughts back to *that* cupboard and *that* game.

"I wonder if Patrick has cubbyholes at his present house?" he asked aloud, getting a peculiar look from Max. "Adult thoughts there, boy. You stick to fantasising over bones and trees."

CHAPTER TEN

*L*eslie didn't write to the abbot that evening, preferring to reread the notebook and not deluding himself it was for investigational purposes. This time it was a case of simple pleasure. The next day would be soon enough to craft a letter, and a delay would help him choose his words. Getting so pragmatic a man as Barnabas to lift the curtain on the truth wouldn't be easy.

By the time he'd pencilled a couple of drafts, torn up one, and heavily edited the other, Leslie was ready to put pen to paper. The degree of candour needed was probably more than he'd mentioned to Patrick, and he'd have to take every measure to ensure it didn't go astray: splashing out on sending it special delivery might be prudent. He began with pleasantries, including a genuinely fond recollection of their chat in the pub, before getting down to business.

I know you've taken a vow not to give away what's been told you in confidence, but you also said my mother and I had been hard done by in terms of information and that the Guv'nor (I think that's what you called Him) had been nudging you. Perhaps He's nudged me too. I believe I know why my father decided to devote his life to God.

That would be the best way to put it, despite thoughts that it might actually have been primarily about getting away from the twin elements of James and the world's system of justice, but he'd let it stand. Barnabas could—and no doubt would—read between the lines if he wanted.

I'm not asking you to confirm if I'm right in so many words, only to give me an indication whether I'm near the truth. I would take a simple lack of contradiction as enough.

I believe my father was attracted to a younger man, one whom I've spoken to recently and who has been, I believe, as truthful with me as he could be. My father unsuccessfully tried to act on that attraction.

An obtuse way to put it, but Leslie couldn't find a better one without risking offence.

As far as I'm concerned, that much is a matter of fact. The following is speculation: my father had a conversation with this man about someone called Fergus Jackson, who was not at all a savoury character and about whom revelations were made.

Leslie, shaking his head, wiped the nib of his pen. It sounded like he was writing to an old maid about an aspect of her investments.

My father became angry and perhaps said things he'd have regretted afterwards, once he'd got his temper back on an even keel. In the weeks following this conversation, Fergus Jackson died in an accident—one that might have been deliberately engineered. Knowing my father's character and history, I believe he may have felt he'd somehow caused the death to happen, especially as he'd previously suffered unjustified guilt about a man's death. It's not such a far-fetched idea if you consider that the person to whom he ranted had a relative who was present at the time the accident happened and who might have had the opportunity to kill Fergus.

The theory appeared so thin set down in such bald terms. Abbot Barnabas might have a right laugh reading it, especially if Leslie was shooting wide of the mark. Still, the fundamental questions had to be asked.

Believing he'd been culpable in causing a murder strikes me as a more likely candidate for what my father sought sanctuary over, than feelings for a young man that ultimately he didn't let come to anything. The young man himself didn't need protecting from scandal, or so it appears, so surely there had to be something stronger behind my father's journey to Combe.

Leslie paused, rereading his words and wondering whether to elaborate, before finally deciding that the letter could be posted as it stood. Only time—and the reply—would tell if he'd said enough.

The days in between were busy at work, with tricky clients who needed full concentration and not a little diplomacy, which meant that Leslie didn't have the capacity for worrying about how his letter had been received. When the response did come, Leslie was so tired it took him a moment to work out who could be writing to him from Devon. He left the letter unopened until he'd made the proper amount of fuss over Max and had taken the chance to have a wash. Reading it would be a welcome accompaniment to his supper, which Mrs. Gray had left for him to warm through, a meal he took with a pang of regret. He hadn't realised exactly how lonely it had become eating on his own until Patrick had come back into his life to remind him what proper company felt like.

When he finally opened the letter and began to read, the warmth of Abbot Barnabas's communication instantly lifted his mood. A friendly greeting and words of both encouragement and concern, for him and his mother, prefaced an assurance that Mr. Cadmore had returned safely from the hospital and was delighted to be back at Combe. Once those important elements were covered, Leslie launched into a typically thoughtful reply to the questions.

Thank you for being as frank as was politic. This is the type of subject that people tend to pussyfoot around and, while it may surprise you to hear a man in my position saying it takes all sorts to make a world, don't forget that I saw plenty of life on the beat. I also take the instruction not to judge others as being mandatory, not optional.

No wonder Leslie's father had found his refuge under this man's wing, although it would be enlightening to know if the previous abbot's view on such matters had been similar. Perhaps, when Leslie had visited, his father's reference to being safe in sanctuary *now* had some element in it of things having changed under the new man's tenure.

I won't argue with your assessment of your father's interaction with this young man, whose name I don't know and don't need to know. As you state, that's a matter of fact so what value would there be in denying it? Whether there is any point in telling your father that you know exactly what happened, I'd not like to say. You would need to balance the benefit to you to have the matter brought into the open with the effect on him of having what he regards as a great and shameful secret exposed.

As to him having assumed guilt for causing that young man's murder, if I may use an expression I was fond of in the past, you're barking up the wrong tree. As you've correctly surmised, he did indeed feel bad about having discussed Fergus—whose name I also wasn't aware of—in such a callous and hostile way on the eve, as it were, of him being killed. But that in itself was merely part of what drove your father here. He'd come too close to doing something he was certain he'd regret the rest of his life, so got himself away from the temptation of doing such a thing in the future. Or indeed anything else which could have been a major mistake. Part of his nature sits uneasily with him.

Leslie wasn't sure that being in a monastery would eliminate all temptation—that monk, Brother Mark, who'd been escorting the scouts had been a fine specimen of humanity and might test the resolve of any man so inclined—but if James was the primary source of forbidden fruit, then he'd be no closer to Mr. Cadmore than the contents of his letters. No surprise, then, that Mr. Cadmore hadn't wanted James to visit him at Combe, and more evidence that the story about being encouraged to take the cowl was nonsense. Still, if Barnabas was speaking the truth, that effectively punctured Leslie's theory about the need for sanctuary being linked to murder, although he felt convinced that getting away from James wasn't the entire story. There had to be some element they'd overlooked or left unconsidered. That viewpoint was strengthened as he carried on reading.

While I've been prepared to confirm or deny what you've outlined, you'll understand that I can't comment further about what still binds your father to this place, apart from his faith, which I can assure you is real. That situation might change if you found the right tree to bark up, as it were, although strictly speaking such a conversation should only be between you and him. All I'll say is that a man and his circumstances change over time, in the wider world or at Combe.

Leslie would need to ring Patrick and hope he wasn't off at a farm doing something unmentionable to some poor animal. *He'd* had the nearest thing to a frank conversation with Leslie's father, so perhaps these words would make sense to him.

Please visit us again soon. I confess that the old me keeps wanting to know all about your friend Fergus's death. If you get to the bottom of it, I'd like to hear the whole story over a pint of The Bear's excellent bitter.

The letter ended with a blessing, one that felt genuine rather than perfunctory. Leslie reread everything, cleared the table, then went to his desk to draft a brief reply of thanks—with a promise to share any results of their investigations into Fergus's accident—before ringing Patrick.

"Are you having second thoughts about coming to mine for Sunday lunch?" Patrick asked, as soon as Leslie had announced himself.

"No, but I'm having second thoughts about our nice 'guilt over Fergus's death drove my father to Combe' theory. While Abbot Barnabas confirmed his wanting to get out of the way of James-like temptation, he said the Fergus thing was, in his words, barking up the wrong tree."

"Damn. Seems like we blew that out of all proportion. Is it a relief to you?"

"Is it hell. It makes the mystery so much deeper."

"I agree. I've kept going back in my mind to that time your father and I met up and mulling over his actual words, as best as I can remember them. I guess what he said *can* be explained by this James business, but I've convinced myself something deeper was going on. It's almost as if he were scared stiff of a particular aspect of himself."

Leslie nodded, then grinned at being so daft, given that Patrick wouldn't be able to see him do it. "That does resonate with a line in the letter. Here. 'So got himself away from the temptation of doing such a thing in the future.' That's referring to the bed failure with James, I think. The very next bit Barnabas writes is, 'Or indeed anything else which could be a major mistake.' There's also a suggestion I get back in touch with the abbot if I find the right tree to bark up. Again, his words."

"Intriguing. Can I see the letter itself? I wouldn't be offended if you say no."

"I don't see why not. Let me think it over, though, because while I don't mind you reading it, I owe it to my mother to envisage what her view on the matter would be. Not that I've any intention of showing the letter to her."

"But you'll have to find a way to broach the subject. Or else it'll stand between the pair of you."

Like so much unsaid had stood between them?

"I know. I'm hoping I'll have an explanation for Fergus's death to offer her at the same time. A sort of consolation prize." Leslie eyed the letter again. "There's something else the abbot says that puzzled me. 'All I'll say is that a man and his circumstances change over time, in the wider world or at Combe.' I don't think he means it as a platitude but rather as a specific reference to my father. Not sure what it implies, except I have a feeling that things were different back in the time of the previous abbot."

"The one who fell down the stairs only might not have done? I bet they were."

"When we spoke, Barnabas made a good case for his death having been an accident—dangerous stairs, behind a locked door and all that—which was the official verdict. Although we both know that the official version isn't always the truth." Leslie stifled a yawn. "Sorry, I'm dog tired. All this doing a full day's work followed by an evening of sleuthing or whatever you'd call it isn't exactly restful. Got to exercise the hound and then I'm off to bed. Alone."

"Glad to hear that. The bed, I mean. Don't overdo things."

Leslie snorted. "Is that instruction so that I'm in peak condition for when we've solved the murder?"

"Only in part. I do worry about you stretching yourself in too many directions. You always were a sensitive flower."

"Thanks." Leslie couldn't manage anything else than that for the moment, the word catching in his throat due to tiredness or emotion or a combination of both. Patrick *did* care, rather than simply regarding Leslie as an opportunity to have his bed warmed again.

"See you at the weekend. Night night."

"Good night, old thing." Leslie put down the phone and called, "Max! Time for a walk. Only a short one, though, because your master's knackered."

As they trod the quiet streets, Leslie's thoughts kept circling round the letter but to no avail. He passed a tobacconist shop on the corner, pausing while Max cocked his leg against a lamppost. A pipe displayed in the window brought back memories of his father smoking an almost identical one, either in the orchard at Larkspur or while on the riverbank. Happy days those had been, trying to tempt trout, with parental words of encouragement pouring out. Then Leslie proudly taking the catch home to be cooked for dinner, after Mr. Cadmore had dispatched it at the water's edge.

Recalling that prompted remembrance of the incident with the escaped mink. The words—*"Evil creatures, Leslie. Best to get rid of them quickly, before they can cause any harm."*—and, more importantly, the exultant expression on his father's face as he did the deed ran through his brain, Leslie stayed rooted to the spot until a sharp tug on his arm jogged him out of his thoughts. "Sorry, lad. Let's get you home."

They walked back automatically, Leslie mulling over the revelation he'd just had, measuring a new, highly disturbing and wildly speculative theory against what he knew, and trotting out a series of clues that could now be seen in a new light.

Sanctuary and his father clinging to it. The walk Leslie had taken with Abbot Barnabas, when he'd said it would be a truly Christian act to forgive his father for what he'd done. The pub landlady saying that her father wouldn't tell her what Abbot John's "nastiness" had consisted of. Barnabas's evident interest in crime and pursuing murders that had been covered over, in contrast to the discussion in the pub where he'd given Abbot John's death relatively short shrift. The strange, troubled glance that Barnabas had given Leslie when he'd raised the topic of whether killing someone was ever justified. The handsome monk who'd come into the abbey to find peace and had done so but only *now*. Leslie's father's need to protect the innocent and his ruthless way of killing that mink. A man's circumstances changing, even within the confines of an abbey, and the part of his father's nature that sat uneasily with him.

There was an interpretation that drew all of those together, and it was far worse than his father having acted as agent provocateur in Fergus's death.

CHAPTER ELEVEN

When Leslie arrived at Patrick's house on Sunday, his thoughts had resolved themselves into a tight theory that needed airing, if only for Patrick to point out—please God—all the reasons why it couldn't be true. He'd brought Max with him, at Patrick's suggestion that the dog would provide a good excuse for them to take a walk together.

Camouflage. In the same way Towser was, back in the old days.

His host came out to greet them not long after he'd pulled up, maybe having heard the car or been watching out for him.

"Is everything all right? You're wearing your worried face."

"I *am* worried. I've had an idea I want your opinion on, although let me get settled first. By the way, you forgot this." Leslie produced the notebook from the car, where he'd been keeping it, out of any risk of Max gnawing at it.

"I suspected I had. I hope it's been useful." Patrick took the notebook, then waved it towards the house. "Come and see my surgery. We can put Max in the garden, so he doesn't think he's at risk of being poked and prodded."

The Pheasantry turned out to be a neat house, comfortable yet orderly. Much as Leslie expected, knowing the personality of its owner. Patrick's clinic was attached, in an extension that had been designed in keeping with the original house.

"Did you have this part built on?"

"No. It was built a while after the Edwardian original, but you'd need an eye for architectural detail to be able to tell the difference in date. This place has always been used for veterinary work, which has been handy for me in terms of continuity of business." Patrick tipped his head towards the front entrance. "It may say *The Pheasantry* on the nameplate, but all the locals call it *The Vet's House.*"

As the tour continued, Leslie recalled his thoughts of the previous weekend and noted the cupboard under the stairs, although he didn't remark on it. That could wait until they'd solved the puzzle or reached the end of their time frame. The delicious aromas permeating from what must be the kitchen were sending his thoughts to his stomach as opposed to any other part of his anatomy. And, anyway, the ideas he'd had about his father were enough of a passion killer.

"What's on the menu? Further backhanders from happy customers?"

"Not quite. In this case, they let me fish their waters. Caught a beautiful pair of trout yesterday afternoon, and they've been sitting somewhere safe." Patrick jerked his thumb over his shoulder. "You see, I've got a small refrigerator in the surgery which I find essential for my work, so they've been in there, keeping beautifully. Puts the larder here to shame."

"Please tell me they haven't been cuddled up against some nasty anatomical specimen awaiting examination?"

"Cheek. I'm not going to give you food poisoning. Word would get around, and it would be bad for business, for one thing." Patrick set about heading and gutting the fish. "There's bottles of Bass in the aforementioned larder or a nice claret if you'd prefer."

"Claret sounds good. Shall I pour us both a glass?" That would allow Leslie to escape from the sight of those trout. While he didn't feel squeamish over their preparation, they reminded him of what he'd need to discuss.

He managed to keep busy, volunteering for tasks, until the food was on the table, and then he bought further breathing space by asking if Patrick had been successful in his search for the chap who'd been embroiled with Fergus.

"Yes. Or at least I've found somebody who should be able to tell us one way or another. I played fair and made sure I didn't obtain an answer until we'd both benefit from it."

"Fair play much appreciated. Anything else wouldn't be cricket. Despite me having bowled a googly when I saw James on my own."

"Your underhand play was noted." Patrick chuckled.

"So, how did you manage to find this somebody?"

"Not without a dead end or two." Patrick carefully filleted the cooked trout flesh from the bones, his skilled surgeon's hands at work. "I originally tried my old CO for the dog-training stuff, but he hadn't kept in contact with any of the people who passed through his hands. He'd lost his own son in the war, so I suspect he didn't want to recall those days if he could help it. Then I tried Eric, who said he'd see what he could turn up from his mate although he's not come back to me yet."

"Other things on his mind. If he gets into parliament, he'll no doubt cut off all ties with us." Leslie took another forkful of potatoes. "Excellent spuds, these. I'd forgotten how good a cook you are."

"Flattery will get you anywhere." They concentrated on eating for a few moments. "While I was waiting for the nonexistent reply, I thought of this bloke I know whose horses I tend. The one I told you about who tells the hair-raising stories of exploits behind enemy lines."

Leslie put down his fork. "Is this another instance of coincidence playing a part? Don't tell me he knew Fergus."

"We should be so lucky." Patrick wagged his head. "No, but he knew someone who was involved in the admin side of things. The boring old pay and pensions and quartermaster type stuff without which no organisation could function, irrespective of whether it's one engaged in espionage or resistance. He offered to get said chap to give me a bell, which he did. While he—Harry, the admin man not the horse one—was cagey about revealing any details, when I explained as much of the background as I felt appropriate, he eased up a bit."

"How much did you let on?"

"I told him about the so-called accident, how I'd been there at the time and couldn't shake off my suspicions, which meant I was investigating the background." He paused.

"Yes? I can always tell when you've a bomb to drop."

"Only a squib, this time. He's coming later today. I hope you don't mind."

"Not at all. Seize the day and all that." Although it would mean Leslie would have to air his thoughts about his father beforehand.

"That's a relief. Harry only lives on the coast so he's tootling up by train on the direct line. He said he's got his own interest in what happened to Fergus. He didn't elaborate, however, and I couldn't tell if that interest was genuine or mere politeness. You can talk freely about Fergus and his pals with this chap, by the way, because we'll be with someone of a sympathetic nature, as it were."

"He's not another member of that ghastly Retainers club?"

"No, but he's apparently the type. As is our mutual pal with the horses. I hope that's not why he engaged me as his vet, though. I'd rather it was professional skills than the dreaded 'boys' network' or whatever you'd call it." Patrick set about his food again, then said, "You seem particularly worried. Is Harry coming here going to be a problem?"

"Only in that it forces me to tell you what's been bothering me without putting it off any longer. It's about my father."

"Bad news?"

"You could call it that. New idea. One I don't like." Leslie pushed away his almost-empty plate. "Sanctuary. Has to be for something serious—Barnabas's letter implies that and him telling me it would be a truly Christian act to forgive what my father had done confirms it." He reached into his pocket. Despite any misgivings about his mother's reactions, he should let Patrick read it. "Here. You'd better see the letter before I start."

While Patrick read it, Leslie studied the man's face, but he remained impassive until reaching the end and giving a whistle. "I see what you mean. I guess you've had an unsettling hunch about what he's referring to."

"Exactly. Funny we've had trout today, because the evening of the day you came for lunch, something reminded me about his ruthless way of killing trout and other creatures like mink when he needed to. Don't laugh, this is serious."

"I'm sorry. It was so stupidly incongruous." Patrick reached over and briefly squeezed Leslie's hand. "I'm sure it's no laughing matter. Go on."

Leslie took a calming breath. "When I thought of that, all the other thoughts came tumbling out. My father's need to protect the innocent, Barnabas talking about a man's circumstances changing, which can apply even within the confines of an abbey, and that horrible bit about the part of Father's nature that sat uneasily with him. Then, I remembered that when the abbot and I were in the pub, I raised the topic of whether killing someone was ever justified and Barnabas gave me this strange look, as though I'd hit on something very awkward. Something that he didn't want to discuss. I'd assumed it was the tricky moral dilemma, but now I'm wondering if I got too close to home."

"You think your father killed somebody, for what he thought was a justifiable reason? And he locked himself away at Combe as a form of penance or punishment or whatever?" Patrick's face showed surprise, although there was no suggestion of disbelief. Clearly the theory wasn't totally outrageous.

"Yes to the first although not to the second. I believe he went to Combe primarily because of the fiasco with James and to get out of the way of further temptation from him. There may have been an element of hiding from this other thing within himself which he hated—this aggression we're surmising—but I think that backfired. What happened to make him cling to his sanctuary, and we're back to the traditional sense of the word, occurred at the abbey itself. We mustn't forget the other so-called accident we've come across and about which there have been rumours." Leslie, whose glass had been refilled, took a steadying sip of claret. "The previous abbot, John."

"Oh, I see." Patrick steepled his hands to his chin. "It's not an unreasonable theory. What have you got to support it? Any solid facts?"

"A few of those and a lot of speculation. Fact: John was regarded as a bit of a tartar, but the pub landlady's father wouldn't tell her what he's supposed to have done to the novices, which suggests it was more than the usual laying out of harsh punishments. His death occurred in the abbey itself, on a staircase the other side of a locked door when Barnabas, who might otherwise be regarded as a prime suspect as he'd have motive and the knowhow, was elsewhere. There's also a remarkably handsome monk who went to Combe to find peace but, my father said, had only done so recently. I'd supposed that it was something to do with the war. Now I'm thinking it's tied up with Abbot John."

"And Barnabas's real view is?"

Leslie shrugged. "On the surface, as I've said, that it was simply an accident and the rumours were wrong. John had influential friends in high places, so they might not have wanted things gone into too deeply if it risked his reputation being harmed, although Barnabas doesn't strike me as the sort who'd be inclined to cover things up for the sake of the abbey."

"But he might keep things under wraps for the sake of protecting the living?"

"Exactly. Every time I think of our chat in the pub, I further suspect Barnabas was trying to divert me away from the topic of John's death." Leslie, eyes closed, put his hands to his forehead for a moment's thought. "So, we come to the question of whether my father could have been the one to give the abbot a push?"

"Do you want me to persuade you it's a yes or a no?" Trust Patrick to be both sympathetic and pragmatic.

"I'm not seeking a particular angle, just an objective assessment."

"Then let me have a few minutes to consider it. I've an apple tart in the larder, if you'd like a slice."

"I think I can manage one, now I've got over that hurdle."

While Patrick cleared the plates and went to get the tart, Leslie rose from the table to peer out at the garden. Well-kept and looking glorious in the sunshine, everything showed evidence of a gardener being employed, at least on a part-time basis, because Patrick had never had green fingers and pressure of work mightn't leave him much time to tend the plot. Leslie's patch might have been small, but it relied on Mrs. Gray's input to present itself as anywhere near respectable. Max was out there, on a long leash, happily dozing in a spot of sun and giving the impression of being both at ease and at home. Perhaps that was a lesson for Leslie to learn.

When Patrick returned, bearing a tray laden with plates and a jug, Leslie helped him lay the food out, although he didn't put his question again. Patrick would answer in his own time, which turned out to be halfway through eating the dessert, although not before he'd praised it. "Rather good, this tart. I could pretend I made it, but you're bound to see through that. Local bakery."

"You're lucky to have them. And a good dairy for this cream."

Patrick smiled. "So, I've been mulling over that theory of yours and, much as it might pain you to hear, I don't see any immediate reason to dismiss it, apart from one element which is generic rather than specific. As an explanation of what's gone on, it brings together a lot."

"Would it be in line with the conversation you and he had? Given that in this scenario he wouldn't have committed violence *before* he went to Combe? Sorry, shouldn't have asked that when you've got a mouthful of pastry."

Patrick chewed, swallowed, and grinned. "Your timing wasn't the best. The answer's yes. Clearly the majority of what he said was about James and about his attraction to men, but that part of his personality he didn't like got an airing, despite it not being described quite so overtly. Violence towards Fergus may well have been in his mind, and the fact he didn't mention sanctuary to me would indicate that he didn't need it at the time."

"What's the one element that might knock the whole theory down?"

"The same factor that would discount anyone from having done the deed: the locked door. How did the murderer get the other side of it?"

"As far as I'm concerned, that's a point in favour of my father being involved. A monk could have asked Abbot John to hear his confession or lend an ear to a crisis of faith. Or even played on John's nature. You know what I mean. 'Brother Gorgeous says if you answer his knock at eleven o'clock tonight, he'll be very kind to you.' Then when John unlocks the door and finds it isn't Brother Gorgeous but Brother Andrew, it's too late, because he's forced his way in."

Nodding, Patrick said, "I accept that, although it's not the part I have an issue with. For a start, how do you get the abbot up the stairs to chuck him down them?"

"Sheer force and threats? Or maybe enticement?" Leslie thrust out his lower lip, trying to envisage the scene. "Make the message from Brother Gorgeous something like, 'Be waiting for me in bed with the door unlocked and the key nearby so I can make sure we're not disturbed.' That could work."

"What about the killer getting out and locking the door behind him?"

Leslie paused. That could throw any murder theory out of the window, unless the death had been engineered in an unlikely fashion so beloved of locked-door mysteries. No, they were missing something equally obvious. "We're both being thick here. Surely there couldn't have been only the one key. In fact, there must have been another or else they couldn't have got in to find John dead, unless they broke down the door. Whether or not that happened, it wouldn't preclude a spare key having been made by someone who got their hands on the original."

"A spare key would eliminate the need for subterfuge too. The murderer gets his hands on it, waits until the abbot has gone to bed and then lets himself in and out again, deed done. Key gets put back where it should live or hidden away if it's a copy. I'm not sure I can buy the latter, though. Unlikely a monk can nip down to the local ironmonger without being noticed."

"True."

"Any idea what time of day this happened? I'm thinking of canonical hours or whatever they call them and wondering if they'd be getting up for prayers."

Leslie shrugged. "I don't know if they say prayers in the middle of the night or simply very early and very late. Maybe it was at one of those services that they noticed the abbot missing. That might argue for a monk committing the crime, if crime it was, because they'd know when the coast was clear, although as we discuss this, I'm doubting if that monk had to be Father, or if he was merely complicit with somebody else. An accessory after or before the fact. That would be less hard for me to bear, so it might be wishful thinking."

Patrick pondered for a moment. "We know that your father is capable of subterfuge—evidence the episode with James—and I can easily imagine him covering up for some poor waif whom he thought had been pushed beyond the point of endurance. What I'm less sure about is him cold-bloodedly planning such a deed to the extent of getting a duplicate key cut."

"I'm inclined to agree. I know that the last few weeks have been another step on my journey of discovery about the old man, but that would be a revelation too far." Leslie sighed. "As a worst case, I can imagine him discovering what had been happening and confronting Abbot John about it. No need for a key in that case, because the abbot lets him in. Father insists the man confess and step down from his position of power. The argument turns heated. Maybe John tries to get away, my father manhandles him, and he falls to his death. Father panics and leaves, locking the door—" Leslie's eyes shot open. "We've been daft. We don't need to overcome the mystery of the locked door. What if it was never locked?"

"I'm not following you."

"Easy enough for the person who 'found the body' to pretend he couldn't get in and had to fetch a key. Or better still—better for the purposes of the murder theory—we have a person who's the one to notice that the abbot isn't at the service, where he's supposed to be. Have you got an encyclopaedia or something else we can look up the canonical hours in?"

Patrick fetched a handful of books, from which they soon had the answer. "Matins is very early morning, Compline late evening. Would either of them work?"

"Better than during the day, I'd say. Said person referred to earlier then volunteers to go and find out what's happened to the abbot and takes the spare key on the pretence that John may have been taken ill and they'll need to access his rooms."

"To a door he knows isn't locked because said person left it so or somebody's recently informed him of the fact?" Patrick rubbed his forehead. "If John was such an old brute, it's entirely possible that two or more people conspired to either dispose of him or cover up the truth. Why not lock that door at the time of the death, though?"

"Because the killer may not have been able to access the key and didn't panic enough to use the one from inside. By which I mean that no key at all would have looked suspicious. If the door was found open, it wouldn't argue against an accident, because an inquest could conclude that the abbot had forgotten to lock his door and had gone to do so when he fell." A logical story was coming together. "Suspicious in itself that John felt the need to lock himself away at night. Did he fear retribution?"

"I think it's equally suspicious that the accident happened when Barnabas—the man who possessed the skill to winkle out villains and might have smelled a rat—was away. Anyway, whatever the details, I'd say you've got a reasonable theory. Not sure how you can test it, unless Barnabas is willing to confirm you're barking up the right tree, this time." Patrick jabbed his thumb in the direction of the garden. "Talking of barking and trees, shall we take Max for a short walk before Harry arrives?"

"Sounds an excellent idea. Or else I'll be falling asleep in my chair. That tart was wonderful, but it's very soporific." As was the relief at finding a theory in which his father wasn't a cold-blooded killer.

Once they were back, sufficiently exercised and more awake, Patrick went to put the kettle on while Leslie and Max settled themselves in the sitting room. He refused Leslie's offer of help, saying that he rarely got the chance to play host and, anyway, two people in a kitchen was never a good idea.

There'd not been long in when a sharp rap on the front door announced the likely arrival of Harry, hopefully bearing inside information on Fergus and his colleagues. Patrick let him in, while Leslie restrained Max, who—given past form—would want to jump all over the newcomer and make him his best friend.

Harry was older than Leslie had anticipated, but he was handsome for his age and immaculately dressed. The blazer he wore was suggestive of a school or university sporting club: cricket, Leslie would have guessed, Harry giving off the air of the wily spin bowler, although given how often his guesses had proved wrong, he wouldn't place a bet on it.

Patrick kept the introductions strictly neutral, allowing their guest to interpret "my friend Leslie" as he wished. After all, that's what they were at present, irrespective of what they had been or might be.

While Patrick finished preparing the refreshments, Leslie and Harry passed the usual bland comments about the weather and the state of the trains, while Max sat at the guest's feet, wearing an angelic expression.

"Ignore him if you want. He's a tart." Leslie rolled his eyes.

"He's fine." Harry patted Max's head. "I'm a cats man myself though, so I hope he doesn't get offended. Ah! The cup that cheers."

"I can offer something stronger if you prefer," Patrick said, as he backed into the room bearing another tray.

"I'll stick with tea, thank you. Need to have my wits about me. Sounds like we've serious business to discuss."

"We appreciate you putting yourself out to come here." Patrick handed Harry a steaming cup, which he received with a nod of thanks.

"I'm making a day out of it. Going out for dinner with Bruce when I've done here. Hence me being in my glad rags."

"Bruce is the chap with the horses," Patrick explained.

"I'd guessed," Leslie said. "I'll echo Patrick's gratitude, though. Fergus was an old acquaintance of ours, and we both suspect there is a story to his death over and above what was officially stated. Only we didn't realise at the time because we lost touch during the war." Leslie, aware that he was starting to gabble, thanked Patrick for his tea and shut up again.

"Better to discuss things at this distance, especially where it concerns work like Fergus was doing. You'd have found yourself locked up if you'd been too free with your words back then. Keep mum, chum," Harry added, blowing on his tea.

"Can you discuss it now?" Patrick asked. "Secrets Act and all that."

"I think we'll be fine. We're not going to be discussing the details of what these agents were up to, obviously. You never know when we might need to use a similar strategy again."

Leslie nodded. Wartime colleagues had expressed a similar viewpoint in 1945, with the threat from Germany and Japan subsiding but increasing concerns about the Soviets.

"Patrick will no doubt have told you what area of work I was involved in during the war. I was a bit too long in the tooth to fly anything but a desk, and anyway flat feet have always made me a bit useless physically. I was doing the boring old administrative work without which no British organisation could function." Harry grinned impishly, implying to Leslie that there had been other aspects to his work than handling pay and supplies. "I remembered the case, although not the specific name until Patrick mentioned it. The seeming futility was what stuck in my mind. You serve your country behind enemy lines without getting a scratch and then get yourself killed on home soil." He took a sip of tea. "I'd have remembered for another reason too. The official input after the event. I was told to get the whole thing sorted quickly from my side and with the minimum of fuss."

Leslie shot Patrick a glance, receiving a shrug in return. "What was that in aid of?"

"Couldn't tell you. When I casually asked why there was all the hurry, I got informed in no uncertain terms that I had no need to know. There were some murmurs about Fergus's work abroad, but I suspect they were a smokescreen." Harry picked up a biscuit from the plate Patrick had left on a table beside him, delicately dunked, and consumed it.

"You felt there had to be more to it?"

"I did. I accomplished what was asked of me, naturally, but you can't stop a man from thinking. Or doing some digging when he's got legitimate access to things which can be dug into. Ever since, I've had moments of wondering what the hell was going on to get the high-ups so agitated about his death, although I'm guessing that the reality is probably much less interesting than the ideas I've come up with. Been a bit too Sherlock-Holmes-like in my invention, I suspect."

Recalling some of the stranger ideas he'd discussed recently—such as his mother's naked man theory—Leslie smiled. "We'd love to hear any thoughts you've had, labyrinthine or straightforward. They may make sense when measured against what we know."

"I hoped you'd say that. Let's get the ridiculous ones out of the way before we head to the mundane. Maybe Fergus was a double agent who was got rid of by our side, in a fashion that wouldn't arouse suspicion, either among his peers or with the German masters to whom he'd given his true allegiance."

"I'd hardly call that ridiculous," Patrick said, "although I think we can knock it on the head. I didn't like Fergus—which is putting it mildly—but I'd damn well stake my practice on him having been loyal to His Majesty. Agreed, Leslie?"

"Agreed. For all that he was a man of very few morals, he was an open book to those in his circle, and that book read 'true patriot.' His father died in the Great War, so he had no love for the enemy."

Harry nodded. "I'll discard that theory, then. Next one. Did Fergus have connections with royalty or a member of the war cabinet, who for whatever reason had the desire and the power to have his death kept hush-hush?"

"You can discount that one too. If he had blue blood, we'd have heard all about it. Open book, as Leslie said, and rather a blabbermouth among friends." If a man could be said to drink tea in a marked manner, that would apply now to Patrick, who'd had to listen too often to Fergus's chatter.

"Hold on, before we shoot that down," Leslie said. "He *did* have a high-ranking contact in the navy, I heard. This chap sailed a desk in the Admiralty."

"I'd forgotten about him." Patrick gave Leslie an appreciative nod. "I think we'd discounted that fact as being connected to his death, but it might have influenced a cover-up."

"When you say high-ranking *contact*?" Harry raised a meaningful eyebrow.

Leslie grinned. "A lover, yes. Mind you, the country's strewn with Fergus's ex-lovers, and he didn't blab about all of them. Simply because there wouldn't have been time."

Harry chuckled. "Bit of a lad, was he? That can either make you very popular or leave you with a string of enemies, if that word isn't too harsh a way of putting it. We all know that it isn't only wartime that generates adversaries. And I have to add, I'm jolly pleased to be having this conversation with you two in particular, because it means I don't have to go round the houses about the next part. You're aware he was lined up for a court-martial?"

"We are," Patrick stated.

Leslie had noted the *you two*. Harry presumably knew about Patrick's nature either via Bruce or from the phone call and had come to an obvious conclusion about Leslie, as well.

"Although," Patrick continued, "we're no clearer about whether such a thing had actually been put in process or was only a possibility."

"As I understand it, and this has been put together from a series of what you might call quarters of a clue, he'd previously been told he was on a last chance. He could do what he liked with the enemy if it progressed the British cause, but any further having it off with this fellow operative and he was for the high jump. He couldn't keep his trousers zipped, so the threat was about to be carried out."

"But they let him participate on the training course?" Leslie asked.

"Apparently the details hadn't been finalised." Harry shrugged. "I believe he said he was innocent, but that means very little."

"Not like the forces to be so inefficient or to necessarily give the miscreant a second chance, although maybe his setup didn't operate by the same rules." Patrick sniffed.

Bletchley had been run on slightly less orthodox lines too, which had rubbed some folk up the wrong way, so Leslie could vouch for such unorthodoxy. "I can categorically say that not every bit of war work operated by the King's Regulations."

"Quite. I suspect the 'friends in high places' card got played as well, to defer or delay any prosecution and therefore buy people some time for thought and action. Fergus up in front of a court could decide to tell all, especially if he had the habit of being loose-tongued when he felt like it. Maybe that Admiralty pal was afraid that names would be named. His, for example. Which Fergus couldn't do if he were dead," Harry added, with finality.

Leslie nodded. That might be a stronger motive than the hapless victim getting revenge. "You need two people for 'having it off.' Was there one other party in particular or was Fergus trying to get into the pants of several of his colleagues? There'd be no surprise in that, by the way."

"Only the one. Or, to clarify, only the one he was caught with. He was a recently arrived agent, one that Fergus was supposed to be nurturing. He took that responsibility too far and in the wrong direction." Harry gave Max a friendly pat. "Us humans, eh? Thoughts never out of our trousers."

"What was the name of this agent?" asked Patrick. "We're hoping it's Dawson. Or at least another name we can link to the accident."

"Nothing doing on the Dawson front. This chap was named Gareth, although I don't know if he lived up to the stereotype and was Welsh, and I'm not revealing his surname."

Patrick shook his head. "The name Gareth means nothing to me. He might have been a colleague of Dawson or one of the people on our list, though. Before you arrived, incidentally, we were discussing another possible accident-that-wasn't-accidental which might have involved somebody taking action on behalf of another person. Sorry to be so vague, but it's all conjectural at the moment."

Harry waved his hand. "Oh, don't worry about that. We've all got our need of discretion, one way or another. I can tell you that Dawson didn't work in the same geographical area as Fergus, which is why—I believe—they ended up on the same training course. I suppose it might have raised German suspicions if two operatives left their area in France at the same time. Still, one never knows how connections can occur, so they *might* have known each other. Look at *us*, Patrick. You know Bruce through his horses, I know him for totally different reasons, and here we are, scrutinising the life and death of an old pal of yours."

"Can you be sure that Dawson and Fergus didn't work in the same location?" Patrick had possibly had the same thought as Leslie: that Harry couldn't—or shouldn't—have known the name Dawson would prove to be relevant, so why had he noted it?

"Because when I did my digging, I found only one other operative listed as working close to Fergus for a while, but that was a woman and she'd moved elsewhere when Gareth came along." Another pat for the dog, who was clearly loving the attention. "Did his tastes run to mares as well as stallions?"

"That's another definite no. I'm impressed that you're telling us this without the benefit of notes." That sounded like a genuine compliment from Patrick.

"I tried not to jot too much down. Doing that can look rather odd in wartime, so I've got it stored up here." Harry tapped his head. "I may not have many outstanding skills, but an almost photographic memory's one of them."

"I wish I had the same facility." Leslie frowned. For the last few minutes he'd had a nagging feeling he needed to air. "I'm sure I've encountered the name Gareth in the past few weeks, but further than that I can't say."

"It means nothing to me." Patrick rose, to fetch the pot and refill any cups that needed refilling. "Anything else you can tell us, Harry?"

"Yes, and it might be relevant. This Gareth chap got injured on Fergus's watch. Nothing too serious, although there was a note on file that it might have been Fergus's fault. I have no idea why. Somebody's suspicion."

How often had that cropped up recently? Somebody's intuition telling them that things weren't as they seemed. Would all of these hunches turn out to be mare's nests?

As if on cue, Harry rolled out another one. "Talking of which, although I'm making an educated guess here, I wonder if that injury may have been the start of their relationship turning from professional to romantic. The old 'tender words at the bedside leading to something else' thing. Anyway, when Gareth recovered, he went back into the field, in another area, but the old wound somehow got infected, and he ended up in a terrible state. Got home eventually, although not in one piece. Not in great shape mentally, either." Harry spread his hands. "Not unknown, in our business."

"Any idea what the injury was?" Leslie asked.

"A wound to a lower limb, although I don't know the detail."

"There's something about all this that's puzzled me," Patrick said. "You may not be able to answer—secrets and all—but most of the trainees on the dogs' course hadn't been in the field yet. Fergus was already experienced, so why did he come back? Come to that, how did he manage the journey, given that transport on and off the continent was strictly verboten."

"Verboten or not, it happened. Officially and unofficially, by sea and by air. Fishing smacks are wonderful things, with a use not limited to Dunkirk." Harry waved his hand; that was clearly all the detail they'd get. "They wanted Fergus and Gareth back for the court-martial and that wasn't going to happen in France, was it?"

"I guess it wasn't." Patrick sat forward, hands clasped. "I suppose that also explains why they both would have come back, when you said that was usually avoided. Was Gareth one of the trainees we had that day?"

Harry shook his head. "I don't believe so. He may well have still been recovering, or they might have wanted to keep the pair apart. So, to use an appropriate analogy, given our proximity to racing country, he's not one of the runners and riders for killing his lover. Not directly, anyway and maybe not in terms of motive or what happened when. The complications to Gareth's injury came after Fergus was dead; otherwise it would have been tricky to get him home. He was very unwell."

"The infection and the aftermath may not have provided a motive but the court-martial might." Leslie paused, struck by an obvious question. "Why wasn't Gareth court-martialled if he'd been brought back for that purpose?"

"Ah, there's another question. It may well be connected to, 'Make sure you get the paperwork cleared up quickly, Harry.' Perhaps *he* also had important enough connections in places where they could affect things." Harry eyed the teapot. "Any chance of wrestling another cup out of there?"

Patrick rose. "I doubt it and anyway, it would be stewed. I'll make fresh. Don't discuss anything important without me," he added, as he went through the door.

"Tell me about Bruce and his horses," Leslie suggested. "We can't get told off for discussing *them*."

"One hopes so. I must mention that Bruce fancies the pants off your man."

"Does he?" Perhaps that should have been, *He's not my man. At present.*

"Oh yes. Often talks about the handsome Patrick. If your chap was a doctor as opposed to a vet, I'd accuse Bruce of inventing illnesses as an excuse to call him out. I suppose one can't induce psychosomatic disorders in horses?"

"I wouldn't know. Although Patrick would be furious if any nobbling had gone on simply to get him into someone's stable."

Harry waved the notion away. "Bruce isn't like that. Worships his horseflesh, especially the racers."

The next few minutes were spent in discussion of said horseflesh's chances in the upcoming season, although Leslie's mind was only half on the conversation. *His* man. He liked the sound of that, and those two simple words had brought the realisation of that hope closer. They had been one and would be again, unless fate scuppered their plans.

Patrick arrived with a fresh pot of tea just as Harry was describing Bruce's upcoming plan to get his hands on a colt that could be trained up for the Welsh Grand National. Once that topic had been aired, they returned to the subject of Fergus.

Patrick said, "It's struck us that men of our nature are perhaps suited to undercover work, despite the risks of being blackmailed because of it. What was Fergus's reputation as an agent?"

"Both Fergus and Gareth appeared to be effective in what they did. The former was regarded—with reservations—as being a brilliant agent, which is another reason his sexual behaviour was tolerated for so long. The reservations were that he could be slightly, um, impulsive. Tended to act on initiative, which was fine when it succeeded but could have been highly risky if he'd failed."

"Was all this on his record?"

"Yes. His return to England was taken as an opportunity for a full debrief. I can't discuss any details I saw, naturally. What I can say, and should have done earlier, is that if you're seeking to bring anyone to book for what happened, you'll have no success with Dawson." Harry's naturally cheerful countenance clouded. "He went missing in 1944, around the time the allies were landing on the Normandy beaches. Simply disappeared, assumed dead, although he popped up once we'd overrun France. His luck finally ran out two years later, when he was the victim of a road accident one dark night. The culprit—or culprits—drove away, but the local police were pretty sure it was members of a group of tearaways who'd got a bit too demob happy and were running riot on the local roads. They never had enough evidence to prove it, though. Fingerprints but nobody they could link them up with. Another bit of irony, to have evaded the Germans and fallen foul of your fellow countrymen."

"That's a shame." Leslie sighed. They'd missed the chance of talking to Dawson by a single year; if only he and Patrick had got on the trail earlier. "No chance it was a real-life version of what you read in books, that the victim wasn't Dawson himself but somebody whose face was smashed up so the identity relied on the contents of his pockets or whatever? Didn't they call it wallet litter? A collection of items that could be planted there to make it seem like somebody else had been killed? I'm clutching at straws, but we both know how much subterfuge went on during the war."

"It did, although not in this instance. Dawson was identified by his commanding officer and apparently there was no doubt. I believe Gareth survived the war, though. As for any other men you think might have a connection, I'm not really allowed to reveal who else might have been involved in the work being done abroad, either in the field or at home. I've probably said too much as it is. The best I can offer is that one of you could read out a list of relevant names and the other one can watch to see if I have any 'involuntary' reactions.'" Harry smiled impishly, then—with a wave of his hand across his face—adopted an impassive expression.

"Well, I know about Chappell, who was helping to run the course, so you can waggle your eyebrow as much as you want for him." Patrick snorted, then listed those who'd been present that day, including Jefferies and other dog handlers whose names Leslie only knew from mentions in the notebook. Unfortunately, Harry's impassive response continued as all the names were recited. When Leslie started to come up with mad suggestions, James Lyth, his own father, Patrick raised a hand. "No point in wasting all our time. There's clearly nothing doing."

"It appears so. If you do make progress further though, I'd be very interested in hearing what you've discovered and not only to satisfy my curiosity. I do have a close connection in the police force who's like mustard about solving old crimes and bringing the culprit to book if he can. This would be right up his street if you had any real evidence to give him."

"We'll remember that, thank you." Leslie glanced at Patrick, who simply nodded and gave his thanks but didn't comment further. It appeared they'd gone as far as they could with Bruce's dapper friend.

"So, it looks like we have to scrub Dawson," Leslie said, standing with Patrick on the step as they watched Harry go strolling away in the direction of the station. Exactly like an old married couple waving off a lifelong friend.

"Do we? Just because he wasn't the chap who was directly involved with the court-martial, he was still best placed to do the deed. That might account for him having made himself scarce when he got the chance. Must have been pretty chaotic following D-Day, depending on which part of France he was in." Patrick closed the front door behind them and ushered Leslie back into the sitting room. "A beer?"

"I'll manage the one." Leslie flopped into a chair, suddenly very tired. "You definitely think it was Dawson killed Fergus, despite the lack of apparent motive? That's not what you said in your notebook."

"I wasn't thinking clearly back then. If you recall, this all took place hard on the heels of the love of my life walking out of it." With a grin, Patrick backed out of the door, before Leslie could comment. When he returned, two bottles of Bass and a couple of glasses in hand, it was as if nothing significant had been said concerning their relationship. Perhaps Patrick thought he'd simply stated a fact, as he might tell a dog owner that their pet had mange, but he'd never told Leslie that was how he felt. He'd professed love, yes, but not such a totality of emotion. Had it been merely a quip, not intended to be laden with the meaning Leslie was putting into it?

Possibly, given that Patrick immediately took the conversation back to the matter previously at hand. "Can we connect the mysterious Gareth with the long-haired Dawson?"

"Cheers." Leslie carefully poured his beer, using the action to get his thoughts onto murder, not romance. "It's this mysterious Gareth business which is really annoying me. I'm sure I've come across someone with that name in the last few weeks, albeit fleetingly, which is why I can't pin down who it was. In my mind it's tied up with work, so that would be another strange coincidence if it's the same man, although it might only be a client—it's not that uncommon a Christian name."

Patrick, whom Max had sidled up to now Harry was gone, took a swig of beer. "The injury doesn't help? A man with a limp or an artificial limb?"

"No, I—" *Of course.* "Make that a yes. That apple tart we ate wasn't merely soporific, it addled my brains. The chap who rang me from Eric's party office, giving me a telephone number for James, was called Gareth. That's why I connected the name in my mind with work, because he rang me there. Add to that the fact that, when Marianne came for tea, she told Mother and me that one of the blokes employed by Eric was lame in one leg. It could be the same man, I suppose. Using the old pals' network to get a job, the same way as Harry ended up sitting here via a mutual connection."

"This Gareth didn't appear to recognise James's name? Although I guess he'd not have a reason to do so if Fergus hadn't mentioned him in one of their bedroom chats."

"He gave no impression he did. Mind you, Gareth told me he'd been asked to pass on the number for a Mr. Lyth, so Eric may have been careful about the James part of the name. I wish I'd probed Harry deeper on where Gareth went on his return to civvy street, but we changed the subject to the timeline of events. Which is important if said Gareth—irrespective of whether he's the Gareth I spoke to—is entangled in Fergus's death." Another drink of Bass. "Let's imagine Gareth was an old lover of Eric's. He ends up working with Fergus because of the old friend-of-a-friend recommendation."

"The friend being the liaison bigwig I met?" Patrick stuck out his lip. "Yes, that's possible, especially if Eric was the person who recommended both of them. My 'I know a chap who'd be ideal for the job' explanation of the coincidences. Only he doesn't turn out to be ideal for the job—or Fergus ultimately doesn't, despite his good work—because they become embroiled with each other. Maybe endangering their behind-enemy-lines operation in the process, which could be why they were shopped in the first place. Whoever they were shopped to decided they'd become a risk."

"I wonder who snitched on them? Another agent out there who sent a message back?"

"That's a point. Fergus wasn't the type to have let anything incriminating slip unless among those he could trust. We're still not clear about what actually happened between the two, though. Fergus getting his leg over with a colleague who later regretted it or an accusation fabricated by said person." Patrick shrugged. "I don't suppose we'll ever know. It wouldn't surprise me if Gareth himself made the complaint when he did his routine reporting."

"It would be easier to straighten out if the people concerned could have communicated through the usual channels and folk like Harry could give us straightforward facts."

"You're a fine one to talk. I still don't know exactly what you did during the war." Patrick snorted. "Anyway, I think the restricted lines of communication narrow the field of who could have reported back."

"Which would help, if the buggers would tell us anything." Leslie took another swig of beer. "Any idea how long Fergus had been home before that training took place? Long enough for the debriefing, we know."

"Couldn't tell you. It would have been logical for Gareth to have come back at the same time, given the transport issues, what Harry said about that looking suspicious notwithstanding. Surely their cover stories could have accommodated that situation? It could have given Gareth the opportunity to bend Dawson's ear. 'If you get the chance, do us all a favour and get rid of him.'" Patrick's attempt at a Welsh accent wasn't impressive.

"You've never been that effective a mimic." Leslie chuckled. "If the chap I spoke to had possessed a Welsh accent, it was long gone. He didn't need to have spoken directly to Dawson, though, if he could have got a message to him via the communication network. Before he left France, for all we know."

"Ah well, we're further forward, despite more work being needed on both fronts. Will you tell Abbot Barnabas your latest theory about your father?"

Leslie nodded. "One final sortie, I think. If he can't or won't confirm what I say—or tells me I'm completely wrong a second time—I think we should admit defeat."

"I'm relieved to hear you say that. Your father's possible motives have eaten away at you too long, and it isn't fair on anyone concerned to prolong the agony. Consign it to one of life's unknowns." Patrick raised a hand. "Easier said than done, I know, but you've got me to help you now. It's not a burden you have to bear alone."

"Thank you." Could Leslie be brave enough to refer to the offhand remark of earlier? Or would it be better to let sleeping dogs lie and tackle the issue once they'd shared a bed? Perhaps a delay would be wiser, because there was no guarantee that a physical reunion would be as welcome in reality as it was when purely in the imagination. That part of their relationship was yet to be signed and sealed.

"Penny for them?" Patrick asked, in a voice so tender it was proving hard to resist.

"They're not worth a halfpenny. I was merely thinking that we need to take one step at a time. Resolve Combe first and then tackle Fergus's death." Leslie raised his glass. "Here's to the inspiration I need to write that letter to Abbot Barnabas."

"I'll drink to that." Patrick did so. "I'll also drink to us. I believed I'd never see you sitting at my fireside again. Even if we only remain friends, I wouldn't ever want to lose touch with you the way I did before."

"Then we'd better have a third toast. To Marianne. She was the catalyst." And maybe Leslie should send her a big bunch of flowers in gratitude. Although not before he'd written the dreaded epistle to Combe.

CHAPTER TWELVE

Sunday evening, Leslie had pencil, pen, and paper to hand, but the most effective words were still to be conjured up.

Leslie would have to take as much care as he'd done with the previous outpouring to Abbot Barnabas, despite the channels of communication having become well established then and left open.

As it turned out, he scribbled, crossed out, and threw away three drafts before abandoning the project, taking Max for a walk and then sitting down to create a fourth and acceptable letter. Evidently his subconscious had mulled over the issue effectively while Max had cocked his leg.

He didn't need to begin with thanks for the previous information, having already sent off a note to that effect, so after the briefest of civilities, he plunged in.

You said I could get back in touch if I thought I had the right tree to bark up. I think I do, now. If I haven't, then I promise I'll give up the wild-goose chase. I've come to the conclusion that I'd rather learn to live with not knowing than further exercise my brain on madcap theories, although I hope this one isn't too madcap. Should I be wide of the mark, then you can have a good chuckle at me being so useless at the Hercule Poirot stuff. Only, there won't really be anything to laugh about if I'm correct.

Leslie tried to imagine Barnabas's reaction to the letter if he and Patrick *were* wrong. Thank God the man seemed to be magnanimous and possessed of a sense of humour. Thank God twice over, because with another man in the abbot's shoes, this level of candour might not have been possible.

When we met in The Bear and Ragged Staff, we spoke about an accidental death of someone I knew during the war. It's the one I referred to in my previous letter. But there was another death we spoke of over that excellent beer, a similar instance of an accident that might not have been accidental. In fact, I think there are similarities on all counts between the two if you consider that both involved a fatal fall and the fact that both victims had a reputation for hurting innocents. I may be libelling Abbot John, in which case I'll pray for forgiveness, but I am suggesting that what Elsie called nastiness towards novices and about which her father refused to enlighten her, was of a sexual nature. We both know that such things can happen in a closed environment, especially where you have someone in a position of power.

Hopefully Barnabas wouldn't be in blissful ignorance of what Leslie was referring to. He must have come across them in his previous employ if not in his present. And if not professionally, perhaps he'd had his eyes opened by hearing from a victim, as Leslie had at Bletchley when a beer too many had led to one of his colleagues pouring out the secrets of his school days.

You don't need to confirm or deny any of the allegations I've just made. The detail is less important than its relevance to my father, who was always a great believer in protecting the innocent. It was that quality which sent me haring off on the wrong scent previously. I also think—although with less evidence of having seen it in action—that my father might be possessed of a violent tendency that he kept well under control. If that was the case, it would be something I know he'd be deeply ashamed of, perhaps even more so than the attraction he felt for that younger man.

A deep breath before tackling the next part.

I will lay before you a scene, which may not be correct in all the details and which could involve other people, after or during the event. My father went to confront Abbot John about his behaviour. Perhaps he asked the abbot to step down from his role and he refused. An argument ensued during which John was pushed down the stairs: accidentally or on purpose I don't know. Appalled at what he'd done, my father may have sought help among his fellow brothers, and it was decided to make the death appear a tragic accident. I have no right to ask about anyone else who may have been involved, because it's equally possible that my father would have helped a killer to cover their traces in such circumstances.

So, a simple question. Right tree this time?

Into the last furlong.

Whatever your response, I give you my word that things will go no further. If I'm correct, then I have a good deal of sympathy with those who would take the law into their own hands, especially if there was a risk the victim would go on to do further harm. Do you recall the question I asked about whether killing Hitler would have been justified? Ironic that question should come into play again. Whatever the truth, Abbot John has gone to face a judge with higher authority than any in our law courts and from whom no evidence can be hidden.

Leslie paused, pen hovering over the page. Had he said enough or too much? Rather than risk dithering interminably, he quickly folded the letter, stuck it in an envelope, and sealed the thing. He could send it special delivery, as previously and let the die be cast. Like Patrick had said, whatever the result, it wasn't something he'd have to face alone.

The reply came on Wednesday, which was as quickly as the post allowed, suggesting Abbot Barnabas had sent it by return. Leslie toyed with ringing Patrick before he opened the thing, so he'd have moral support, then decided that would be cowardice of the highest order.

"Shot at dawn, I'd be, if I did that," he said to Max, who'd come to greet him in the hallway while he picked up his post and who merely gazed blankly. "Let's get it over and done with."

He slit open the envelope, to find a single sheet on which Barnabas got straight down to business.

Dear Leslie,

Since your previous letter, I've been thinking how I could best make an answer that satisfied both my duty and conscience, in the event of you hitting on what really happened. Part of me hoped you'd give up the chase so I wouldn't have to tackle the task, but the Guv'nor reminded me that would be spineless. Therefore, I'll simply state that Hercule Poirot wouldn't think you useless, although he might pick you up on some of the detail.

Leslie suddenly felt the need to sit down before he fell down, so made his way shakily to the living room. He'd expected to feel pleased at having his suspicions confirmed, albeit pleasure tinged with sadness, but his overwhelming emotion now was flat exhaustion. He reread the words, making sure that he hadn't misinterpreted Barnabas's confirmation, but there was no other interpretation possible. He and Patrick might not have every part of the story correct—and they'd better restrain themselves from trying to work out which part, because that way lay madness—but they'd got their answer.

I may be putting words in your father's mouth but I think he'd be grateful if you visited again. He'd never say so, being still painfully aware of the lack of respect he showed you and your mother. The thing is, when he went to get his leg x-rayed, they turned up some matters of concern, and he's been having further tests. While we're not entirely certain what's going on, it might be as well that you don't put off your visit for too long.

Your friend,

Barnabas

What the hell was meant by that? And had Barnabas hinted at it in his last letter, with his nudge about visiting Combe again soon?

Leslie read the letter a third time, trying to work out if the next step was to ring Patrick or his mother or his boss—the last to get the next day off so he could go straight down to Combe. In which case, he'd also have to get in contact with Mrs. Gray and pray that the person she shared a party line with wasn't using it.

As it happened, any decision was taken out of his hands, the phone sounding sharply while he vacillated.

"Hello?"

"Leslie." His mother's usually mellow voice carried a note of agitation.

"Is everything all right?"

"I don't know. I've been out all day with Mrs. Watson and got back here to find a letter from your father, addressed to both of us. He hasn't written to me since the month after he went to Combe, and I'd not expected to hear from him again." She sniffed loudly. "Sorry. I didn't expect I'd get so wound up."

"I'll come down. Now."

"No, that would be too much bother. It's . . . Well, he's ill. I think he's putting a brave face on it, but he wouldn't have written if it wasn't serious, would he?" The sound of a nose being blown. "Did you know?"

"Only five minutes ago. In a letter from the abbot." Leslie rubbed his free hand over his brow. "If you're considering going down to Combe, we really should talk beforehand. That letter contained some information Father might not have shared. Nothing to do with his health, so don't panic."

"Oh. Well, if you can get away, I won't say I wouldn't be grateful to have you here, although don't get into bother at work for taking leave at short notice." The relief in her voice was palpable. "I'll get your bed made up, in case."

"Thanks. I'd hate to have to sleep in the hammock. As for work, I'm in Mr. Rokeby's good books. Been working like billy-o the last few weeks so he should be sympathetic. I'll get matters organised now, and if you don't hear from me in the next twenty minutes, I'll be knocking at the door later. You'd better have a sandwich made up too."

Once his mother had gone off to complete her jobs, clearly happy to have something to occupy her, Leslie rang his boss. Rokeby proved sympathetic as expected, telling Leslie to take all the time he needed and not to put work first as *his* brother had done, leaving everything too late in terms of seeing Mr. Rokeby senior before the end. While the remark was no doubt intended to be kind, it didn't do anything to help Leslie's peace of mind.

Mrs. Gray proved more soothing, assuring him that the house and the dog would be fine under her care and that she'd be round in twenty minutes to do what was needed. She focussed on the practical—where he might find a roll to eat before the journey and newly pressed clothes for his case—and left him feeling calmer and better able to focus on the task in hand.

As he packed a case for an unknown number of days away, Max all the while observing him with an expression of mixed curiosity and disdain, he made a mental note to ring Patrick before he went out of the door. Not least because they'd agreed to meet on Friday night and there was no guarantee Leslie would be home by then.

But when he got round to the task, Patrick wasn't at home so the news would have to wait. What his mother would make of him ringing the man from her house was another matter.

Leslie pulled his car up at Larkspur, the place where the recent sequence of events had started. Or, to be accurate, where the journey to finding the truth had begun in earnest, starting at that chance encounter with Marianne on the common. Funny how she'd acted as a catalyst for so much of what had transpired, both in the subterfuge she'd employed in getting Leslie and Patrick round the same table again or by the information she'd shared.

As he got out of the car, his mother opened the front door, welcoming him with a warm hug, such as they'd not shared since he was a boy.

"Thank you for coming. Mr. Rokeby was happy to let you have some time off?" she asked, still in his arms.

"Yes. Everything's organised, and I've as much time as I need. As we need." He took her arm, picked up his case, and steered her into the house. "I'm gasping for a cuppa and a sandwich. I won't be fit to discuss anything until I'm sat down with them."

Once he was ensconced safely in the drawing room with much-needed refreshments to hand, Leslie said, "Father. The abbot asked me to visit him soon. He said that something had shown up when he'd had his leg x-rayed, and while I don't know what that was, it must be serious."

His mother, cradling a cup between her hands, nodded. "That's all I know, as well. Kind of the abbot to write to you about it."

"He didn't write specifically about that. It was part of a correspondence I've been having with him recently. Trying to get to the bottom of why Father went to Combe." Leslie eyed his mother over his cup. "I believe I have an answer to that, but don't feel obliged to have to hear it."

"It would be a relief, I think, because I've locked my own ideas away too long. I may possibly be able to hazard a guess myself, and if I'm wrong, you can have a laugh at an old woman's foibles."

"I said much the same to Abbot Barnabas when I wrote to him. I'm sure you can't have come up with anything as daft as some of the theories I had for what had happened." Leslie gave his mother a reassuring smile.

She went to take another drink of tea, eyed her cup, then laid it down with a watery grin. "This calls for a sherry. Or a stiff gin. Would you like one?"

Leslie nodded. "I'll keep it here for when my tea's gone down."

Perhaps the drink was less for Dutch courage than to provide a prop—something to occupy her hands and eyes while she bared her soul—because she launched into her ideas as she poured. "I loved your father very deeply and I know how much he loved me, but I'd always had a feeling that his eye sometimes wandered elsewhere. Does it sound odd to say I suspected I wouldn't lose him to a woman?"

"Not odd at all," Leslie managed to get out. He took the glass his mother offered, trying to steady his hand on it. "You've hit the nail right on the head. It's not uncommon. Several chaps I worked alongside during the war had the same inclinations, or had possessed them in their younger days." Despite what Leslie had said about his tea, he took a sip of his drink. A stiff gin indeed and exactly what was needed, especially after that revelation. "You pour them strong, Mother."

"I reckoned you could do with it."

He forced a grin. "A chap needs Dutch courage when the conversation turns the way this has. I don't think you'd ever have lost Father to a chap, you know. His eye may have roved, but I'm sure it was nothing other than that. Oh, Mother." Leslie wasn't the only one with trembling hands: hers were trembling so much they risked spilling her drink. Leslie left his chair, put both their glasses safely on a small table, then took her hands in his. "You're being terribly understanding. Plenty of women would have been livid if they'd discovered such a thing about their husbands."

"Bless you." The reply came out as barely a whisper. "I told you a terrible lie when I said I'd moved beyond the point of wanting to puzzle out why your father did what he did and that he was dead to me. It still hurts that he felt the need to go, because he could have stayed here. I'd have understood. We'd always been great pals, as well as anything else, your father and I."

Leslie had already suspected his mother had been putting on a brave face all this time, but he wouldn't confess that: it would seem too unsympathetically smug. "Have a good cry. You'll feel even better for that than for having a gin."

"Oh, you silly boy." Laughter punctuated the tears, until she could summon up a smile.

"If it's any reassurance, his going to Combe wasn't about his leanings alone. I'll tell you about that too, if you wish, although first there's something else I need to say. I'd hate you to be hurt any more than you already are, but I think there's been too much dissembling and secret keeping and now's as good a time as any to get things aired."

She squeezed his hand. "At the risk of offending you, if you're about to tell me you're in love with Patrick, then I've known that for years."

Leslie dropped his mother's hand, gobsmacked. They could have aired this long ago and eliminated all need of pretence, although admittedly his mother had never dropped any hint previously. Perhaps she'd not been sure or ready to risk stating her belief in case she'd got it wrong. How many mothers were in the same position, suspecting but not daring to speak, especially if their husbands wouldn't approve? "Mother, you continue to astonish me. This is clearly an evening for revelations."

"It's an evening for honesty, possibly." She let go Leslie's hand and took a sip of gin, giving him the chance pick up his own glass and return to his chair, in need of a drink, too. "And I'm so pleased to see you happier than you've been the last few years. You must have cleared up whatever misunderstanding happened between you two boys. I met Marianne, and she said you boys had been meeting up to work on Fergus's death."

"She should know, as she manipulated us into doing so." Leslie had known some formidable women at Bletchley, but this pair would have given them a run for their money. Rather than employing young men, Churchill should have parachuted a platoon of mothers and other strong-willed women behind enemy lines. They'd have wheedled out all of Hitler's secret plans and barely drawn breath in the process. "Yes, there was a misunderstanding, which was partly because we'd both got upset at Fergus's death, partly about other things, and entirely concerned with us being idiots. I think we've sorted most of it out now."

His mother nodded. "Will you tell me what the other thing was? What you referred to earlier?"

"I think I should. It's concerned with a theory and a long story about how I came up with it." Some details of which Leslie wanted to avoid if he could, or at least defer given how quickly disclosures were coming. "Easiest if I take you through my thinking. Firstly, I got it into my head that Father may have felt he'd contributed to Fergus's death." Leslie raised a hand at his mother's exclamation. "It made sense to me at the time because I knew he'd heard about something Fergus did and got angry about it. When Fergus's death happened so soon after that conversation, I thought he might have felt guilty and convinced himself he was to blame. Like he did when the tramp died in the churchyard."

Mrs. Cadmore stared at the fire, perhaps lost in memories of earlier days. "Yes, that makes sense. He often had times when he felt he'd not done enough to help a person or situation." She turned to face Leslie again. "But you said this theory was incorrect. How do you know?"

"I asked Abbot Barnabas. He's a good sort, an ex-policeman, believe it or not, so he understands how things are in the wider world. We had a chat over a couple of beers when I went down to Combe and struck up a rapport. I'm sure he'll make a point of being there to meet you—us—when we visit. I don't promise he'll ply you with drink, though." Leslie was pleased to see the quip raise a smile. "As a result, I felt I could write frankly to him and while he'd made a solemn vow not to divulge certain things, a vow he wanted to respect, he was happy to drop hints about whether I was on the right track. I wasn't with my Fergus theory."

"Have you discovered what happened to *him* by the way?" Her face had begun to gain its usual colour, now bearing the same inquisitive expression she'd had when they'd first discussed the accident. A conversation that seemed ages ago now.

"Not yet. We—Patrick and I—have bashed ideas about like footballs and missed the net plenty of times while we've been at it. We still both feel sure his death wasn't an accident, although any supporting evidence is highly circumstantial. And it can wait, for the moment, can't it?"

"Yes. This news has rather put things into a different perspective, all round." His mother sighed deeply. "As long as you promise to tell me if you *do* end up on the correct track."

"Of course." Irrespective of whether her favourite, James, turned out to be involved up to his pretty neck. "Let me tell you the other bit of what I put to Abbot Barnabas and which he's confirmed in his roundabout way. Which is as near confirmed as I'm ever going to get. Father had two reasons for going to Combe, both linked to his personality. We've discussed one, which came as no great surprise to you, so I wonder if the other will. Did Father have a violent streak, if that's not putting it too harshly, which he felt he had to keep suppressed? I've seen his face when dispatching a mink and he seemed a different man, and I also recall the story about him roughing up one of your old beaus." That couldn't be all, given how Leslie's mother was showing as little outward emotion as if Leslie had been reading the cricket results.

"A violent streak might be putting it too strongly, but while he never displayed the slightest hint of aggression towards us, I know exactly how protective he could be. You've heard the story about my admirer and how it was two young men squaring up to each other and throwing a few punches. It was actually far more serious."

Leslie frowned. "How serious?"

"Not long after we were married, this ex-suitor wrote to me, via your grandparents. They passed the letter on, not realising the contents, which were worrying. This chap said I'd made a mistake in not accepting his hand—I jolly well hadn't—and he was desperate to whisk me away. Don't laugh. I was thought quite a catch in those days."

"You still are, Mother. Go on."

"I told your father, naturally, and wrote back to tell this man I wasn't interested. He persisted, and I'm afraid things came to a head. Your father went round, and while I never was told exactly what happened, the communication stopped."

"Did Father belt him one?"

His mother unexpectedly grinned. "That would be one way of putting it. He did confess some time afterwards that he lost control and might have been too heavy-handed. Whatever he did, he felt very bad about it and swore he must never let himself get into a similar situation. We had to tell you a bowdlerised version of the story when you asked about an old photograph and why your father had a black eye."

Now Leslie knew why his mother had looked particularly pained when Marianne had mentioned boxing and he'd referred to the rival. Had this unwanted admirer been knocked down the stairs as Abbot John had?

"He so wanted to protect the innocent and the vulnerable, you see, and he included me in that," she continued. "He might have been afraid he'd do something similar again one day, especially under the strain of the war."

"Yes. I see that. That and James—" Hell, he hadn't meant to mention him.

"James?"

"You might as well know, Mother, that your little pal James was probably trying to get my father embroiled with him." Leslie hadn't intended to sound so bitchy, either. "It didn't happen, but it puts his open invitation here in a different light."

"And his visiting me. The toad." She knocked back the rest of her gin, then peered into the empty glass. "I think I'd like another one."

"I'll get it for you." The pause in conversation would allow them both to think. No doubt his mother would want to know further details about James when she'd had a day or two to consider things, but in the meantime there were other hurdles to jump. Leslie gave them both a top-up. "Something happened at Combe after Father became ensconced there. The previous Abbot, John, was killed falling down a flight of stairs, and I believe Father was somehow involved in the death—before, during, or after the event. That's why he's determined to stay at the place, because it's literally his sanctuary. Barnabas has hinted to me that I'm not far from the truth with that theory, despite him being away from the abbey at the time it happened, so has clearly been informed since. Perhaps when hearing a confession."

His mother nodded slowly, eyes on the fire again. "What was Abbot John like?"

"A cruel man, especially to his novices. Tongues were wagging locally, as you can imagine, saying that he'd been murdered, but that was probably covered up at the inquest. Barnabas isn't unhappy about the coroner's verdict, and he doesn't strike me as the kind of man to prioritise protecting the abbey. His flock he might go the extra mile for."

"So, perhaps Barnabas was complicit in having the death ruled as accidental. Leave judgement in the hands of a much higher authority."

"Quite. We must pretend we don't know any of this, when we're at Combe. Apart from with Abbot Barnabas himself. I admit I'm going to struggle to keep a blank face if Father wants to confess to me."

"Do you think that's why he wants to see us, or does he merely want to say a final farewell?" She got out her handkerchief, perhaps expecting the tears to flow again.

"I have no idea. Didn't he give a hint in his letter?"

She shook her head. "Only that he wanted to see us both. Hopefully all will be clearer when we get down there."

"Hopefully." Leslie wouldn't hold his breath. "Would it be all right if I ring Patrick now? I'm supposed to be meeting him at the weekend for another session of Fergus-sleuthing and even if we're back by then, I'm not sure my mind would be in it." Too much of a risk of falling straight into his bed, too, for the sort of comfort only Patrick could provide.

"Certainly, dear. Although I think we should leave making any proper plans until the morning, when we'll be able to think more clearly. Accommodation and the like."

"I know a smashing pub with rooms. They'll take good care of us." Leslie drained his glass, then went to give his mother a good-night kiss. "I'll be off to my bed once I've made my call, assuming I can get through and he's not dealing with a pregnant mare."

"I won't be long after you. No point in sitting here dwelling on the past or wondering about the future." His mother ran her hand down Leslie's cheek. "I hope you'll be happy, dear, as we were once. I've suspected for a long time that you'd never marry, despite men like you and Patrick doing so. I simply want you to follow your heart wherever it leads, whether that's to Patrick and his animals or into a place like Combe." Her eyes began to well.

"You're an angel."

Smiling through the tears, she flapped her hand at Leslie. "Go and ring him. That's an order."

"Yes, sah!" Leslie gave a mock salute, planted another kiss on his mother's cheek, and went off to the hallway.

This time his call was answered by a weary-sounding Patrick. "I'm glad it's you and not another call-out. I'll be glad when the junior's back."

"I bet. Still, chances are you'll have Friday night free to take a rest, I'm afraid." Leslie quickly gave a precis of the letter from Barnabas, the news from Leslie's mother, and their likely subsequent plans. "I'm ringing from Larkspur now. I guess we'll be off to Combe tomorrow, and I won't know when we'll be back until we find out exactly what's wrong with Father."

"Take as long as you need, and if there's anything I can do, let me know. Only not tonight as I'm knackered." As if on cue, Patrick produced a yawn. "How's your mother taking things?"

"Very well, considering. And not just the news from Combe. I've had what might be termed a full and fairly frank conversation with her about my correspondence with Barnabas. She'd had her suspicions about my father's preferences, so that aspect wasn't as great a shock as the news about his health was. I've got a story to tell you about an old flame of hers too, which backs up our theory, although the details can wait. The most interesting thing is that she'd already guessed. About us." Leslie automatically glanced over his shoulder, but the door to the drawing room remained shut, his mother perhaps ensuring his privacy.

"Blimey. You've not been chucked out or read the riot act?"

"Not at all. She's been remarkably understanding." Although how much of that was tied up with not wanting to lose another loved one, Leslie wasn't sure. He'd happily accept what had been offered. "Anyway, we'll discuss it further when we meet up."

"Sounds like we won't be short of conversational fodder." Patrick yawned again. "Sorry. Got to get to bed. Night night, Leslie Lad."

"Good night Paddy Boy."

Leslie replaced the receiver, shouted to his mother that he was finished, then headed up the stairs. Despite the many shocks of the previous few hours, he couldn't help experiencing a small glow of something like relief. If he could get through the next few days and still feel as positive, all would be well.

CHAPTER THIRTEEN

Thursday morning seemed to fly by in a whirl of planning, packing, and booking. Leslie felt he'd hardly drawn breath until he found himself a second time in the train heading for Combe, after several line changes and a slightly hair-raising ride to the station. He'd forgotten how erratic the local car service tended to be.

Leslie had anticipated that one of his roles during the trip would be to keep up his mother's spirits, but as it turned out, she'd needed little support, throwing herself into all the practicalities, clearly finding activity therapeutic.

She'd brought a book to read on the journey, although it got as scant attention as Leslie's crossword once they were west of Salisbury, a conversation starting between them about memories of childhood holidays. By the time Combe station appeared, they'd settled into an easy silence, his mother no doubt as wrapped up in thoughts of days past and days to come as her son.

Despite their tiredness, she insisted they go straight to the abbey once they'd deposited their luggage at The Bear and Ragged Staff. The redoubtable landlady Elsie summoned a car to take them, a journey that proved much less terrifying than the Kinebridge equivalent. Barnabas wasn't tending the lodge this time, but the monk who acted as porter said he was under instructions to let the abbot know the moment they arrived and to ask them to wait for him to come down. He found them a comfortable bench in the sunshine, then scurried off, returning a few minutes later in Barnabas's wake.

Leslie effected the introductions, then Barnabas offered to take Mrs. Cadmore up to the sick bay, where Brother Andrew would be pleased to see her, and Brother Francis had refreshments on hand. The abbot promised Leslie to come straight back for a little chat soon and to be bearing tea and cakes should they be required, an offer which Leslie politely declined. He wasn't sure he'd enjoy them in his present state of mind.

With a wan yet brave smile, Leslie's mother let herself be led off, while Leslie took his seat again. Not far away, Brother Mark and a couple of other monks were heading towards a large grassy area, carrying what looked suspiciously like a cricket bat, stumps, and other items essential for a knock around. Life going on normally and in a bubble of peace. That aspect must be very appealing, especially for a troubled mind; Leslie wouldn't have minded trying a weekend of it himself, if they offered retreats.

The abbot's voice brought Leslie out of his contemplations. "She strikes me as a courageous woman, your mother."

"She is. A remarkably understanding one, as well." Leslie shifted along the bench so Barnabas could sit beside him.

The abbot waved in the group of monks' direction. "I see we're about to have an outbreak of the Ashes. Brother Luke came to Europe with the Anzacs and decided to stay. Another man who's found peace here."

"I hope Brother Mark doesn't indulge in bodyline. That would break all the harmony." Leslie breathed deeply, drawing in contentment with the air of the place.

"I haven't told your father about our correspondence." Trust Barnabas to cut straight to the point. "So, it'll be up to him what he says or leaves unsaid."

"In contrast to which, I've told Mother pretty well everything. I thought that would be for the best. She'll keep a straight face in the sick bay." Leslie snorted. "Probably better than I will."

"I think you've been wise. There have been too many secrets between the three of you."

Leslie gave the abbot a sideways glance then decided to take that remark at face value. Surely it wasn't a hint at his own secrets?

"I have a confession to make to *you*," Barnabas continued, "although I'd be grateful if it went no further. After Abbot John's tumble down the stairs—and if you snitch on me, I'll plead I was merely discussing the chronology of events here—I returned and found the abbey . . . not quite in turmoil, because things had been handled efficiently, but tense, let's say. Your father was particularly upset, although I didn't immediately get to the bottom of why. At one point he wanted to take what you might call the easy way out."

"The old 'Do the honourable thing, Carruthers. There's a bottle of whisky and a pistol in my study'?" Leslie, emotion welling up, focussed on the game of cricket that was underway in the distance.

"Exactly. The old-school way. Tempting for any man to go down that road to avoid facing the consequences in this life and relying on the mercy of God in the next. But he changed his mind, not least because I told him that would be supremely unfair. It would also have been terribly cruel on you and your mother because he'd have been, in effect, running out on you again. No doubt I could have concocted a story, told you he'd died of natural causes—heart failure or some such—but that style of deliberate lie, white or not and whatever the good intentions behind it, wouldn't be right."

"I appreciate your honesty and your actions." A sudden, disconcerting thought. "He's not been tempted to take the 'honourable' way out since?"

Barnabas gave him a puzzled glance. "Not that I know of. Why?"

"I was thinking about my father's leg. I guess his falling down the stairs was coincidental to Abbot John's tumble, rather than being a deliberate act of emulation, if that's the right word."

"I hadn't thought of that." The abbot mulled it over briefly. "No, I'd say it was nothing other than a consequence of the staircases here being old and unforgiving." He eased himself forward. "I'm afraid I'll have to leave you, as I've other business to be about. One of the older monks died a couple of days ago, and

I've his niece to meet, but your mother says you might stay here a few days, so please come and see me if you do."

"We'll buy you a pint at The Bear and Ragged Staff, if you're up for it."

The abbot chuckled. "Tell young Elsie to get a barrel of her best ready." He shook Leslie's hand, then went off, humming something that sounded suspiciously like a music hall song.

Watching the monks play their reduced-numbers version of cricket kept Leslie occupied while he waited. While the bowling wasn't quite as vicious as Larwood's, no quarter was being given on either side, so the time flew past until Mrs. Cadmore's heels could be heard clattering on the flagstones of the path. Leslie rose to greet her, pleased to see how calm and collected she appeared.

"How did it go?"

"As well as could be expected." They sat together for a moment. "He's received some bad news in terms of his health and has decided he doesn't want to have any treatment. Not that there's a lot the doctors could do if they've got their diagnosis right. I would imagine your father feels that's part of his penance for doing what he did."

"He mentioned that?"

"Not in as many words. I asked him why he didn't want treatment, but his answer was simply that it wouldn't be the proper way forward. When I played innocent and said it seemed a bit harsh on himself, he took my hand and told me that I didn't know the half of things and he hoped I never found out." Leslie's mother gave him a surprisingly bright smile. "Just as well that you and Patrick had done all your digging and shared what you'd learned. I dread to think how I'd have come away feeling if I hadn't been prepared." She took his hand, squeezed it, and said, "Your turn now."

With uncanny timing, Brother Francis came strolling down the path, greeted Leslie like a long-lost friend, and took him off to the sick bay.

"Brother Andrew's been moved to a different bed, but he's still my sole patient," Francis said as they walked along. "Unless and until that cricket game turns nasty and I have some sore heads to deal with. No quarter being given or asked for."

"I can imagine." There'd be nothing particularly godly in not trying one's best.

"You'll notice a change in your father since you were last here. It's not only his physical condition. He's been very worried about today, and you can read it in his face." Francis patted Leslie's shoulder. "I hope it will prove therapeutic for all three of you."

Mr. Cadmore certainly did appear worse than the previous time, with a pallid face and distinct lines of strain. Although if Francis hadn't mentioned the change in him, Leslie might have blamed that opinion partly on his own overactive imagination, trying to see what it thought it should see. He shook his father's hand warmly, then eased himself into the chair by the bed.

"Well, this is a bit of a turn up," Mr. Cadmore said, with a welcome hint of the humour he'd displayed in times past.

"Indeed."

His father went through what sounded like a well-rehearsed account of how his diagnosis had come about, the choice he'd made about treatment, and the likely prognosis, ending with, "I'm well looked after here, so don't worry about me. I'd only ask that you take special care of your mother over the next few months, which I know will happen anyway, so you don't need an old buffer like me instructing you."

"I will." This meeting was less tense, something closer to the chats they'd had when out fishing, the man and the growing boy.

"It was lovely to see her again. Lovely, yet painful for both of us and probably more for her. I know how hard it's been for you both." Mr. Cadmore winced, whether at the thought of the hurt he'd caused or pain he was now suffering, Leslie couldn't tell. "I shan't embarrass you or her by sharing the details of what we said, but I hope we've taken a step further forward towards finding an acceptable peace. I was surprised how chatty she became by the end."

"She's a good woman. An understanding one. Probably to an extent neither of us realised."

His father shot him a sidelong glance. "She says you and Patrick are trying to get at the truth behind Fergus Jackson's accident. I wish you'd mentioned that last time." His hands played over the bed cover. "I, of all men, should know that a supposed accident isn't always what it appears."

Leslie waited for further detail but none was forthcoming. "Father, you should know that I've not stopped trying to work out why you came here and what continues to bind you, apart from the obvious." He gestured at the crucifix above the bed. "Although I understand at least some of it, because unlike Patrick, James Lyth has a loose tongue."

"Ah. I should have guessed he'd be a broken reed." Mr. Cadmore passed his hand across his brow. "Let me be honest: I've had many a soft spot for young men through the years, although I truly thought it was purely paternal. That I saw them as almost another son or someone to take under my wings."

Leslie nodded but didn't interrupt the flow.

"However, it began to be plain to me that the reality was something far deeper. That temptation was starting to grow. When James came along . . ." The pain etched on Mr. Cadmore's face brought a lump to Leslie's throat. He'd come to Combe in part convinced that he shouldn't make the interview easy for his father—his mother's tears had influenced that—but now all he could see was a man who'd been torn in too many directions to cope.

"You don't need to say anything further unless it would help you to do so."

"Then I'll leave it unsaid. Too personal." Mr. Cadmore turned, reached for a glass of water, and took a sip. "Would you like a cup of tea?"

"Yes, please. I'm absolutely parched, although I refused one earlier, so I might be in Brother Francis's bad books."

When Francis arrived, summoned by the ring of a little bell on the bedside table, he informed them that he had some tea already on the brew so two cups—and a plate of small biscuits—appeared within minutes.

"Good service at this hotel," Leslie said, after he'd taken the chance to quench his thirst.

"I'll let the management know. Francis does make an exceptional cuppa."

Another sip: the tea was refreshing Leslie's wits as well as his throat. "You said earlier that you wished you'd known we were suspicious about Fergus's death. Why?"

"There's something I've been pondering since your mother mentioned it. I'm not sure how best to explain."

"Say it as it comes to mind, no matter what order it tumbles out in. You're not Agatha Christie telling a story." Leslie stroked his father's arm. "It can't make less sense than some of the harebrained ideas we've had." At least one of which he'd never confess to the man, no matter how little time he had left.

"Then let's start at the time I came here. I thought such a move would take me away from temptation, monks being older men like me. Surprisingly, that's proved to be the case, despite the unexpected presence of people like Brother Mark."

"He's the chap who likes playing cricket, isn't he? I think I saw him today."

"That would be the one. Poor chap, to be burdened with such a handsome face. Anyway, I suspect my . . . encounter . . . with James made for a bit of a sickener on that front. I arrived here with a clean slate, to a place where I thought none of the worse parts of me could be exposed." Mr. Cadmore took another drink of strong tea. "I have little doubt that would have remained the case had I not begun to hear terrible rumours. The previous abbot may have called himself a man of God, but he didn't act that way."

"John? I heard about him when I was here previously. The landlady at The Bear and Ragged Staff had plenty to say on the subject. A nasty man from all accounts."

"*Nasty*'s about the right word. Domineering with his novices, and not here alone. That overbearing nature came out in horrible ways, physically and—" Mr. Cadmore pulled a disgusted face.

"Sexually? I've heard of such things, especially where one man has power over young men or children."

"Then you'll know how appalled I was when I discovered it had happened. Was still happening." Mr. Cadmore's voice wavered again, before he took a deep breath and resumed the tale. "It could have been you he was preying on. Someone's beloved son, who wouldn't fight back because of the position the abbot held and the duty the monks owed such a man. So, when we learned that Barnabas was going to be away for a few days, three of us spoke together. It led to a long dark night of the soul for us, but in the end a decision was reached. The innocent had to be protected, and we seemed to have no choice over what we should do. Please don't tell your mother any of this." His words faltered, giving way to tears.

"I won't." Leslie, holding his father's hand, was happy to make the promise. It was nothing she didn't already know. "What we say here stays here."

When the tears dried, Mr. Cadmore—still with his hand in Leslie's—continued. "As a result of all this, I know that decent people can take matters into their own hands and do things they'd never contemplate otherwise if they believe it's for the greater good."

Leslie nodded. "Is that what you think happened with Fergus?"

"Possibly. I have to confess that when James told me how ill-used he'd been by the man, I felt a great desire to go and deal with him myself. Ironic that he died so soon afterwards. I racked myself with remorse when I heard, thinking that in my raging I'd somehow heaped burning coals on Fergus's head, but I decided that was silly." No sign of dissembling: Leslie's father had clearly overcome any guilt he might have felt. "However, James made some odd comments that evening, ones which maybe I should have probed at the time, but I was too wrapped up in my own emotions." A helpless sweep of his hand. "He spoke about Fergus having enemies. I believe—using hindsight here—that James had the intention of making sure I ended up numbered among them."

"That appears to be James's way. I don't think any of us noticed until now."

"Then he's probably left a trail of dupes behind him. Anyway, he said that Fergus would be getting what was coming to him, one day, and it was simply a matter of who did the deed." Mr. Cadmore shrugged, which clearly caused him discomfort. "I don't believe he had any intention of delivering the blow."

"I'd say you were right. For a start, unless he's deeper than we all realise, he wouldn't have had the guts to stand up to Fergus." Persuading someone else to do the deed was another matter. Was there a chance he'd known Dawson? "James couldn't have been there, so you can eliminate him. Did he mention any specific names when he spoke of Fergus having enemies?"

"Not that I can recall, even though I asked him, so he was either protecting a particular individual or talking in general. What he *also* said, and it means very little to me but it might to you and Patrick, was that Fergus could cause a lot of embarrassment to people if he chose. He knew things folk wouldn't want made public."

That didn't narrow the field. "Did that include at a court-martial? One was hanging over Fergus, so James might have meant that his evidence could be embarrassing. Or he could have used it as a platform to condemn others if he felt he had nothing further to lose."

A shake of the head. "No. I'd have remembered a court-martial. The strangest bit wasn't so much the words James used— affecting a man's standing, which is all of a piece with public embarrassment—but his expression when he said it. As though he knew a great secret and wanted me to know the fact, though he wouldn't divulge to me what it was."

"James probably knew lots of folks' secrets, either directly or through Fergus informing him. Some of them would be men of standing who wouldn't want the truth to emerge." Leslie finished his tea, trying to hide his disappointment. It would have been too much to hope that his father would suddenly come out with the vital clue that would clear up the puzzle completely.

They ended their chat much as it had begun. Mr. Cadmore, looking desperately weary, produced what sounded like another prepared speech, saying that Leslie and his mother were welcome to visit him at any time but not to feel constrained to do so. They had their chosen lives to lead as he had his. Leslie kissed his father's brow, squeezed his hand, and left with a choked, "Until next time."

Back in the fresh air, he made an effort to compose himself before facing his mother, although when he reached the bench where they'd been sitting, she was nowhere to be seen.

"She's been scooped up by one of the cricketers," the porter said, emerging from the lodge. "They didn't want her getting bored, so they've invited her to watch the game from a better spot. I'll take you down to the pitch."

That had the stamp of Barnabas all over it. He wouldn't have wanted either of them to sit moping. As he followed the porter, Leslie thanked God that Abbot John wasn't still in command at Combe. Although if he had been, perhaps his father would have come home already, having no need of sanctuary.

CHAPTER FOURTEEN

Over breakfast on Friday, his mother had insisted that Leslie return home that day, if he wanted, so he could keep his appointment with Patrick. She'd remain at Combe for as long as she needed, having found a surprising level of peace there.

"I'll take my time, dear, not having any commitments that can't be broken," she'd said as she buttered her toast. "I've got Barnabas and Elsie to keep me under control."

"Don't you go thinking of taking the veil." It was only half a joke: Leslie didn't want to lose his other parent to the cloister.

"I promise I won't. Although I can't say I'm not tempted by the life Elsie lives. And the thought of the scandal it would cause in Kinebridge if I took up a job as the landlady of a public house is very appealing." She'd given Leslie a roguish smile, one he'd not seen on her face since his childhood, when she'd devised some innocent little prank to play on the Sibley twins. Perhaps worry about his father had gradually subsumed that side of her personality and only now could it blossom again.

"If you did, I'd pay to see some of the faces in church. The wedding at Cana upsets them enough." Leslie had thought of a couple of men's clubs in London where his mother would be perfect to run the front of house and how much greater a scandal that would cause if she did so. Kinebridge society would never recover. He'd decided to accept the offer of an early return to London, though, taking the opportunity to visit his father again that morning before heading off.

After a journey blessedly short of incident, he found himself back at home, awaiting Patrick's arrival. They'd be going out for a fish supper and a few pints, but Leslie was relishing most their time alone together, which would bookend the evening.

On Patrick's arrival, as soon as Leslie had ushered him in and closed the front door, he drew his ex-lover into a hug.

"This is nice," Patrick said. "You've clearly survived, if—I'm guessing—a bit emotionally bruised."

"Not as much as I thought I'd be. Glad to be home, though." Leslie nestled for a few moments, then broke the clinch, determined that there'd be nothing else at present. "Thanks for that."

"Dr. Sibley's hug medicine is always available to you, free of charge and without prescription." Patrick smiled. "How is your father?"

"Not well, but stoic about it. I'm not exactly sure of the medical details or how long he's got, especially as he won't have treatment. He's got some form of cancer, so it's serious, though."

"Is the 'no treatment' bit a touch of self-punishment?"

Leslie shrugged. "Maybe it's a spot of penance. Although he might feel any extension of life wouldn't be worth the discomfort involved, not that I've much of an idea what the doctors could or couldn't do."

"Don't ask me to enlighten you. It's all a bit different with animals." Patrick rubbed his arm. "Your mother hasn't returned with you?"

"No. She loves it down there. Seems to have found some peace and reconciliation."

"And you? Did you achieve reconciliation with him?"

"As close as we'll get, I suspect. I spoke to him about James, which he was pretty candid about, and the Abbot John business got quite a mention. I promised I wouldn't tell Mother what was said, but that doesn't apply to you." Leslie repeated that part of the conversation almost verbatim, the words etched into his memory. The bit about Fergus could wait for the moment. "I think we're all feeling better for our conversations, despite things being left unsaid. It isn't hard to fill in the blank parts."

"How long do you think your mother will stay down there?"

Leslie shrugged. "As long as she feels it's doing her some good. It's ages since she had a proper holiday, so however extended a break she takes won't do her any harm. My main hope is that she doesn't get it into her head to take the veil, although she's more tempted by the life of a pub landlady."

"You jest."

"I don't." Leslie recounted what his mother had said over breakfast and her pleasure at the thought of shocking her friends. "They'd make a formidable double act, her and Elsie, the present landlady of the pub we stayed at. They'd keep The Retainers or their equivalents in line, and they could indulge their inner Miss Marples while they were at it. Discuss accidental or purpose killings to their hearts' content. Which leads me to something that might be relevant to *our* mystery." Leslie consulted his watch. "We should be getting down to the restaurant. We can discuss it on the way."

"Are we taking Max?"

"No. He's still with Mrs. Gray, being spoilt. The only being I have to walk today is you. No cocking your legs at lampposts."

"I gave that up in the blackout." Patrick grinned and headed back towards the door.

Once out on the street, Leslie said, "Father said he wished he'd known we were interested in Fergus's death and not only because of the similarities to Abbot John's *not-accident*. He'd been mulling over some of the things James said to him that last time they met—he's had his eyes opened on the bloke's feet of clay, as well, by the way."

"I wonder if Fergus had too. Categorised him afresh from someone to be led astray to a quiet manipulator." Patrick kicked at a stone on the pavement. "Maybe we've underestimated James's role in all this."

"He certainly knew more about the darker aspects of Fergus's life than he let on to any of us. He told my father that Fergus had it coming to him and it was only a case of who did the deed. And that Fergus could embarrass plenty of people if he let his tongue wag."

"That hardly makes the field smaller, although it could include James himself if he still had lingering aspirations to take the cloth."

"That's what I thought. The largeness of the field, I mean," Leslie clarified. "But it strikes me that James might have had someone particular in mind. Apparently, he pulled 'that' face when he spoke about affecting a man's standing. You know the one I mean. The smug, 'I know a secret and *you* haven't any idea what it is.'"

"I remember that little grin, because it made him appear to be aged about nine. I always suspected he learned it off Fergus and tried it on all the old men, especially the dirty ones."

"Probably." Leslie shuddered at the thought of James using it on his father and what his motive might have been. "Right. We're back to whichever of Fergus's many conquests had so much to lose that he might have persuaded Dawson or Jefferies to take drastic action. Your pal the dog handler didn't start splashing money about afterwards, did he? Are you listening?"

"I'm not aware that Jefferies was suddenly awash with cash. See? I was listening to every word." Patrick cuffed Leslie's shoulder, none too gently. "I was mulling over a thought I'd just had. Affecting a man's standing. What if your father didn't quite quote James verbatim? Or the little sod was making a bit of a play on words as part of being a smart aleck."

"Both of those are possible, but I'm still not with you."

"I wondered whether 'standing' was meant as a verb rather than a noun?"

"Now you've totally lost me." Leslie shook his head. "Am I being thick?"

"Possibly, although I should make myself clearer. What if James wasn't talking about a person's reputation. There's another way a man can stand."

Of course. "Standing for parliament. It's obvious now, isn't it? Eric, who was connected to one of the men involved with the training, so might have been able to influence the outcome of any enquiry. Eric, whom we discussed in regard to manipulating the make-up of those present on the course and then discarded. Too soon, probably."

"Quite. Eric, who might employ the mysterious Gareth and who may have known him before or during the war. I never did get to the bottom of what Eric was doing on Churchill's staff, but when I hear some of the stories about how we misdirected the enemy, it wouldn't surprise me to discover a connection to the secret operations people through his war service. Assuming it's the same Gareth."

"It doesn't have to be the same Gareth, though, does it? Not if the motive's shutting Fergus's gob rather than some elaborate revenge for the hurt he's caused people. Or if it *is* the same Gareth, his role in all this simply reverts to telling Eric that Fergus is likely to shoot his mouth off at the court-martial or afterwards."

"Why not James in that role? Fergus lets something slip—pillow talk and all that—then James hares off to tell Eric. Not caring a jot what the consequences might be." Patrick slapped his hands together, then wagged his finger excitedly. "Which is why the pair of them have been so keen to spread the story that the wound was self-inflicted. A nice smokescreen for one and a sop to the other's conscience."

"I wonder how much of a conscience James actually has. I know that sounds bitchy, but really . . ." Leslie snorted.

"Bitch as much as you like. Anyway, the self-inflicted wound bit would also give a suitably noble excuse for Eric to get his mate to ensure the death is quickly dealt with, sans anyone poking into it too deeply. 'Honour of the service, old chap. Accident much better on the record than a suicide or implications of cowardice. Poor bloke, worried about the court-martial. Never knew he was like that. My sympathies are with his mother.'" Patrick's impersonation of Eric may not have captured the voice, but the intonation and choice of words was spot on.

"If we're correct—and I'm trying not to get too excited, because we've been wrong too often before—do you think the bloke who ran things had a wider role in events? Chappell? Hold on." They'd reached the restaurant. "Don't answer that until we're at the table. Walls have ears."

"'She's not so dumb, chum'?" Patrick's grin suddenly disappeared. "Actually, you're right. A bit too close to our friend's home turf, which means that anyone could hear us potentially slandering him and report that back. I want to be able to enjoy my dinner, not be looking over my shoulder every two minutes."

"Then we'll have to hope we're given a table out of earshot."

Luckily they were. The waiter was apologetic that he could only offer a table tucked away in an alcove, but they accepted it with alacrity.

Once they'd ordered, Patrick evidently felt secure enough to continue the discussion. "Talking about looking over my shoulder for unfriendly ears made me think of something else. Could our mutual friend have persuaded Chappell to get Dawson to kill Fergus?"

"He could have, but what reason would he give? Preserving his reputation wouldn't have been enough."

Patrick lowered his voice. "What if this was all planned in advance. Eric goes to his mate and says he has evidence that Fergus is a traitor, endangering the whole operation. Maybe he offers the fact of Gareth getting injured as part of that evidence."

Leslie considered the theory. "That could explain him being brought back not only for that training, but for the sudden court-martial. What did Harry say? That Fergus's sexual behaviour had been tolerated up until then? Something clearly changed."

"Yep. And it might explain the bizarre bit about him still being trained for duty while that court-martial loomed. I know you're innocent until proven guilty, but these things don't always seem to hold fast in time of war."

"Are you thinking he was only on the course because it provided a useful setting for his death?"

"Why not?"

Why not indeed. "Right. So, Eric pours words in his mate's ear. 'Traitor in the ranks. Needs sorting.' I can't do as good an impersonation as you can."

"I realised who you meant." Patrick paused as the waiter arrived with their drinks. "Cheers."

"Cheers." A chinking of glasses. "Chappell arranges to be there in a liaison role, which could cover a multitude of activities, official and unofficial. Say he gets hold of young Dawson beforehand and says, 'Jackson's a danger to us all. If you get the chance to dispose of him, like you would any other enemy agent, you'd be serving your king and country.'"

"He had a Scottish accent, did he?"

"Behave." Leslie jabbed at Patrick's arm. "As a theory, it makes as much sense of what we have as any other we've put together. Eliminates any need for naked men running amok or members of the royal family getting things covered up. Not quite an example of Ockham's razor but along those lines."

"It has a pleasing simplicity, certainly. Bear with me for a moment while I try to remember Chappell's reactions when I first brought news of the accident." Patrick sat back for a moment, sipping at his beer, evidently lost in memories. "No. Nothing. He was pretty poker faced, but that might go with the business these people were in. He appeared grim, I'd say, rather than shocked."

"Hmm. We don't have a scrap of evidence, then. Not a hint of a confession from anyone involved, like we have with my father."

"There's Fergus's odd remark about falling on his sword, but that's hearsay. From James, whose reliability we now see in a different light. Right." Patrick tapped the table. "Let's concentrate on nothing other than this here meal. A pint of beer, fish and chips, what more could a man want?"

The glint in Patrick's eye suggested he knew exactly what else any red-blooded bloke would want to make his evening complete, but Leslie would ignore that for the moment. While they technically had a solution, they'd no proof it was *the* solution, so the promise he'd made couldn't be called in for payment. Yet.

As the pair walked back to Leslie's house, they found the air had turned distinctly nippy. Tightening his raincoat around him.

Leslie wished he'd had the sense to wear a thicker one. "Does this Eric theory count as a solution, then? Given there's not a cat in hell's chance of proving it."

"*Could* we ever prove any theory? Unless Dawson happens to be alive and would spill the beans."

"He can't, because he was run over, remember? Harry assured us it couldn't have been mistaken identity because— Damn and blast it. His commanding officer identified the body, and if that officer was Chappell, he might have wanted to help Dawson start a new life."

"Or been persuaded to. Dawson tells him he's in deep bother and threatens Chappell. If the bloke won't help, Dawson will reveal what actually happened on the course. How he was acting under orders. As a result, this car accident gets staged and some poor sod cops it in Dawson's place, leaving him free to do whatever he did." Patrick drew his gloves from his pocket and put them on. "Why is it suddenly brass monkeys' weather?"

"Because we're in England, not the south of France. From where, if you'll excuse the terrible link, Dawson already did one disappearing and reappearing trick during the war. Still, if he's gone to ground again, that's as completely useless for our purposes."

"Supposing we somehow managed to find him, I doubt he'd be willing to testify. If he's got away with things for so long, why rock the boat? Which also applies to anyone else involved."

Leslie, frustrated, felt the delivery of justice slipping through his fingers. Maybe they'd have to rely on that higher judge, as would apply to Abbot John, but that thought didn't help. "I suppose that an anonymous tip off to the *Daily Tripe* or some other newspaper wouldn't work? Eric would only deny it and want to discover the source of the story, so we'd all probably end up on the wrong end of a libel case, which takes us back to the lack of evidence that this is anything other than wild speculation."

"I reckon a libel case would be a better outcome than another I can think of. If Eric covered himself once by killing Fergus, he could cover himself twice in the same way. He already might suspect we're on his trail, given that I contacted him for information before we got it from Harry." Patrick heaved a sigh.

The words hit like a punch to the stomach. "I'd forgotten that."

"I hadn't. He wouldn't necessarily have to go as far as physical harm to cause us damage. If he felt himself under threat, he could spill the beans on you and me and James and bring down the whole boiling with him. Murdering our reputations rather than actual murder."

Leslie shivered and not simply because of the cold. The notion of Eric as a cold-blooded killer, while hard to swallow, had grown all evening but only now were the ramifications clear. Including one that had sprung into his mind. "Paddy Boy, it's for the best we've cut out our careers as a vet and a solicitor, because we'd be absolutely rubbish as detectives, amateur or otherwise."

"Yes, we've hardly covered ourselves in glory. What bleeding obvious thing have we missed this time?"

"To start with, how an officer was called on to identify the victim of the road accident, whoever he was. Think of Harry and all his 'need to know' type stuff, how he couldn't possibly give us names and all that. Why would the police have gone to *that* particular person to confirm the identity of the body?" They'd reached Leslie's house now, the conversation carrying on as they entered and discarded their coats. "It's not like they could have found out his name from Dawson's landlady."

"What if the dead man had a piece of paper on him, listing Chappell as contact in the case of emergency because he didn't have any close family still alive? Or maybe Dawson had a letter addressed to Chappell that he was due to post, so the police latched on to that?"

Leslie ushered Patrick into the kitchen, where he set about getting the kettle on the hob. "That would work if it *was* Dawson, although . . . no, it could work for a stranger too, if the person who ran him over went back to put the note in his pocket."

"And to check he was dead. Maybe finished the job off using a method that accorded with an accident. *Another* accident that wasn't."

"Exactly. But let's consider it another way, one that eliminates any notes in pockets or the like. Dawson *was* the victim, although he was deliberately killed, because he knew too much and was maybe threatening to tell all. Like Fergus was."

Patrick, who'd taken a seat at the little kitchen table, drummed gently on it. "Presumably Chappell gets one of his gang—an ex-agent or an active one, if he's still involved in that game—to do the deed. Easy enough to use the traitor story again because plenty of folk are still worried about quislings. Then what?"

"Chappell turns up at the relevant police station, probably playing the security card. 'Worried about one of my agents. He's threatened to throw himself in front of a train or under a lorry. I want to stop him.'"

"To which the village copper says, 'Oh, ah, zir, I think ee be too late.'"

"That's miles worse than the accent I attempted. You're right with the idea, though. Only I don't think Chappell was behind it." Leslie absentmindedly spooned tea into the pot, then tipped it out. "Bugger, lost count."

"You didn't warm it, either. Mrs. Gray will *not* be impressed."

"Then don't tell her." Leslie, with a smirk of defiance, spooned the correct amount of tea from the caddy into the cold, earthenware pot. "Right, what if it was Eric who got Chappell to do for Dawson? On the grounds that he might say what had really happened to Fergus? Eric threatens that he'll expose Chappell's complicity in that death if he didn't play ball a second time."

"What if Eric himself did the killing? Maybe with some help from Chappell, who could easily have lured Dawson to a meeting, then bundled him in front of the car. A risky business to try to kill someone outright at first impact, although if the driver reversed back . . ." Patrick paused. "What were the fingerprints on?"

"Eh?"

"Harry said that the police had fingerprints from the scene of the accident. But if it was a hit and run, where were they found? Not like you'd have a weapon left at the scene."

"A part of the car that hit him? One that the driver didn't know had dropped off until it was too late to go back and get it?"

Leslie suggested. "Not that my car's bumper would have many fingerprints on it and it would take a hell of a whack for it to fly off."

"Exactly. So did those fingerprints exist or were they a convenient part of the story, meaning the death couldn't be linked to any specific person by mistake?"

"That does sound awfully like the subterfuge that was going on during the war." Leslie grinned. "Creating the illusion that something was about to happen in a certain place in a certain way when the reality was totally different."

"I'd heard stories along those lines, many of which are no doubt true. Surely people wouldn't go into civvy street having forgotten the principles of staging deceptions, whether well planned or opportunistic." Patrick shrugged. "Desperate men do desperate things and sometimes fortune favours them."

"It's certainly favoured Eric if he was involved with both killings and has got away with them for so long." Leslie wouldn't have been surprised if the war years, and those immediately after, had seen chances taken by other men and women. How easy to commit murder and make it seem like a result of the conflict, directly or indirectly. He filled the teapot, leaving it to stand while they planned their next move. "Well, what do we do now? Call up your mate Harry and offer him our thoughts to pass on to his pal the policeman? Risking, naturally, that we get laughed to scorn."

"I think there's a step to take before that. One we should have taken when Harry came to visit." Patrick drummed on the table again. "Mea culpa, but when we were listing names and watching for a reaction, I cut you off. Too soon, I now reckon. We offered him James Lyth but not any of the rest of the clique. We should ask if Eric Hazletine means anything."

"He won't be able to hint by raising an eyebrow if we talk to him on the phone. Well, he could, but we wouldn't see it."

"He'd have to find another manner of letting on, then. Although if our luck's in, then Eric was somebody he came across who isn't covered by the need for secrecy." Patrick fished in his pocket. "I've kept a note of his number in my wallet. For exactly this eventuality."

"Excellent. I admit I'm getting to the point my patience is wearing thin and I want answers now, one way or the other. Although I've got time for this cup of tea, first. Hate it to stew or go cold."

"That would be a travesty."

Once they'd wet their whistles, Patrick put the telephone call through, fingers crossed—literally—that Harry would be at home and not out gallivanting. When the man answered the phone, it did sound as though he had a party in progress, although sharing the instrument didn't make it easy for Leslie to hear clearly. He concentrated hard on the merry voice coming down the line.

"Ah, Patrick. Lovely to hear from you. Got some of the gang round, so let me shut the door."

Orgy? Patrick mouthed silently, making Leslie mouth, *I dread to think,* in response. He thought he heard an injunction to keep the noise down, followed by a door shutting, before Harry came back on the line.

"Me again. Have you made a breakthrough?"

"You might call it that, if you count hearing something that's made us reassess all our ideas. Got a question for you, about a chap whose name we omitted to mention. Eric Hazletine."

"Oh, yes?" Harry instantly sounded both more sombre and more sober. "Friend of yours?"

"Acquaintance. A friend of Fergus." Patrick shot Leslie an intrigued glance: they'd evidently scored a hit.

"Do you know what he did during the war? Apart from rescuing children and getting himself a reputation as a hero?" Harry's question had a waspish edge. "I'm assuming he's the same Eric Hazletine who's being touted for parliament."

Leslie leaned closer to the receiver. "That's him. He was one of Churchill's inner sanctum. Fetcher and carrier, he told us, but it could have been a different role."

"Let's say glorified fetcher and carrier. Remember I asked you if Fergus had a connection to a member of the war cabinet or other important personage?"

"Yes, and we said no. I never thought of Eric as a potential connection." Leslie shrugged at Patrick, then let him answer too.

"Same here. He and Eric were friends and they'd been lovers although in both cases that's pretty meaningless. Cast of thousands. Almost." Another *What the hell's going on?* look at Leslie.

"Hmph? Well, whatever they were to each other, Eric Hazletine was one of those who came to see me to make sure I didn't cause any trouble after Fergus died."

Patrick gave Leslie a triumphant smile, such as might accompany a winning try for his team. "Can you recall what he said when he came to get things sorted? Anything that aroused your suspicions?"

"Not that I can recall. He implied that the order came from the highest level, although I can remember taking that with a pinch of salt at the time."

"We've got a lot to explain to you, but there's no point in doing that now. Get yourself back to your party and we can ring you again over the weekend. We don't want to commit ourselves to paper. Libel and all that." Patrick puckered his lips.

"Quite. I'm intrigued to hear what you've got to say, so give me a ring tomorrow afternoon if you like. I may have a sore head in the morning. Actually, it might be an idea if you can get down to Brighton. One of my guests is the policeman I mentioned last time, and I bet he'd like to hear what you've got to say. I'm afraid I've already whetted his appetite with an account of my visit to yours. You can name names with him. If what you have to say isn't worth pursuing, he'll conveniently forget it. You won't be liable for slander."

"That's a relief. I can make it down tomorrow."

"That would work for me, too." Leslie nodded. "I'll see if my dogsitter will have my pooch a while longer."

They finalised the arrangements with Harry, checked that Mrs. Gray could have Max for an extra day or two, and made for the sitting room.

"That went as well as could be expected," Patrick said as he took his seat. "Unless this police chap thinks we're mad."

"I doubt he will. Harry's clearly been giving him chapter and verse, and you'd have thought he'd have put the tin lid on it already if the official opinion was that we had nothing to go on. And I'm guessing—although given the accuracy of some of my recent guesses that's no guarantee of anything—that if he's at that party, he may well be staying over, which adds to the likelihood of us not having to hold back about The Retainers."

"Yes. We can give him plenty of facts about those old days, even if we're short on them for the rest of our theory."

"I bet Harry can fill in some blanks for the bloke, whether or not he wants to do so for us."

They'd taken the same fireside chairs as previously, when Leslie had gone through the notebook; the same air of domesticity had settled in. This was a workable solution to the mystery, so was there any reason not to fall back into the relationship they'd had before?

"You're going off into your thoughts again. Penny for them?"

"You've asked me that before. In the same come-to-bed voice. Which is what I was thinking about, actually."

Patrick raised an eyebrow. "Time to clinch the agreement we made?"

"I'm tempted." The attraction between them had become as strong as ever, and they'd proved over the last few weeks that they still connected. Their relationship wasn't simply about bed and what they'd do in it. "It would feel like cheating, though, because we haven't put our latest theory to any sort of a test."

"Who would we be cheating, though? Only our consciences, and they're robust enough to cope, surely. Haven't we got over the great argument at Waterloo and all the misunderstanding then and since?" Patrick wasn't pleading: he sounded like he might when explaining a diagnosis, rather than a suitor attempting seduction.

He was right about their consciences being the only judges, and while the fact of the great argument happening would always be there, as part of their history, it had long ago ceased to be a barrier. And with this revelation about Eric, the last remnants of doubt about Patrick's role in Fergus's death—remnants Leslie hadn't realised he'd still clung to—had dissipated, taking their burden with them. That argument could merely serve as a lesson that their relationship could survive heated words, as many a married couple's did, as long as they remembered to say sorry and to talk, rather than let matters fester and boil over.

"You're quite correct. It's only some half-baked principle I'm clinging on to. I said we'd do it when we knew about Fergus, and I don't think we know yet. It's not cold feet, honest." If it were, he'd have packed Patrick out of the door by now. "I always keep my promises."

"You always did, Leslie Lad. Nobody whose word I could trust more than yours. That's why I thought I'd screwed it all up at Waterloo. When you told me to bugger off, I thought that was that, permanently. Pleased to find there's redemption, though, even if it isn't necessarily tonight." Patrick's sympathetic smile spoke volumes.

"That's why I love you, Paddy Boy. You understand me on the occasions I don't understand myself." Leslie shook his head, struck by the absurdity of the conversation. "What a pair of clowns we are. Could have had these chats ages ago."

"We're not clowns. Merely human." Patrick took a sip of tea. "Anyway, maybe we couldn't have talked like this so soon after the event. Everything was too raw. And we didn't have the benefit of what we've heard from other people since, to round out the story. We weren't ready to admit any misunderstandings."

Leslie wasn't sure he'd ever be ready to admit the extent to which he'd had Patrick in the frame for murder. Maybe when they were in their seventies, creaking at the joints and sitting either side of the fire with a cup of cocoa, it might be time for such candour. If they lived to their seventies: hadn't the past few years taught them that you never knew how much time you had left?

"Oh, to hell with pledges. Mrs. Gray won't be here until ten o'clock tomorrow. Plenty of time to muss up the spare bed and pretend we've done a bad job at remaking it." Leslie vacated his chair and plonked himself on Patrick's lap, as he'd done so often in the past.

"You're sure?"

Patrick's words about the love of his life sounded in Leslie's brain, clear as if they'd been spoken only seconds ago. He stroked Patrick's hair. "Surer than I've been about anything in a long time."

CHAPTER FIFTEEN

Harry's flat was as neat and tidy as the man himself, with no hint of whatever excesses had taken place the night before, not even stale tobacco smoke. Jack Martindale, the police officer—a great bear of a man—turned out to be a chief superintendent, which was at least a rank higher than Leslie had anticipated. Little doubt that he'd prove an ideal sounding board for their theory. Harry offered tea or lemonade, saying that his liver would never forgive him if he got the sherry out again.

"Tea suits me," Leslie said, taking his place on a comfortable sofa next to Martindale. "I want to keep my wits clear."

They made small talk with Jack while Harry tinkered in the kitchen, not needing to mind their words, because Harry had apparently made clear to the officer that their guests were a couple, as he'd assumed from that first meeting at Patrick's. Perhaps such an explanation would actually have been unnecessary, because Leslie was certain he and Patrick were both glowing from what had transpired the previous night. Patrick seemed positively shimmering with satisfaction, and Leslie suspected *he* looked similar.

Any lingering worries he'd had about their reuniting had disappeared as a result both of a glorious encounter in his bed and a shared breakfast that could have been a replay of any shared breakfast from the days before the argument. Albeit they were older—and, Leslie hoped, wiser—now, so the sense of things having come right was no doubt genuine. They'd gone beyond merely slaking their lust.

Jack clearly felt himself among friends, because he made no bones about his relief at being among people with whom he could be the person he really was.

"If only parliament would have the common decency to take men in our situation off the list of criminals, we could rid ourselves of the scourge of blackmail and those who commit it." Jack raised his hands. "Sorry. I'm knocking on an open door, saying that to you two."

"Saying what?" Harry said, reappearing with his laden tray.

"That the law as it stands is a blackmailers' charter."

"Hear, hear. Maybe Fergus would still be alive if it wasn't." Harry poured the drinks as he spoke. "Since I gave Jack some preliminary information about this case, he's been peppering me with questions, most of which I couldn't answer. Thank goodness you can help him out."

"An eyewitness is worth twenty folk who had the information at one or two removes. Thank you." Jack took his cup, then ladled a spoon of sugar into it. "You were there when Fergus's death happened, Patrick. Talk me through everything as though I know nothing."

"I'll tell you the tale as I might have had you asked me in the fortnight following the course. I'll add nothing we've learned since." With that proviso, Patrick launched into an account that was as logical and lucid as any police officer could have wished for. He began with the background: the group of five men, their habits and foibles, and how others fitted into that set up. Leslie chipped in to clarify points as required, not sparing the interaction his father had had with James or the details of Fergus's dubious investment schemes. Harry contributed what little he felt able to say about Fergus's activities in France, and then Patrick concluded by telling as much as he knew about the setup of the training, the events of the day itself and what had happened in the aftermath. Harry then chipped in with his account of the clampdown surrounding his investigation of Fergus's death, an account that Jack had clearly heard part of before.

"Patrick, did you always suspect there'd been foul play?" Jack asked, when they'd all reached a natural break.

"Not at first but it began to nag at me. As I said, rumours flew from the start about self-inflicted wounds. Has Harry told you about the court-martial?"

"Yes. You knew Fergus. Was he the kind to take his life rather than face trial?"

"No," Leslie and Patrick said at the same time, before sharing an embarrassed glance.

Patrick waved his hand. "Go on, Leslie. I've spoken enough for the moment."

"Fergus didn't lack courage, despite him lacking judgement at times," Leslie said. "He was the sort who'd go down all guns blazing. The sort who enjoyed getting his own way."

"Neither of you liked him?"

Leslie smiled ruefully. "You're too astute, Jack. Speaking for myself, I couldn't bear him, and Patrick's of the same mind. In part that's because we couldn't tolerate his leading people astray, although with the benefit of hindsight, we can say James didn't go unwillingly. We thought he was mixed up in Fergus's death somehow, because he was related to Jefferies, the dog handler, but we've discarded that notion. Feel free to pick that strand up if we were premature in dismissing it."

"I will." Jack's brow puckered. "I've not taken notes so far, but I'm feeling increasingly like I need a permanent record. Once we've finished airing everything, can you jot the main points down for me to peruse at my leisure? Allusions would be fine where you don't want to commit to paper. I'll know what you mean."

"I'd be happy to do so," Patrick said. "Do you want us to give you an outline of all our tortuous thought processes, as well? Or would you prefer to be unsullied by them?"

Jack snorted. "The latter, please. While you would both make excellent witnesses if called to court, I'm not keen on amateur detectives. I would, however, appreciate you telling me what you think Eric Hazletine's involvement is in this, given that he couldn't have done the actual deed. I know he came to see Harry about not rocking any boats, but that's not enough."

Would anything else they had to say be more persuasive? "We'll start with some facts. Eric's always wanted to get into parliament. He's also always wanted to get into the pants of anyone available. While applying that to his wilder youth with the females of the species would likely do no harm for his reputation, it's a different thing when it comes to having chased the males."

"Agreed." Jack drummed the arm of the sofa. "No amount of saving children would strike that off the account, alas."

"Quite." Leslie continued. "Since not long after Fergus's death, Eric's been the main source of information about it. He's been telling people about the impending court-martial and possibly promoting the notion that the wound was self-inflicted. Eric also has a chap called Gareth working in his office; whether that's the same Gareth as was caught up in the court-martial as the seduced party, we don't know."

"What's his surname?" Harry asked.

Leslie racked his brain. "Biggs? Briggs? Something like that."

"Now," Harry said, with a little grin, "you know I can neither confirm nor deny that in words. But I could raise an eyebrow if either name was correct." He did so.

"He's such a tease." Jack shook his head fondly. "Still, we know where we stand on that one, and I'll force some further information out of Harry later. He can't evade His Majesty's Constabulary. Any other facts for me?"

"Eric was pally with the chap who was acting as liaison from the secret-agent side of things for running the course. Chappell," Patrick said. "That's where we think he got his info from. The question we have for Harry is whether that's the same chap who identified Dawson's body after the car accident."

"I'm happy to verify that it *was* Chappell. It would be a matter of police record, anyway." Harry cast Jack a quizzical glance. "The accident wasn't on your patch, was it?"

"No. But I do remember it because I saw you not long afterwards and you said you thought the victim was one of your old contacts. Most suspicious, young Harry, at the time." Jack raised an eyebrow at his friend, clearly giving him a cue.

"That's why I was able to reassure you two that it wasn't a case of mistaken identity," Harry said. "I'd had the same idea myself, that Dawson's death might have been staged, although Jack was very helpful in giving that theory the lie. I'm having second thoughts about it, now, however. Not so much that it wasn't Dawson, but how convenient it was that Chappell got called on to identify him and possibly reduce—again—any chance of matters getting out of hand. Dawson does seem to have been the person best placed to kill Fergus, doesn't he, Jack? Which, if he was acting on orders, made him a man in possession of a dangerous secret."

Jack nodded. "That's how it strikes me. I'll be finding out all I can about that car accident, although I do know that there was some pressure from the cloak-and-dagger boys to get things sorted without mention of what Dawson did during the war. A colleague I spoke to after my conversation with Harry also expressed his surprise at how blasé said boys were about no culprit being brought to book. He'd assumed that security was more important than justice. It all strikes me as highly suspicious, nevertheless."

"What were the fingerprints on?" Patrick asked. "The ones you told us about, Harry, that were found at the hit-and-run scene and couldn't be linked to any of the local hooligans."

"Let's ask the expert." Harry deferred to his friend.

Jack rubbed his chin. "Offhand, I couldn't say for sure. Something like a pole or metal gatepost next to the body. One of the coppers who'd dealt with the case suspected that whoever did it—and his money was on that group of young ex-soldiers who didn't care what they did or who got hurt—stopped and came to find out whether the person they'd knocked down was dead or alive. The print consisted of a palm and fingers, as though whoever it was had steadied themselves on the pole as they bent down." Jack tapped the sofa, having evidently come up with something. "Chappell reckoned the fingerprints might have had nothing to do with the case. A drunk supporting himself as he waited to cross the road, maybe. The commanding officer could have been right, or history could have been repeating itself and he might have been taking the same role Eric played when he chivvied Harry along."

"If Eric had been the man driving the car, or had someone else do it for him, he'd have wanted there to be no doubt that

Dawson had been killed." Leslie glanced out of the window, to where a gull had flown past, soaring into the sky. That bird would have a magnificent view of everything happening on the ground; if only there was an equivalent for the police to draw on when crimes happened. "It's not much, is it? To form a case on."

"Men have hung for less." Jack raised a hand. "To clarify my meaning, I should say that the road to hanging a man has begun on sparser evidence. You get a tiny chance of a connection between victim and killer, and once you start to explore, you find enough to sway a jury. In this instance, we've got our first step in terms of connections to the dead man, direct or indirect. If we could link that handprint to either Eric or Chappell, we've got a second, firmer step in the right direction. While they could dismiss those connections by legitimately saying people were simply working together in a time of war, it would be less easy to present a genuine excuse for their presence at a crime scene. With any luck, we might find one—or both—or them willing to shop the other. The notion of honour among thieves, or murderers, doesn't always apply."

That sounded encouraging, although Leslie had the feeling the words were intended to paint a rosier picture than might really apply.

"It's all so damn circumstantial, though." Patrick's lips tightened. "James uses the words 'affect a man's standing,' and we take that to mean standing for parliament. That won't impress your jury, will it? Come to think of it, I'm not sure James himself would create much of an impact in the witness box. First impressions would be favourable, but once he let the veneer of an innocent led astray start to peel . . ." He shrugged. "A shame we haven't got my sister Marianne to call on. I'd like to see any defence barrister try to get the better of her."

"Ring her," Leslie said, suddenly keen again. "Ring her now. I've had an idea."

"Happy to oblige if Harry's willing to let us use the telephone. Although not until you explain." Patrick's frustrated look had begun to disappear.

"Marianne told me that Eric has tried to seduce her on and off for years. That's no surprise to us, Harry and Jack, because he tried it on with everyone, up until he got married. As part of his chatting up, he'd plied Marianne with secrets to impress her, including information about Fergus's death. We all know that she's not the sort of woman to spread gossip, so he could have been relatively free with the tittle-tattle. The inside info couldn't only have been about Fergus, though, because there had been subsequent attempts, with—what were her words—low-value coinage. Half secrets about parliament and other stuff." Leslie ran his hands through his hair. "Maybe that *other stuff* included something that would help us."

"If she possessed a vital piece of information, wouldn't she have mentioned it to you?" Harry asked, aiming his question at her twin.

Patrick, grinning, shook his head. "You don't know her. If she didn't think it relevant, it wouldn't get discussed and, anyway, she might not have realised that a particular thing Eric had said *would* be relevant. I bet if she'd ever suspected him of direct involvement in anyone's death, she'd not only have told me, she'd have cut contact with him."

"Terrible to have to ask this," Jack said, "but we policemen have wary minds, born of bitter experience. Is there any possibility that if we ask your sister about this matter that she'll let Eric know that we're on his trail?"

"Given what we've said of her character, are you really asking if she's having an affair with Eric and hiding the fact from those close to her? Not a chance. Strictly entre nous, she doesn't particularly like men. Not in *that* way. Eh, Leslie?"

Leslie nodded, despite the fact he couldn't one hundred percent confirm that Patrick was correct.

Harry glanced inquiringly at Jack, got a thumbs-up, and said, "Then feel free to avail yourself of my telephone. It's in the hallway."

"Thanks. I'll leave the door open, although you'll only get my half of the conversation, which I know is frustrating." Patrick headed off, notebook and pen in hand, leaving Leslie and the other two men readying themselves to try to guess what was being said at the other end of the line.

After the usual exchanges, Marianne evidently sought an explanation for the call, which Patrick answered neatly. "It's ultimately your fault, old girl, for having conned Leslie and me into meeting again. We're on the Fergus Jackson murder trail. Yes, I'm deadly serious. There's a policeman in the next room—friend of a friend—who's very interested in the matter. He also wants to make sure that if I ask you something, you won't go all blabby knickers on us and tell the people involved that we've been enquiring about them."

Leslie chuckled at the use of the childhood phrase. *Blabby knickers.* Like *silly pants*, it was one of the names the three had called each other so often.

"All right, all right, keep your hair on. Just asking. You'd have done the same in my position." Patrick laughed.

Typical twins, Leslie mouthed to the others.

"Anyway, Leslie says you were telling him about Eric trying it on with you. Feeding you titbits of information in order to impress. Any chance you can tell me *exactly* what those titbits were? They may mean something to us in the greater scheme of things, even if they're meaningless to you. Go slowly, because I need to jot them down." The conversation entered a particularly frustrating stage for the listeners. Up to that point, Leslie could have made educated guesses at what Marianne had said. Now he was in the dark. Patrick ummed and then said, "Yes, got that. About what happened on the training course. Did he put any slant on it? Hm-phm. That's what we thought. Played the self-inflicted wound card."

Leslie glanced at Jack, who appeared to be taking his own notes. Did he, too, suspect that Patrick was deliberately clarifying what was said for their benefit?

"Parliamentary tittle-tattle? Of course I would. We want to know everything. May not mean anything to me, but our constabulary mate might make something of it."

Jack's eye roll and pretend yawn showed what he thought of such stuff. The next part of the conversation—from Patrick's end, anyway—seemed to consist of confirmatory noises, until he said, "Ah, we'd thought he'd had a finger in the get-it-done-and-dusted-quietly pie. Oh, an unofficial as well as an official finger? Most interesting. Well put, old girl. He *is* a slimy sod."

"Cover-ups?" Harry whispered, with a shrug, to which Leslie shrugged. So far, despite the potential confirmations, they didn't appear to be breaking new ground. Perhaps it had been a vain hope that they would.

"Well. I had no idea."

Leslie's ears pricked up at Patrick's words. Not only the implication of them but the eager tone in which they'd been spoken.

"I'm glad you said no to his suggestion, unlike Fergus. Too bloody dangerous by half. I bet a lot of them never made it home. We had a suspicion Eric was embroiled in recruiting for the cloak-and-dagger mob, so it's gratifying to have it proven. Did he mention a bloke called Chappell? He did? Excellent. Yes, yes, I do know I sound like a parrot, but there's three pairs of ears listening in and I'm trying to give them a clue, before they come and rip the telephone off me in frustration." Patrick snorted. "If you've got anything else to tell us, particularly about the secret-agent stuff, you'll have devoted worshippers for life."

"She'll have magnum of champagne, as well," Harry shouted.

"That's Harry. He wants to ply you with alcohol but only out of gratitude. You'll have to earn it, though. No, it doesn't matter if the information isn't from the horse's mouth, as long as the source is reliable. Which means James Lyth is counted out. Eh? I'll tell you why when we next meet. Suffice to say we think his true colours have emerged."

Leslie hoped he might be included in that meeting because he'd contribute plenty on the subject.

"Dougal?" Patrick asked. "That's encouraging. There'd be no counting him out on the honesty front. Straight as a die. Yep. Oh. Slow down a bit, I can't keep up." A long pause, and the sound of notes being scribbled. "Let me clarify: 'was in danger' not 'felt he was in danger.'" Another pause. "Well, old girl, that's worth every bit of champagne Harry can get his paws on. Yes, we'll keep you updated, although if this business leads where it might, it could be all over the newspapers. No, I'm not going to say anything else at the moment and neither, I hope, will you. To anyone. I'm not joking when I say we could be dealing with someone who's killed twice. Patience, child." Patrick ended the call with further thanks and a promise to meet his sister for lunch soon, then came back into the sitting room.

"Result?" Leslie asked.

"In spades." Patrick, waggling his notebook, slumped into a chair. "Any tea left in that pot?"

"I bet you could do with a glass of something stronger. I've some bottles of beer that weren't drunk yesterday." Harry rose to fetch them, with an impassioned "No sharing the clues while I'm away."

Once he was back and everyone had a glass of refreshment, Patrick said, "I don't know how much you gleaned from my part of the conversation. A lot of what Marianne said was nothing new, simply confirmation of what we'd surmised, such as Eric being involved with the cover-ups. She also said that in the early part of the war he was engaged in recruiting people for his pal Chappell, to get them to join *your* mob, Harry. She knows that because he asked *her* if she was interested. He approached people he thought would make good agents, including Fergus, and had recognised qualities in Marianne which could have been useful. Only she had the sense to refuse."

"How did he take this refusal?" Harry asked.

"In good part, as he'd taken the snubs she'd delivered when he'd made a pass at her." Patrick drank some beer with evident pleasure.

"I wonder if Eric helped recruit either Gareth or Dawson," Leslie mused. While it was useful to have several of their suspicions corroborated, they weren't much closer to linking Eric to the key figures in the case or having a third step along the road to a conviction.

Patrick shrugged. "Marianne didn't mention either of those names. Frustrating, although she redeemed herself with what she had to say next. I'm afraid she's quoting somebody who can't be interviewed, because we lost him over the channel, but Dougal was the kind of chap whom you'd have called a good witness."

"The Dougal who was one of your Retainer clique?" Jack asked.

"Not *my* Retainers, but yes, the same. He was the one who brought James into that set, although Dougal began to drift away from the rest of them, pretty much from when the war began. He was another of those who was sounded out by Eric for a secret role, although not with any great pressure, because he'd already signed up for the RAF. He did have a mate whose name he put forward for 'special duties' as Marianne termed them." Another draft of beer. "The mate took up the offer. *He* was actually on the course when Fergus died, although I didn't know which of the trainees he was at the time. Fergus told me about the connection but didn't provide a name."

Jack, fingers steepled to his chin, was evidently considering the information. "Was Dougal still alive at that stage in the war? Would he have had a motive to kill Fergus and could he have persuaded his pal to do the deed?"

"He was alive, if up to his neck in fighting Messerschmitts." Leslie stuck his lip out in thought. "And he certainly once vowed he'd swing for the bloke, but if you jotted down all the folk who said something similar about Fergus, you'd need pages and pages for your list."

"I'd be on it. Of which Leslie is acutely aware." Patrick swiftly carried on. "As for Dougal, the dates work, but he wasn't the kind to kill anyone except in fair combat. However, he did tell Marianne a couple of things that didn't bear any significance until our telephone conversation. She saw Dougal not long before he flew his final mission. He told her he'd seen Eric speaking to Dawson only a few days before Fergus died, although Marianne didn't have the chance to delve into that, even if she'd known it was important."

"To clarify, for my poor, addled wits. You have a reliable witness to Eric and Dawson speaking?" Harry asked, to which Patrick nodded. "How did Dougal know Dawson?"

Patrick raised an eyebrow. "Because *he* was the pal that Eric had recruited."

"How obvious." Leslie heaved a sigh. "Fergus was right about you not guessing that. He'd have won his bet and his pint."

"Quite. I don't think Marianne ever knew the name of the person who supposedly found Fergus's body, or if she did, she never connected him to what Dougal had told her. She only remembered the surname because it was the same as a teacher's whom she'd hated at school. Anyway, Dougal had arranged to have a drink with Dawson not an hour later. He denied any such meeting had taken place and stated that he'd not seen Eric since he'd been recruited. Dougal knew he hadn't made a mistake but assumed the lie was due to one of two things: either they'd been discussing stuff so confidential that he couldn't acknowledge such a conversation had taken place or it had involved Eric's Retainer-like activities so was not for general consumption."

Jack cut in. "I hate to spoil the party, but despite the fact that it does sound suspicious, that's not really strengthening the case against Eric except by adding to the circumstantial evidence. If he recruited the man Dawson, Eric could argue he'd have valid reason to be talking to him once the agent was back in this country. Not like he'd be able to contact him safely otherwise."

How obvious and how depressing. Was Patrick's great news going to turn out to be a damp squib?

"You told us you had a *couple* of points," Harry said. "What's the other?"

The question reignited Leslie's hope. Could there be another rabbit pulled out of the hat at the eleventh hour?

"I've got to admit I've kept this until last because it's—for me—the best part. Again, it bore no significance to Marianne previously, although I bet she's now puzzling over it for all she's worth." Patrick stroked his chin. "Leslie, Marianne told you over the phone that she'd seen Dougal with his fiancée. The meeting I referred to earlier."

Leslie nodded. While he couldn't yet see the whole rabbit, surely there was a hint of ears over the hat brim? "Yes. It was a bit awkward for her because he'd started talking about old pals and the fiancée didn't like it. Marianne, being the prudent woman she is, cut the conversation short and left them alone."

"Always has been sensible, my sister. She remembers everything he said because it was the last time they spoke, even if the words bore no link in her mind to Fergus's death. Don't forget, this happened a couple of years afterwards. Anyhow, Dougal had received a letter from Dawson, one smuggled out of France in 1944, saying he was scared and going to ground. Marianne had made an offhand remark about it being for the best that she and Dougal had declined the offer to serve as agents. You can imagine how guilty she felt about that quip when he was killed shortly afterwards. That's why the conversation stuck with her. But he also mentioned that Dawson was as much in danger on home turf as he was on the continent."

"We heard you clarify the wording for that bit. Did Dougal say why that danger applied?" Jack asked.

"No. What with his fiancée getting crosser by the minute, he left things by saying they'd have to discuss it another time. Another time that never came. My dear sister assumed"—Patrick raised an eyebrow at Leslie as he used that deadly word—"that it was the old story, the same part of a man's nature that threatens any of us four and drove Fergus to his court-martial."

Harry nodded. "I always wondered why Dawson disappeared after D-day and guessed it was because his cover was about to be blown. But he returned to England at the war's end, didn't he? That hardly accords with Dawson thinking he was still in danger."

Leslie suddenly knew why Patrick would have been excited at his sister's news. "Eric was at death's door in 1945. Everyone thought he was a goner, including the doctors who gave him penicillin. Dawson may have thought he was safe at last."

Jack blew out his cheeks so loudly it sounded as though he might be about to burst. "It's still not real evidence, though."

"No, but I have an idea where you can find some." What had Marianne said over the phone about letters? "Dougal's mother kept every letter he ever sent her, from when he was a boy. If she still has them, there might be a reference to Dawson in there. Dougal knew how slim his chances were of surviving the war, so he clearly wanted to discuss something he'd discovered but he wasn't able to do so with Marianne. He may have committed that something to writing in case he didn't make it."

Jack, who'd perked up at the mention of Dougal's mother, nodded. "That sounds highly promising if I can get my hands on those letters. I can no doubt get the mother's name and address from the war office, and hopefully she'll be amenable to letting me have a look. Regardless of that, we've made a start, and while we may not seem too much closer to a resolution, any long journey starts with a few steps."

Leslie nodded. It might have been a platitude but he'd accept it. "This feels less than a long walk than a relay race and we're passing on the baton."

"Well, I'll try not to drop it. In the meantime, Patrick, please thank your sister from all of us for her contribution."

"I'll do that with pleasure. I only hope," Patrick said, "that if you ever get enough evidence to corner Eric, he doesn't think he's nothing left to lose and decide to bring us all down with him. We've been cagey enough about ensuring he doesn't get wind that we're on his trail given that he's standing local to Leslie and walls might have ears."

"We won't let anything untoward happen, Patrick," Jack assured him. "I've not survived in the force this long without having a string or two to pull. If Eric started getting frisky, we could play the national security trump. He was one of Churchill's own, don't forget, which might necessitate any trial happening behind closed doors. We have our options, don't we, Harry?"

Leslie dreaded to think what those options were or the extent to which Harry was still involved with such clandestine matters. *He* felt he'd never truly be retired from Bletchley and all its associations. "Then we need to leave it in your capable two hands. Four, if we rightly include Harry."

"I—we—won't betray your trust, I promise." Jack gave them a reassuring smile.

Leslie and Patrick shared a glance. Their lap of the relay had clearly been completed and they'd have to hope Jack kept a tight grip on the baton for the next.

On the way home, they had the unexpected pleasure of a compartment of the corridor train to themselves.

"Do you think Jack's pledge will come to fruition?" Patrick asked. "The one about not betraying our trust?"

It was the first time the matter had been discussed since leaving Harry's. Leslie had wanted a bit of time to compose his thoughts and Patrick must have felt the same.

"If it doesn't, I don't think it'll be for want of trying. Impressive chap, Jack. Mustard at his job, probably."

"Probably." Patrick drew his fingers down the window, as though doodling on it. "Whatever the outcome, this feels like an end of things, as far as our input is concerned. We can do nothing else."

"I think you're right." Leslie stared out at the countryside, feeling a bit like a limp lettuce. He'd experienced the same elation followed by a combination of tiredness and emptiness when they'd solved a tricky problem at Bletchley. The difference was that back then there'd always been a fresh issue to get their brains around, whereas now, the only challenge would be not to let his relationship with Patrick slip again. Maybe that would be plenty to concentrate on.

He felt a tap on his leg. "You're miles away."

"No, I'm not. I'm very much here. Where I should always have been. Where *you* should always have been. And it shouldn't have taken a murder—two murders—to get us here."

Patrick grinned. "If we're counting influencing factors, don't forget the interfering sister."

"I hadn't. Marianne deserves a whole case of champagne." Leslie nudged Patrick's foot with his. "You probably don't know, but I've got a walk-in cupboard under my stairs. Unfortunately, it's accessed from the kitchen so is full of Mrs. Gray's things and other items in storage."

"An under-stairs cupboard?" Patrick's eyes lit up. "I have fond memories of one of those."

"So do I. Although I'm not sure we could devise an adequate reason for clearing it out, and at present you couldn't fit a gnat in there."

"Let alone two grown men?" Patrick returned the foot nudge. "Then maybe it's as well that I've got an *unused* one in my house. I don't mean the one in the hallway, because that's almost full. You've never graced the upper floors, but if you had, you would have noticed another, under the little staircase to the old servants' bedrooms."

"Empty, is it?" Prickles of excitement ran up Leslie's spine. "As in room-enough-for-two empty?"

"Precisely." Patrick suddenly appeared to find his shoes of immense interest. "I've rather made a point of keeping it so. As a reminder of times past."

A sharp quip—along the lines of asking whether Patrick went in there and played *let's pretend*—died on Leslie's lips. This confession deserved the proper degree of respect. "You daft old sausage. I think that's made me love you even more than I already did."

Patrick looked up, smiling. "Then I think you need to come down to Surrey for a game of hide and seek. Soon."

Leslie held out his hand to shake. "You have yourself a deal."

EPILOGUE

Three months later, things had gone very quiet on the Brighton front, apart from the occasional phone call from Harry to say, "Jack's still working on it. Those letters could be the key, if you read them knowing what we know, but he wants to get as much evidence as he can in his armoury before tackling Hazletine. He reckons Chappell won't be hard to crack, though, despite his war service. Or maybe because of it."

It was frustrating, yet Leslie and Patrick's parts had been played. They had their jobs to get on with, their relationship to keep developing, plus the final days of Mr. Cadmore's life and Leslie's mother's imminent widowhood to occupy their minds. A final visit to Combe had been more important than any thoughts concerning either Fergus Jackson or Eric Hazletine.

So, it was a bit of a surprise when, a week after their return from Devon, they received a letter from Harry. The contents were addressed jointly, and said he'd been trying to ring Patrick but had been told he was in the West Country on personal business. Events were on the move, and while Harry couldn't break the trust Jack had placed in him, they should keep their eyes on the newspapers over the next few days because a certain aspiring politician might be finding himself arrested. Harry made a special request for confidentiality until the news appeared. While he would sympathise with the pair wanting to inform some of their family—Marianne in particular—about what was afoot, he'd rather they restrained themselves until the cuffs were on. Whether metaphorically or literally.

"We'll need to tell both her and your mother what's what when the story *does* break," Patrick said, as he reread the letter. "Especially as they've been key to us making such progress."

"Yes. I wonder what's changed with Jack's investigations? Has another letter come to light that names Eric directly? Or did Chappell turn coat?"

"Possibly either or both. It would have to be something significant to get past all the possible excuses of 'in the interests of national security' or other nonsense." Patrick ran his hands through his hair. "Maybe Eric's the turncoat and he's hoping to get a lesser charge. I don't know enough about the law to be able to say whether you can keep your neck out of the noose if you were simply an accessory. Although if what we think is true, they were in it up to their eyeballs."

Leslie nodded. If you made someone else commit a murder, you were surely as guilty as the man who did the deed. "It's all out of our hands, now."

"Our friendship isn't, though. Thank God for this business and us both wanting it cleared up or we'd still be at daggers drawn." Patrick slid his hand into Leslie's. "If I promise I'll never make a stupid assumption in the future, will you promise the same in return?"

"Already done so. In my mind if not in the spoken word." Leslie gave him a kiss.

"Thank you. And if we're talking things that are solely in the mind and should be said aloud, then I should make a proper apology to you."

"I'm not aware you owe me one, Paddy Boy."

"*I* am. I was horribly short with you when we first met up again." Patrick cradled Leslie's face in his hands. "My mind was all mixed up with your dad and everything. But seeing you walk into that bar was the start of a new life for me."

"You sound like Celia Johnson. Stop it, or we'll both be in tears."

"You can stop my mouth with another kiss."
Which was precisely what Leslie did.

ACKNOWLEDGEMENTS

Many thanks to my family, who all encourage me and keep my feet firmly on the ground in equal measure. And to the members of We Write Stuff, who are great for bouncing ideas around with. Every author needs good pals.

Dear Reader,

Thank you for reading Charlie Cochrane's *The Deadliest Fall!*

We know your time is precious and you have many, many entertainment options, so it means a lot that you've chosen to spend your time reading. We really hope you enjoyed it.

We'd be honored if you'd consider posting a review—good or bad—on sites like **Amazon, Barnes & Noble, Kobo, Goodreads, Twitter, Facebook, Tumblr,** and your blog or website. We'd also be honored if you told your friends and family about this book. Word of mouth is a book's lifeblood!

For more information on upcoming releases, author interviews, blog tours, contests, giveaways, and more, please sign up for our weekly, spam-free newsletter and visit us around the web:

> **Newsletter**: riptidepublishing.com/newsletter
> **Twitter**: twitter.com/RiptideBooks
> **Facebook**: facebook.com/RiptidePublishing
> **Goodreads**: tinyurl.com/RiptideOnGoodreads
> **Tumblr**: riptidepublishing.tumblr.com

Thank you so much for Reading the Rainbow!

RiptidePublishing.com

RIPTIDE
PUBLISHING

ALSO BY CHARLIE COCHRANE

Novels:
Best Corpse for the Job
Jury of One
Two Feet Under
Old Sins
A Carriage of Misjustice
Lock, Stock and Peril
Lessons in Love
Lessons in Desire
Lessons in Discovery
Lessons in Power
Lessons in Temptation
Lessons in Seduction
Lessons in Trust
All Lessons Learned
Lessons for Survivors
Lessons for Idle Tongues
Lessons for Sleeping Dogs
Broke Deep
Count the Shells
The Case of the Grey Assassin
The Case of the Undiscovered
Corpse

Novellas:
Lessons in Loving thy
Murderous Neighbour
Lessons in Chasing the Wild
Goose
Lessons in Cracking the
Deadly Code
Lessons in Playing a
Murderous Tune
Lessons in Following a
Poisonous Trail
Lessons in Solving the Wrong
Problem
Lessons in Keeping a
Dangerous Promise

*Standalone novellas and
short stories:*
Second Helpings
Awfully Glad
Don't Kiss the Vicar
Promises Made Under Fire

ABOUT THE AUTHOR

Because Charlie Cochrane couldn't be trusted to do anything grown up, she writes cosy mysteries. These include the Edwardian-era Cambridge Fellows series, the contemporary Lindenshaw Mysteries, and her 1950s Alasdair and Toby series where two actors play Holmes and Watson both onscreen and off. Multipublished, she has titles with Carina, Riptide, Lume, and Williams and Whiting.

Charlie is a member of the Crime Writers' Association, Mystery People and International Thriller Writers Inc, and regularly appears at literary festivals, reader conventions, and author conferences.

Where to find her:
Website: charliecochrane.wordpress.com
Facebook: facebook.com/charlie.cochrane.18
Twitter: twitter.com/charliecochrane
Instagram: instagram.com/cochrane.charlie2

Enjoy more stories like *The Deadliest Fall* at RiptidePublishing.com!

Back to You

A shocking truth threatens the future they could have together.

ISBN: 978-1-62649-575-3

Pressure Head

Some things are better left hidden.

ISBN: 978-1-62649-713-9